The Blue Witch

J. L. Apollo

The Blue Witch is an original work of fiction.
Names, places, and events are of the authors imagination
or are used fictitiously. Any resemblance to anyone
living or dead, or actual events is purely coincidental.

Published in the United States by
Shades Hollow Press
Overland Park, KS

Identifiers: LCCN

Library of Congress Control Number: 2020924717
9781736320501 (ebook) ISBN
9781736320518 (hardback) ISBN
9781736320525 (paperback) ISBN

Cover Artwork & Design by Jeff Brown Graphics

Copy/Line Editing by Aja Pollock

Final Editing and Proofreading by Michelle Hope

Table of Contents

Chapter 1 1

Chapter 2 24

Chapter 3 36

Chapter 4 47

Chapter 5 54

Chapter 6 61

Chapter 7 66

Chapter 8 73

Chapter 9 79

Chapter 10 85

Chapter 11 91

Chapter 12 102

Chapter 13 108

Chapter 14 114

Chapter 15 117

Chapter 16 127

Chapter 17 135

Chapter 18 143

Chapter 19 148

Chapter 20 154

Chapter 21 158

Chapter 22 163

Chapter 23 167

Chapter 24 172

Chapter 25 179

Chapter 26 185

Chapter 27 192

Chapter 28 197

Chapter 29 204

Chapter 30 210

Chapter 31 216

Chapter 32 222

Chapter 33 227

Chapter 34 232

Chapter 35 236

Chapter 36 241

Chapter 37 248

Chapter 38 252

Chapter 39 258

Chapter 40 266

Chapter 41 271

Chapter 42 279

Chapter 1

Brendan Pandane lowered his stance, his hand drifting to the familiar comfort of his sword's grip. A half dozen senses, if you included an experienced gut, sounded their warnings within him as he entered the Great Hall of Andavar. Brendan cast his gaze about, searching for whatever was bristling the hair on his neck. But he could find nothing.

Brendan straightened, stretching his arms high over his head, before running his fingers briskly through his long dark-red hair. He then slapped himself firmly in the face, and promptly did so once again.

"Shade me!" he muttered, gently rubbing his face. The lingering sting of his self-inflicted assault brought no relief from his misgivings.

Try as he might, he could not escape the dreadful feeling's embrace or its fingers crawling across his skin. Nor could he ignore the foul, pervasive presence of death within the Great Hall. Brendan wiped away beads of sweat from his brow with the back of his hand, shivering unexpectedly. Searching for some haunting specter of the dead, Brendan stepped but a few feet farther before the hair on his arms rose and a chilling new sensation washed over him, stopping him dead in his tracks. He could feel lifeless breath on the back of his neck.

Brendan spun about, drawing his sword, but found nothing there. His keen eyes immediately began scanning the hall in earnest from top to bottom as he moved forward. Nearing the center of the floor, he gazed up at the Great Hall's massive stained-glass ceiling.

The stunning work of art covered the entire length and breadth of the expansive hall. Its thousands of vibrantly colored glass panels honored the world of men with a vast array of scenes depicting past kings. Some had passed into legend; others had been all but forgotten. Glowing as the morning's rising sun penetrated it, the intricate stained-glass ceiling was an impressive sight to behold, one that could take the breath of even the most jaded first-time visitor to the Great Hall.

Brendan's eyes roved over the hall's white marble floor. Dancing colors swirled and floated like a fine mist upon a gentle breeze above the polished surface, a product of the skillful design and magic of the hall's glass ceiling.

Brendan scanned the towering white marble statues serving as the hall's pillars. Each one had been hand-carved into a great beast straining to hold the cavernous glass ceiling and its expansive framework in place. But once again, he could find nothing to justify his ill feelings. He noticed several of the king's council members milling about, waiting to take their seats. He could see Vander Ray, the captain of the King's Watch, standing with the king at the far end of the hall. Vander seemed at ease as he laughed at something their king was saying.

A member of the Watch nodded to him as he approached, and Brendan returned the gesture before continuing uneasily across the massive hall. He found it rather odd he was the only one sensing this, whatever this was. *Perhaps I'm out of sorts,* he thought, trying to explain the feeling away, knowing he hadn't gotten any sleep the night before. He'd been hurrying, without stopping for rest, to return to the palace after fulfilling a command from the king.

He'd chosen to forgo a peaceful night's sleep in his own bed in order to spend time visiting his family's grave site on the way back. Instead of the short visit he'd envisioned, he'd lingered there in the dark for far too long, as crickets and frogs sang to him their night songs, devoid of harmony. The headstones and monuments of the dead had watched over him like silent sentinels as he'd lost all track of time reflecting on his young life and the loss of his family.

Brendan's mother, father, and older sister had all been killed in a mining accident when he was only five years old and his younger sister, Aria, was not yet a year old. His parents had toiled in the crystal mines, along with many others of their small community, most of their adult lives. It had provided them a modest living, but one that allowed them to care for their family's needs adequately enough. Over five hundred lives had been lost when an unexplained explosion collapsed the mine.

Their uncle on their mother's side had reluctantly agreed to take Brendan and Aria in. Their aunt and uncle had provided for them, but it had never been a pleasant situation or a loving home. Brendan, upon turning sixteen, had decided it would be better for all involved if he and Aria lived on their own. His aunt and uncle had made no attempt to dissuade him from his chosen course of action.

Brendan's uncanny skill with a sword was already evident, and he managed to support Aria and himself with it. It was his friend Vander Ray, after the passing of his own father, who'd convinced Brendan the two of them should join the King's Watch.

They were both young—too young, really—but showed such skill with their swords they'd been accepted on the spot. It hadn't been long before it was generally acknowledged the two young men were the best swords not only in the Watch but in the ranks of the army as well.

On occasion, and usually at one of their superiors' request, they would put on displays of their skills against any who wished to challenge them. The most competitive of these exhibitions were when the two sparred against each other. These matches had become nearly legendary among the men and women of the Watch and army.

The two had moved up the ranks quickly. Vander had been promoted to captain of the King's Watch shortly after Brendan's unmatched skill with a blade had caught the attention of King Tennington and led him to declare Brendan his High Sword.

It was Brendan who'd recommended Vander be promoted to captain when the position became available, and King Tennington had made it so. Some thought them still too young and lacking in the leadership experience needed for such positions, but nobody could deny their skill. Clearly, the two friends had impressed King Tennington, and none would challenge his decisions. They quickly proved their worth, excelling in their leadership roles during the kingdom of men's rigorous war games. They had each won over the doubters and gained the unquestioned support and respect of their men.

"Brendan, come join us!" The king's voice boomed across the hall, drawing Brendan's attention from his fruitless search. The king had moved to take his place at the end of the High Council's long stone table, and he and his council members were about to be seated. The polished table and its high-backed wood and leather chairs sat on the main level of the hall to the left of the throne. The throne itself sat twelve steps above the main floor, offering the king a commanding view of the Great Hall.

Brendan had only recently turned nineteen, but his long red hair and skin kissed by the summer sun gave a bit of fierceness to his youthful appearance. His dark-green eyes and the short, thin beard hiding some of the light smattering of freckles on his face gave him a serious look not often found in someone so young.

Brendan took great pride in the fact that he had never failed his king and never lost a fight. He felt King Tennington Ashford expected nothing less of his hand-chosen High Sword. Tennington, the beloved graying king on the far side of his prime, had become like a father to Brendan in their time together.

As High Sword, Brendan answered only to the king. He had earned a place at council, though by design, he rarely attended; he hated politics and the rhetoric that often came with such meetings. Nevertheless, it was widely known Brendan had the trust and the ear of the king. None dared question the complete loyalty to each other they shared, now grown even stronger after the recent attempt on King Tennington's life.

As the council meeting dragged on, Brendan sat quietly, a hostage of protocol. His thoughts, however, were free to fix on the haunting presence he'd felt earlier. And though he could no longer sense it, he could not be sure that it was gone either. His focus and attention elsewhere, he quickly lost all interest in the meeting at hand.

Weary from his travels and lack of sleep, his thoughts eventually drifted to the assassination attempt at the palace. It'd taken place upon his return from a mission to

Datton, a small city at the foot of the Shale Mountains, two days' ride northwest of the capital city of Andavar in the kingdom of men. There, he'd sought out, killed, and returned the body of a Sintin to the family who'd lost a small child to the black-scaled demon of nightmares.

The Sintin had dragged the boy away from his home but kept him within sight of it. He'd perched himself comfortably upon a large boulder as he held the boy captive, and the panic-stricken family could do nothing to save him. Those men and women who had been brave enough to attempt to rescue the boy lay scattered in pieces before the invading demon.

The Sintin would allow the screaming boy to crawl through the pooling blood, over the dismembered body parts of his fallen rescuers, toward his family, only to drag him back to thoroughly lick the intoxicating mix of blood from his smooth skin. He'd done so repeatedly and without mercy, toying with his young victim and the boy's distraught family. The Sintin took great pleasure in taunting the townsfolk and remaining family members who were watching from a distance. He mocked them for their cowardice and challenged them to come save the boy.

The boy's mother had to be pulled away as she fought desperately to reach her son, crying out and pleading for someone to help him. The young boy's father had rushed forward with the others, thinking to charge in and save his child. But seeing those far stronger and faster than him torn to pieces before him, he knew he could be no savior for his son. And so, he'd reluctantly stopped while others lay dead or dying.

Fear and self-preservation had frozen him in place. He could only watch, unable to look away, as his son began to quiet. No longer screaming, the child started to sing ever so softly. Tears fell freely from the father's eyes; he knew his son was singing to comfort himself. As he listened to his son's song, he realized it was one his wife would often sing to him as she put him to bed.

Moments later, sound no longer came from the boy's mouth as it opened and closed silently, his voice imprisoned by fear. As the terrified father had watched, horrified by the sight before him, his son's eyes had opened wide and fixed upon the Sintin. There, cradled in the arms of the Sintin, the boy had stared up at the demon, unblinking, as it took its first bite of his flesh. At no time while the demon fed upon him had the boy looked away, not even in death.

Brendan remembered his shock at hearing the details of the Sintin's attack. Its cruelty had been made abundantly clear to him. It was Tennington's command that the demon be hunted down and receive a merciless re-death for what it had done to the boy. It was a dangerous charge, and one most at the palace thought would surely bring an end to Brendan's life.

Sintins were not only cunning, ferocious creatures but they were bred from ancient demons as well. Nightmares from another time, they were humanlike in form but had massive claws and teeth the size of small daggers. The Sintin Brendan defeated had possessed large blood-orange eyes set deep in its oversized head above angular jowls. Its body rippled with muscles under a thin layer of fine, smooth scales, giving it the appearance of being slick and wet. A row of short, curved spikes protruded from its spine, and it would have towered over even the largest of men.

Nobody living now had actually seen a Sintin before this attack. They had thought Sintins were creatures of the old world, demon spawn that no longer existed in the world of men. Where it had come from, and why, nobody could be sure.

Brendan recalled the moment he'd come upon the Sintin and the terrible fight that had ensued. Even the lightest touch of his sword seemed to cause the Sintin great pain. He could find no justification for it, but as he fought the Sintin, his sword felt like a living thing. Finally, gaining the upper hand, he carried out King Tennington's orders. Though he took no pleasure in it, he spent a great deal of time fulfilling his charge.

He would poke at the Sintin with his sword, causing small, piercing wounds in its cursed flesh. The demon had spat vulgarities at him while dragging its body along the ground, desperately trying to escape its fate. Brendan had made sure to laugh at the Sintin, as it had at the boy's family. He would pretend to leave, only to return again and deliver to the creature more pain and suffering. Finally, after the Sintin had taken an untold amount of punishment, it begged for a quick re-death. Brendan had responded to the Sintin's pleas without the slightest hint of mercy, as the demon had with the boy's mother and father.

Brendan thought of the boy's grief-stricken parents and how they'd thanked him for exacting a revenge they could not. He remembered being with the family as they'd ritualistically burned the Sintin's body so the demon could never rise again. And he remembered how the boy's mother had hugged him, clinging to him and trembling for the longest time as she wept. He thought of the boy's father and the haunting, vacant look in his eyes as he'd shaken his hand before leaving.

Brendan had been giving an account of his battle with the Sintin and its punishment to a very attentive King Tennington in the palace gardens when the assassin made his move. The assassin had posed as a gardener in order to get within striking distance of the king. He had been quick, but not quick enough.

The man's presence in the gardens had caught Brendan's eye, and he'd been paying close attention to him. He'd noticed the man was far more interested in the king than his work and was pruning—very poorly—only the shrubbery nearest to the king. Tennington, so interested in his report on the Sintin, and apparently very comfortable under his protection, had not seemed to pay the gardener any real attention.

Brendan had seen the flash of a wicked-looking dagger, and in one fluid motion, he'd removed it from the assassin, along with the hand wielding it. He'd done so with blinding speed, his sword feeling a part of him and reacting with him. It was a sensation he'd felt a great many times when using his sword but could never explain.

He would have preferred to capture the man alive, to question him, but the assassin, showing speed and agility of his own, struck out at him with a second weapon. It was a short-handled device with multiple blades springing out from within it. It sliced through the air just past his head as he pushed Tennington safely away before engaging the assassin once again.

Brendan opened a nasty gash across his opponent's chest with a powerful slicing blow, knocking the man to the ground and sending the strange weapon flying from his remaining hand. The assassin rolled away and came back to his feet, throwing three blades so fast that he could not avoid them all, and one stuck deep in his left shoulder. He withdrew it and flung it back at his attacker so quickly, there was no chance for him to escape it either, and the blade buried itself to the hilt in the assassin's right side.

The assassin grunted in pain but wasn't slowed as he countered, this time with some kind of flashing explosive. It detonated in front of Brendan, sending small shards of shrapnel tearing into him as he avoided the greater part of the blast. Even then, the force of it threw him back into King Tennington, knocking them both to the ground.

Brendan gained his feet and was charging after the fleeing assassin when the man came to a sudden halt, blood spraying from a wound in the back of his neck. Brendan could see the tip of a sword jutting out through the wound. He saw the sword draw back through the wound and the assassin fall. There, standing over him holding the sword, was Vander Ray.

"You want to get here a little quicker next time?" Brendan quipped at Vander.

"I would have thought you could handle one lone assassin without my help, High Sword," Vander shot right back, cocking an eyebrow at him.

Brendan could not help remembering, as his mind replayed those events, how King Tennington had approached them grinning as he carried the severed hand of the assassin. "Could either of you use a hand?" he'd asked.

Unconsciously rubbing his wounds through his tunic, Brendan allowed himself a small smile as he remembered that day and Vander's pride in killing the assassin before he could. He and Vander had known each other since childhood, and they'd been in more than a few scrapes together. Vander was about the same height as he was, but with wavy dark-blond hair and pale-blue eyes. Vander was a bit leaner yet just as muscular, with the kind of rugged good looks that the young women of their realm seemed to love. And unlike himself, Vander was a charmer and very comfortable with those of the opposite sex.

Vander's father had spent a great deal of time and effort training the two of them in the use of their swords and how to size up and fight an enemy. Vander's father had been a celebrated commander in the battle unit known as the Elite First. Their legendary battle cry, "First to charge! Last to die!" had been heard at the beginning of every great battle since the Elite's inception.

Brendan's thoughts turned to his encounter with the young blue girl the night before. Why had she seemed so frightened? Or was it sad?

"Brendan! Brendan! We must speak after this session," King Tennington said not-so-discreetly into his ear. Brendan jerked his head up, jolted from his wandering thoughts. He nodded wordlessly to his king and then made every effort to focus upon the meeting at hand, more than a bit embarrassed that he'd been caught daydreaming.

Brendan's attention was not held long, however. He caught a flash of movement across from where he sat. Something in the shadows had shifted—or had it? He could not be sure. It was there and gone nearly instantly. Either way, he was wide awake now.

Following the council meeting—which, as usual, had involved far too much talk and not nearly enough decisions made or actions taken—King Tennington and Brendan sat alone.

"I must ask you to do something for me, Brendan. Though I will not command it of you. It has been suggested that the assassin may have been a minion of the Blue Witch."

The Blue Witch? Brendan thought. *How could that be?* "I find that very hard to believe, Your Majesty. If she wanted you dead, she would not need the hand of an assassin."

"The hand?" Tennington smirked as he gave Brendan a wry look. Brendan, suddenly realizing what he'd said, shook his head. The two looked at each other and burst into laughter. "I thought as much myself," King

Tennington continued. "But it is not a possibility I wish to ignore either. She could have used the assassin for some yet-unknown reason."

Brendan pondered the possibility for a moment before responding. "Okay, let's suppose this theory is correct. What reason would she have for wanting you dead? She's never disputed your right to the throne and has never been an enemy of yours or your kingdom. Though I must admit, we know almost nothing about the blue girl." Brendan paused and took a deep breath before continuing. "She showed herself to me when I was returning home last night. I was at my family's grave site when she came to me. I have not had the opportunity to speak to anyone about it. Not even my sister."

"Ah yes, your sister, and how is Aria these days?" Tennington asked.

"Good! She turns fourteen tomorrow, and she's as obstinate as ever," Brendan replied with a smile, shaking his head.

"I don't believe I've ever known a child quite like her. Aria is as beautiful a young girl as I have seen, but I believe her to be the most headstrong, dangerous thing I have come across in all my days," Tennington said, smiling, before laughing out loud. "And she still owes me a fine horse!"

Aria had always had a mind of her own, and usually it was coming up with some sort of mischief. Tennington was correct, of course; Aria was indeed very beautiful. Brendan could not deny that. Aria had long flame-red hair and bright-green eyes, and her smile was infectious. Her body was maturing into that of a young woman quickly now, and she'd stolen the hearts of many young would-be suitors. To their chagrin, Aria was more interested in her weapons training with Brendan and working on her fledgling magic skills.

Aria possessed magic but was still struggling with the use and control of it. Their mother was believed to have possessed magic, but she had refused to use it herself, considering it too dangerous and unpredictable. Aria had experienced this firsthand when Brendan had brought her on a visit to the palace. She'd quickly become bored and started playing with her magic to occupy her time. She'd tried to show off her newfound powers to King Tennington and accidentally turned his favorite horse into a large raven that flew off over the city walls, never to be seen again. The king had been impressed, but was none too happy at losing his favorite horse.

"You know, I've never seen the Blue Witch myself," Tennington admitted. "Is she truly blue? You must tell me about her."

Brendan thought about his encounter the night before and did his best to describe her. "She's the most fascinating thing I've ever seen. Her skin is light blue, and what would be the whites of her eyes are an even lighter blue, with a deeper blue in the centers that has a captivating sparkle…like light on unsettled water. Her hair is long and flows nearly the length of her back. It is of a very light silver blue and seems to have a shine all of its own, though that may have been moonlight reflecting off it; I can't be sure. She's young in appearance, my lord, fifteen or maybe sixteen years old at most. She's slight of build and has a way about her that suggests she's more woman than child. She wore black robes unlike any I've ever seen. I could see in the darkness last night a very faint elaborate pattern of light blue glowing softly throughout them."

"Yes, I have heard that said before of her robes. I'm told there is not a seamstress in the land who could have created them. I'd guess elven made, but nobody's seen an elf in hundreds of years. What purpose did she have with you? Did she speak to you?"

"I do not know her purpose, my lord. She spoke only my name, but her voice was sad and haunting. She seemed lost within herself and fighting to control her emotions. It is thought, as you may know, that her mind is disturbed. We know she does not seek the company of others and is rarely ever seen. Though I must tell you, I saw something in her eyes, my lord, that I believe was not meant to be revealed."

"What? What did you see?" Tennington asked, leaning in closer to Brendan.

"I wish I could be sure. I think fear, or possibly a deep sadness. Perhaps even both."

"Fear?" the king repeated under his breath. "This encounter may help with what I am about to ask of you, Brendan. I want you to lead a small delegation into the Blue Witch's realm. I need you to find her and convince her to come speak with me. The Blue Witch may have answers about the evil that's coming into our realm more and more often these days. And she may be able to tell us who sent the assassin and why. Though I believe the concerns about her involvement in the attack to be falsely placed, there are those on my council who remain skeptical of the witch. I think it has been made to look as though she is our enemy, but by whom? She may know this."

Tennington reached forward, brushing something only he'd seen from the table's surface as he paused in thought. "I spoke with Willow on the matter. She's very concerned that there's a dark power at work here. But Willow's been blinded by something and cannot fully use her abilities to help me. The question I fear most is, who is so powerful they could keep Willow from using her special gift of sight and would dare cross the Blue Witch in order to kill me? I fear we are dealing with a threat we will not be able to understand or defeat without the Blue

Witch's help. Something has changed in our realm, Brendan. Something truly evil is at work here. I can feel it in my bones, and I need answers. That is why I need you to find her and convince her to speak with me. I am afraid for our people. We are blind, and we need the Blue Witch's help. She knows your name, and it seems she knows something's wrong."

"She'll kill me!" Brendan blurted out. "It's one thing if she comes to you, here in this realm, but you dare not enter hers! No one has ever done so and lived to tell of it! You know this! She's made it clear nobody's to ever dare attempt crossing the Dead Bridge. It's certain death to do so!"

It was indeed well known that the Blue Witch had made such warnings against crossing the Dead Bridge. Though, in truth, some fools had, of course, tried, thinking themselves special and fearless, only to find they were neither.

King Tennington cocked an eyebrow at Brendan and cleared his throat. "That's why I don't want you going alone. She'll be far less likely to kill an entire delegation under my flag, representing me and this kingdom, than a lone intruder in her forbidden land."

Brendan hesitated a long time before answering. "It is a difficult thing you ask, my lord. But I've never failed you, and I would not wish to in this. I'll make this journey for you, and I will find a way to succeed if it's possible to do so. Though, if I may, I would be so bold as to ask these things of you in turn: I choose those who are to join me. Forgive me, but I do not need politicians, my lord. I need those who can best help me succeed in times of trouble. I would also ask that while supplies are readied, you allow me enough time to see Aria before I depart. As I said, it's her birthday tomorrow, and I've been away from her a great deal of late."

"Of course, Brendan," Tennington replied. "Who would you choose to go with you?"

Brendan did not hesitate, already knowing his mind. "I want Vander, and I would like him to choose two—no, make it three—of his most trusted and capable men. I would like Drake Fallon to serve as our scout, and I want Willow to join us. We'll need her gift of sight if she regains it. If you'd have Vander put that group together along with our supplies, I will see to other matters here, then go see Aria. I'll return before first light. We'll leave as soon as everyone can be gathered. Though I hope all will be ready by the time I return."

"I'll send for Vander at once and have him do what is needed to be ready."

"One more thing, my lord. I must be in charge fully, and all, including Vander, must know this."

"Agreed. It shall be done, so long as Willow and the others agree to go willingly. As with you, I will not command any of them to go, not on this journey."

Brendan stood, bowing deeply to his king, and then he hugged the man. "They'll all agree. Much like myself, they love you too much not to."

Brendan left the palace after seeing to other business. It was a comfortable ride outside the city walls to the small cottage he shared with Aria in the country. Though it was considerably later than he'd intended, he appreciated the natural beauty of twinkling damp leaves reflecting the moonlight of a particularly bright night sky. The clear, star-filled heavens, combined with the mild weather of the season, added to the calm, pleasant ride.

As he approached his home, Brendan saw a flash, then flickering red and orange light through the windows, and heard screams coming from inside the cottage. He leapt from his horse and ran up the stone pathway to the front door. As he reached for the latch, the door flew open and an older, heavyset woman came barreling out with her hair on fire. She ran right smack into him, sending them both sprawling to the ground. Brendan knew immediately who it was.

He quickly gathered himself, grabbed a handful of dirt from the flower bed at his side, threw it over the woman's head, and patted out the last bit of fire. Zilda Frahn stared at him wild-eyed as tendrils of smoke continued to waft from the top of her head. Her unfettered anguish could easily be read through the dirt upon her face as she sat on the ground looking up at him in utter bewilderment.

As her temperature rose and her color changed, Zilda wrinkled up her dirt-streaked face and announced in her low, stern voice, "I quit!"

Aria, stepping through the doorway grinning mischievously, stopped short upon seeing her brother. "Welcome home, Brendan!" she said, looking at the two before her. "This, of course, was a complete accident." She swept her open hand back and forth across the scene innocently.

Zilda, brushing the dirt from what was left of her hair, let out a defiant, "Hah!"

Zilda was their housekeeper and watched over Aria when Brendan had to be away for any length of time. Zilda had threatened to quit many times before, so this was nothing new. Brendan had always managed to convince her to stay on, usually with an increase in pay or a lot of groveling. Sometimes, it took both. Though, looking at her smoldering head, he was pretty sure he would not be able to convince her to stay after this fiasco. Zilda reached out toward Brendan, and he took her hands, helping her to her feet.

"Do not say one word to me, Brendan Pandane, not one word!" Zilda snapped before stomping off into the cottage, muttering as she went, "That girl's going to be the death of me!"

Brendan turned to his sister, looking for answers, as he brushed the dirt from his hands. "What happened this time?"

"It wasn't like before, I swear. It was a simple mistake, really. I was working on creating fireflies, and, um...well, things just spiraled out of my control. It was truly an unfortunate accident," Aria said, shaking her head and staring at her bare feet. She wiggled her toes before peeking up sheepishly at Brendan.

Brendan grabbed her, pulling her quickly to him, and gave her a big hug as he lifted her off the ground and spun her around laughing. "I love you, sister, but I don't know what I'm going to do with you!" He winked at her and set her back on her feet.

Zilda Frahn stormed out of the cottage at a fast pace—well, fast for her, anyway—her things stuffed unceremoniously under her arms, and headed down the path leading to the small road that passed in front of the cottage. With her hair singed so much that she was nearly bald and her face still streaked with dirt and rage, Zilda shouted over her shoulder without looking back toward the two siblings, "You may send me my final pay, Master Pandane! And be a good lad and include something extra for my hair!" With that, she waddled off down the road disheveled and grunting as she struggled with her items. A rather large pair of white bloomers waved in her wake, as if signaling her surrender.

"Well, Aria Pandane, you've put me in a bind once again!" Brendan said, laughing anew. "Pack up your clothes and anything you'll need for an extended stay, then get yourself to bed. We leave for the palace very early in the morning. I'll wake you when it's time and explain things along the way."

"I love you," Aria said, flashing a quick smile before heading off to do as she was told.

"Oh, how I pity the man who marries that girl," Brendan muttered, shaking his head.

It was very early, and still well before daylight, when Brendan woke Aria. The cottage was soon put in order and locked up tight. Their horses were saddled and they were ready to depart when Brendan handed his sister a small package wrapped in brightly colored cloth.

"Happy birthday, Aria!"

Aria squealed with excitement and opened her gift. She stopped and stood silent, her hands trembling as she held it. Aria looked up at Brendan, her eyes filling with tears. "Mother's?" she asked, her voice shaking.

Brendan nodded, afraid to speak with the lump in his throat. Aria held up the pendant and looked at it closely, admiring its beauty. It was pure silver and finely detailed with engraved symbols and a clear dark-red stone set in its center. It hung from a silver chain necklace that was delicate looking but incredibly strong.

The pendant had been in their family for generations but had been missing from their mother's body after the explosion in the mine. Aria was aware of this, but Brendan would never tell her the real story of how he'd gotten their mother's pendant back. Brendan was determined that Aria would never know of his part in the Rooster Massacre. He'd decided that immediately afterward and saw no reason for her to ever know the awful truth of what he'd done. Nor would Aria ever know any part of what the thief had done to their mother as she lay helplessly trapped in the mine begging for the man's mercy.

"I came across it quite by accident in a small shop in Datton and purchased it for you." This was the white lie he'd decided to tell her. "I originally planned to give it to you on your sixteenth birthday."

Aria looked at her brother knowingly. "But something has changed."

"I'm going on a journey at the king's request. I will be leaving as soon as we arrive at the palace, and I expect I'll be gone for an extended period of time. You'll have to stay there until I return. I thought it would be nice for you to have Mother's—"

"You're concerned, and far more than usual, that you won't return."

"I always have, and I expect I will this time as well," he said, even though he didn't believe it to be a reasonably sure thing himself.

"You're a terrible liar, Brendan, you haven't the knack for it. You're concerned, very concerned, and you know it. Maybe you'll tell me someday, if you do manage to return, how you really got mother's pendant back. I know you didn't just buy it in some shop," she said, cocking her head. "Keep your secrets if you must." She sighed. "I would beg you not to go, but I know it would be pointless, so I will say only this." Tears began to fill her eyes once again. "Please return to me." She moved toward him and hugged him as tightly as she could. "You are all the family I have, and I could not bear to lose you. Do not leave me alone in this world, I beg you." She released him and looked up at her brother, her tear-filled eyes meeting his. "Thank you for Mother's pendant, it is the perfect gift." Aria turned away and pulled herself up onto her horse. With a gentle nudge, she started down the road toward the palace without looking back.

They arrived at the palace a short time later to find everyone Brendan had requested, along with three of

Vander Ray's men, making final preparations to leave. Vander, seeing Willow approaching Brendan, quickly grabbed his younger brother, Starlin, by the arm.

"Watch this, Starlin!" Vander pointed across the way to Brendan and the young girl approaching him from behind. "The seer is about to tell him."

Brendan, feeling a light touch on his arm from behind, came to a stop and turned about. "Willow! Good morning! I'm glad you're joining us."

Willow was very young. Brendan believed her to be eight years old now. Her auburn hair, spilling down far past her shoulders, had always had a wild look about it, and this morning was no different. It was not that it was unkempt or even windblown; her hair simply looked like it belonged to a wild animal. He found the child's large hazel eyes and soft features a bit out of place beneath such wild hair.

Though she was so young, Willow's gift of sight could not be denied; it had been proven accurate far too many times. Nobody knew who Willow really was or where she'd come from, not even Willow herself. Willow had been found abandoned on the palace grounds as a much younger child, along with a simple note stating her name and asking for her to be cared for. King Tennington himself had unsealed and read the note. He'd taken her in, seeing to it she was well cared for. Willow had been a favorite among the palace staff ever since.

"Good morning, Brendan. I must speak with you. It is most urgent," Willow said.

"Of course. Walk with me," he replied. "How may I help you?" Brendan asked as the two strolled just out of earshot of the group preparing to leave.

"I cannot see the Blue Witch. I cannot assure you we will find her, or that she'll help us if we do. I'm afraid, Brendan. I'm afraid I may be of no value to you on this journey."

"I'm hoping you'll see more when we draw nearer to her; that's why I requested you join us."

"It's my hope as well. I still see some things, though, and you are not going to like what I have to tell you."

"I asked for you," he said, "because I need your special sight to help me make the best decisions I can for the success of this journey. Please do not hold anything back from me, no matter how unpleasant you may think it to be. Can I count on you for this?"

"As you wish." Willow took a long pause before speaking again. "There are two others who must make this journey with us. I have already informed Vander, so that we may be as prepared as possible. The first is Starlin Ray. Vander refused at first, but I convinced him he must summon his brother here, and he has. I know you intend to leave Aria at the palace while we're gone," Willow continued. "That can't happen. She must come with us."

Brendan shook his head defiantly. "No! Absolutely not!" he said, louder than he would have liked, drawing looks from those closest to them. He glanced back at those who were now watching and noticed Vander and Starlin staring directly at him. "I'm concerned enough about bringing you along. But at least if you have your sight, you can see danger coming."

"Hopefully. Brendan, there is an evil presence here at the palace, but its form is hidden from me. I know this much, though: Aria must come with us. Vander has put the King's Watch on high alert and has briefed his second-in-command about my concerns. You must not leave Aria behind. I believe she'll play an important part in what's to come, though I do not yet see how. I know there's great danger in making this journey, but I assure you, for Aria and Starlin, it would be far more dangerous for them to stay here. You must trust me on this, Brendan. Our king is concerned about my going as well, and even had second thoughts and tried to convince me I shouldn't. But I wish to go, and I've convinced him that I should," she said.

"Yesterday I felt something evil, something of death, in the Great Hall, but I couldn't find the source of it either. I must agree with your concerns; I'm afraid they confirm my own. So. There you have it, Willow!"

"Have what?"

"You have already proven your value to this journey, and we haven't even taken our first step. Well done! I'll let Aria know she's going to be joining us," Brendan said with a warm smile. Willow, beaming with pride, strolled away with a noticeable bounce in her step.

With all preparations made and Aria thrilled to be joining them, the small group's members made what introductions were needed among them. They then said their goodbyes to those they would be leaving behind and mounted their horses. As the sky before them showed the first signs of brightening with the dawn of a new day, they began their journey to the Dead Bridge.

Chapter 2

Brendan had seen to one other detail before departing Andavar. He'd asked King Tennington that all pay due to him be delivered to Zilda Frahn instead. It was a hefty bonus for her hair and troubles. He smiled as he rode away thinking about how surprised she'd be. Though he still didn't have any illusions it would change anything when and if they returned.

Brendan rode beside Vander as the two led their party out of the capital city of Andavar west toward the Shale Mountains and the coastline beyond. The members of the group had packed and dressed for the unexpected. They all carried warm travel cloaks, though they were not expecting to need them, even in the mountains, at this time of year. All, including the two young girls, were dressed in travel pants, boots, and soft tunics. Aria and Willow were the only two of the group who were not heavily armed.

"We'll ride to Datton before crossing through the Shale Mountains and on to the Sea River," Brendan said to Vander. "We'll hire a barge to take our party south out of Ravens Burg as far as we can convince them to take us, hopefully all the way down to Inlet Bay. But first, there's a healer in Datton that I hope will join us. He's as good as I've ever seen. He worked on my wounds from the Sintin. He's young and adventurous, and seemed quite intrigued by how I'd come by such wounds. He confided to me he has no family he knows of and no plans to stay in Datton. He wants to see and do things he would never have a chance to experience there. I believe he would be willing to join us."

"I hope you're right. A healer could come in handy," Vander replied.

The journey to Datton was uneventful, and the young healer, Drae Tine, did indeed join them as Brendan had hoped, completing their party. Brendan and his group set off for Ravens Burg, moving quickly and stopping only for brief meals and a little rest as they rode southwest through the Shale Mountains.

They camped at night but did not stop until it was late, and they continued on early each morning. Brendan assured them all there would be plenty of time for rest once they were aboard the barge and heading south on the Sea River.

Brendan expected the journey downriver to take three full days if all went well and he was able to secure a barge to take them all the way to Inlet Bay. Sending the barge back up the coastline would be easy enough. The barge would be towed behind a sailing ship, but it would be costly. Fortunately, Tennington had provided them with plenty of funds.

Aria and Willow spent a great deal of time riding together. They'd met on a few occasions prior and now bonded quickly. The two girls were enjoying the journey and each other's company immensely. It made sense, Brendan thought; they were, after all, the youngest in the group, and the only girls.

The group's scout, Drake Fallon, spent most of his time riding alone, and was more comfortable doing so. Drake was, however, quite charming and friendly whenever another member of the group approached him. He was simply used to spending long periods of time alone and was very content to do so. Drake was a lean man with hawkish features and as tough as knotted leather. His skin, weathered and scarred by both time and exposure to the elements, left no doubt that he'd spent years traversing the wilds of their lands.

The group settled into an order comfortable for all soon after departing Datton. Vander and Starlin rode out front with Vlix Bade, a man hand-chosen by Vander for his vast experience and intelligence. He was an impressive man with the look of a grizzled veteran yet still very much in his prime. His dark skin and his hair, which showed no signs of graying, gave no hint of his true age. Brendan assumed he was nearing fifty years old. Willow and Aria rode behind them, followed by Brendan and the young healer Drae Tine. Brendan did not ask, but he thought Drae was two or possibly three years younger than himself. He found, as they rode, that Drae was quieter and a bit more reserved than he remembered from his first encounter with him. Drae's short brown hair and gray eyes contributed to his studious look, fitting for a healer.

Asten Sten and Trite Mantay, the other two men hand-selected by Vander, rode in the rear. Asten was also an impressive man of note, and had a regal look about him. With dark eyes, long black hair, and a neatly trimmed beard to match, Asten was the tallest of the group. Trite was far younger than the other two men. He was bright-eyed, with softer features and the slighter build of a fit, youthful man. His long, flowing light-blond hair and stormy blue eyes were striking features of the gregarious young man.

Brendan was very pleased with the men Vander had selected. He found each one to be engaging, well spoken, and well respected by his peers. His traveling companions, with the exception of Aria and Starlin, had been selected not for what they knew about their own kingdom but rather for their unique skills to help face what none of them knew of the Blue Witch's and what dangers they might encounter there. Brendan and Vander had made one thing abundantly clear to all of the men: if there was any trouble, they were to protect the two girls above all.

Brendan knew he would be relying on something rather thin when it came time to face the Blue Witch. She had come to him only days before and somehow knew him by name. How could that be? Either way, she had done him no harm then, and something in her voice and eyes had made him believe that she would speak with him before simply destroying them all for entering her forbidden land. It was all he could truly place any hope in. That, or she would forgive their trespass and agree to the king's request to speak with her, for her own purposes.

One night after they'd made camp, to keep everyone loose and get a better measure of the men Vander had selected, Brendan decided to train with him and his men. He found he was even more pleased with Vander's choices; Vlix, Asten, and Trite were very advanced in their weapons training and skills. He also spent some time working with Aria at her request. Aria impressed the company, demonstrating her speed and agility, as well as a fair amount of skill with a blade for someone so young. Though she never wished to carry a blade herself, she loved training with her brother.

"She's taught me everything I know," Brendan joked. When they had finished for the night, Brendan pulled

Vander aside to speak with him. "Well done, Vander, I am very pleased with the men you selected."

"To be honest, I thought about bringing three particularly friendly chambermaids I know of instead, since we are most likely going to die soon," Vander replied with a smirk. "At least we may have had a little fun on this death march!" He laughed out loud at his own joke. "So, tell me, my friend, what's your plan when we get to the Dead Bridge?"

"I don't know what we'll find when we cross over the bridge, but we will stay together, and all will stay behind me. I will bear the king's flag. I have reason to believe the Blue Witch will at least hear me out before she decides what she will do with us. I've given it a lot of thought, and I don't believe she'll harm us if I'm given the chance to speak with her."

"Well, from what I know, if you enter her realm, you never return. Let's hope you're right, for all our sakes," Vander said, looking back toward those of the small group who were laughing and talking among themselves around the campfire. "Or those good people there, along with the two of us, will become a cautionary tale about undertaking a fool's mission. To my knowledge, the Blue Witch has never harmed a citizen in our realm. But she's killed every single one who's tried to enter hers. Or"—he paused in thought—"something there has."

Brendan looked to the rest of the group and then back to Vander. "I know, my friend, I know. We have no idea what we'll be walking into."

When the group arrived in Ravens Burg the next day, it was late afternoon. They'd made good time, and Brendan hoped to cut another day from their journey south. If they were lucky and could make the arrangements needed to head downriver first thing in the morning, there was a good chance they would.

"Drake and I will see about the barge. Vander will oversee our other needs with your help," he said to the rest of the group, "including securing rooms for the night at a suitable inn. Let's meet back at that big fountain over there by sunset. I wish for us to share a nice meal together this evening. Until then…" Brendan said to the group. He gave Aria a hug and Willow a wink before heading off to the docks with Drake.

Brendan's mind began to focus on what was needed from the barge company, and on a stop he wished to make before leaving Ravens Burg. Brendan and Drake arrived at their destination a short time later and entered the office of the Sea River Barge Company.

"Welcome! Welcome, my friends!" a large, very fit man with a thin beard shouted out from behind a long, narrow counter at the back of the room. "I am Baird Prow. I am known in these parts as Bear. How may I assist you gentlemen?"

"Well met, Bear," Brendan responded. "We seek passage for a party of ten, including as many horses and three additional pack animals, to Inlet Bay. We wish to leave at first light. Can you accommodate us?"

"I can, but it won't come cheap, my friends. There's a lot of downtime on the return trip, and I'd have to contract with a ship to get my barge back up the coast. You're in luck, though, this day, my friends! My newest and largest barge is available to you and your party. It's the finest in the land, if I do say so myself. And she's without equal in size and comfort, I might add. I designed her myself."

"What would you have to charge your new friends here for your services?" Brendan asked with a smile.

"I would not feel right sending my prized new barge that far unless I made the trip personally, and my time does not come cheap. Hmm." He stroked his beard for a moment. "I would want my best crew; that's five additional men. They do not come cheap either, of course."

"Of course," Brendan agreed.

"We would need supplies for three days and an emergency supply for three additional days," Bear added. "And all the supplies needed by my men and me for the return trip, of course."

"Sounds about right," Brendan agreed once again.

"Very well, let me write up the order, and we shall see where we stand."

Bear had it tallied up and an agreement ready in short order. He slid the agreement across the counter to Brendan and waited. Brendan took the paper and studied it closely. He found the price was no more than he'd expected, neither outlandish nor in any way unfair. He could not help but notice Bear's use of "Premium Service" in the order's wording.

"Bear, I find the charges agreeable. Therefore, I will not haggle with you. We will pay half on departure, the balance on arrival. We are paying a large sum for what you state is premium service, and we will expect nothing less. I must assume that you are a man of your word, and one who deserves our trust, until it is proven otherwise. But so that there is no misunderstanding, I warn you: We are in the service of King Tennington and are acting on his behalf. There will be no games played and no excuses or impropriety of any kind. You will be held responsible for your actions, as well as the actions of those in your employ. Are we agreed on this?"

"We are indeed, my friends. I pride myself on my service and my honesty. Please feel free to inquire about my reputation anywhere you wish. If you are not satisfied with what you hear, we will part friends, and you may take your business where you please."

"Well spoken, Bear. We shall see you on your dock by first light." The two men shook hands on their agreement, and as they did, Brendan noted the size of the big man's powerful hand, which nearly engulfed his own.

"Until then," Bear said, clasping Brendan's shoulder with his free hand.

Brendan and Drake left Bear and headed back toward their designated meeting spot. After they'd walked some distance, Brendan asked, "What is your measure of the man, Drake?"

"Dangerous!" Drake answered. "My guess is he is not only respected but feared in this area, and none would dare speak against him even if he wasn't an honest man, which I believe him to be. Baird Prow; I'm not sure, but I think I've heard his name before."

"I think you're correct on all counts. If his barge and men are as capable as I believe him to be, we should be in good hands. We have plenty of time to spare, and I would like to stop at that armorer we passed. I wish to make an inquiry about some weapons and possibly a purchase, if you'll indulge me."

"I had intended to ask you myself," Drake responded with a gleam in his eye.

The two reached the shop they were heading for in short order. The sign out front read, *The Raven's Sword.* The shop sat on the corner of two of the busier streets in Ravens Burg. It was an older shop to be sure, but it was well tended and featured a curved stained-glass window in front that wrapped around the corner following the contour of the building. A large raven perched on a sword with a golden grip, with its wings spread wide as if it were about to take flight, graced the window.

Brendan and Drake, however, wasted little time admiring the shop's window before entering. The boy tending the shop gave them a friendly wave as the bell above the door signaling their presence settled. He then swept his arm wide, indicating they were welcome to look around as they pleased.

The two men quickly became engrossed looking at the vast array of items displayed in great glass cases. A variety of swords in different sizes and even shapes were displayed. Some featured strange curved blades, but most were more traditional in appearance. Some were very ornate, others all business.

A rather large assortment of other weapons was also on display in the shop. Daggers of all sorts and sizes, bows, arrows, throwing knives, and a great many more were available to be purchased. Brendan, after looking for some time, spoke with the young shopkeeper. He learned the boy's name was Davron, and his father, who was away on business, owned the place.

"Davron, I'm looking for something small that would fit in your hand and could be thrown, exploding on contact. Do you offer such a thing?" Brendan inquired.

"A flash pod," Davron replied. "We do, sir, but I'm afraid we only sell those to customers we've had a long relationship with. Wouldn't want just anybody running around with those things."

"Davron, I have not properly introduced myself. I am Brendan Pandane, High Sword to King Tennington. My companion Drake Fallon and I are here on the king's business." Brendan got the response he was looking for, as Davron straightened himself and his clothes with a look of concern upon his face.

"I've heard of you, High Sword, and I assure you, my father and I are loyal to the king and have done nothing to warrant a visit from you."

"My guess is you'll survive this visit, Davron." Brendan glanced to Drake and winked before turning back. "So long as you answer my questions truthfully, that is."

"I'm at your service, High Sword," Davron managed to say before exhaling the breath he'd been holding.

"I recently came across a man in possession of one of these flash pods. I believe he may have purchased it here."

"He almost certainly did. I know of no other armorer in the kingdom that offers what we do when it comes to such things. What was his name? Perhaps I know him."

"I don't know his name. The man was tall, with dark hair and eyes, and in excellent physical condition. He wore two small silver rings on his right hand. Didn't have any facial hair but had a large scar above his left eye."

"I know the man you're speaking of. His name is Zantan. I know little else about him except he makes purchases here with an account he does not feel obligated to pay. My father hates Zantan but fears him terribly and won't say anything about the balance to him. He'd be furious knowing I spoke of it, but I hope we never have to see Zantan again."

"Oh, you won't," Brendan replied, casually looking about, "unless he has the ability to rise from the dead. A good friend of mine put his sword through the man's neck."

"What a shame," Davron quipped, clearly pleased by the man's demise. "I will inform my father not to expect payment of his account."

"Our king would not want your father out what he is due from Zantan. How much does he owe?" Brendan inquired. After receiving the number, Brendan paid the bill in full, to the great pleasure of Davron.

"Many thanks to King Tennington, and to you, High Sword. My father will be most pleased when he returns."

"Very well. Now that we have that settled, I wish to purchase those flash pods. How many do you have?"

"I've got an even dozen available now. How many do you want?"

"I want them all, of course," Brendan said, smiling.

The Blue Witch

After Davron carefully showed both Brendan and Drake how to use the flash pods, the two departed to meet with the others. They reached the fountain to find their group had arrived only moments before them. Vander and the others had managed to secure rooms for the group, stable their horses, and even replenish a few supplies.

"We won't be able to eat at the inn this evening," Vander announced as he sat on the fountain's edge, splashing his fingers in the water casually. "Their chef's getting married tomorrow, and he's out of town along with most of the help. Sounds like it's gonna be a pretty big wedding. Anyway, we're on our own for dinner."

They strolled down the street to find a suitable eating establishment and soon came upon an inviting tavern named the Raven's Nest, which offered meals. There, they were provided a suitable private room in which to enjoy their dinner. They found the tavern to be clean and the food surprisingly good. Their meal was served to them family style at a long single table. The fare featured a variety of meats and warm bread, with plenty of honey and fresh butter. Large bowls of mashed potatoes, flavored rice, and vegetables were placed on the table as well. An assortment of small cakes and pies was brought to the table afterward and consumed quickly by the group. Brendan had ordered that no strong drink was to be served, so plenty of water and enticing fruit drinks were provided instead. When they'd finished their meal, Brendan stood and addressed the group.

"Everyone knows where we're heading. It's uncertain what we'll find once we cross the Dead Bridge, but we'll stay together when we cross. I'll lead us. I'll share with you now that the Blue Witch came to me recently and spoke my name. I believe if she sees me, she will at least hear me out. The Dead Bridge is a long day's ride from Inlet Bay, and we will make for it immediately after we dock. So, rest up while we're on the river. Are there any questions?"

There were none, and the group soon departed for the inn they would be staying at for the night. The streets of Ravens Burg were bustling now under the oil lamps lining them. The shops were still open for business, and their patrons were giving them a reason to be so. The evening air was filled with the rich, pungent scents of a merchants' row. Sounds of singing and music could be heard from performers busking on the streets, and occasionally from those entertaining patrons within an establishment.

Brendan's group did not stop as they weaved their way through the crowded streets on their way to their inn for a much-needed night's rest. Then Bear appeared on the street ahead, working his way toward them through the sea of people.

"We've got to get your horses and supplies. We need to leave here immediately."

"Why?" Brendan demanded.

"You have powerful enemies, my friend, and they're here looking for you!"

Brendan, heeding Bear's warning, wasted no further time with questions. There would be time on the barge to ask more. The group, with Bear's help, retrieved their supplies and horses and headed straight for the docks. Bear's crewmen were already there, preparing the barge for their departure early the next morning. As they approached, Bear began shouting orders to his men.

"Get it all on board now, we leave immediately!"

To their credit, the crew jumped into action. Some finished hoisting supplies from the dock onto the deck, while others went to the lines and prepared to cast off. Bear did not slow, leading Brendan's group and their animals straight up the wide gangplank onto the barge. They were away and floating safely down the Sea River in mere moments, leaving the docks and lights of Ravens Burg behind.

Chapter 3

B ear looked Brendan up and down as if he were seeing him for the first time and shook his head.

"I've briefed my men and given them their orders," He said shortly after their harried departure.

"Sounds like we should talk," Brendan replied.

"I was not aware my men and I were signing on for anything inherently dangerous."

"I wasn't aware there was any inherent danger until you told me of it. What else can you tell me, Bear?"

"My sources, and I have very good ones, told me the High Sword tortured and killed a Sintin recently. And he and the captain of the Watch killed Zantan. Apparently, Zantan was the assassin who made the attempt on Tennington's life in the palace gardens recently. I was also told the Sintin and Zantan were thought to be in the service of a powerful being. No one knows who it is for sure, but the Blue Witch may be behind it all. Though I doubt that myself."

"You are well informed, Bear. You must have very good sources indeed."

"Indeed I do, my friend. Here's the interesting part: it's thought the Sintin's attack on the boy was designed with the express purpose of drawing the High Sword away from the palace. My sources believe it was intended the Sintin would kill you, giving the assassin a better chance of killing Tennington. No one knows why Zantan was delayed in his part, but it allowed you to return before he could carry out his assignment. Perhaps he assumed the Sintin would kill you and he would have more time. Perhaps something else detained him. The point is, you spoiled somebody's plans, Brendan, and they've come looking for you."

"I've unknowingly put you and your men in peril. That was not part of our agreement."

"No, it certainly wasn't. But my men and I will defend this barge and your party with our lives if necessary. We're loyal to the king and would never consider refusing help to those in his service, no matter the danger. Now, I must confess something to you we have not had a chance to speak of yet. When I found you and your party on the street in Ravens Burg, I realized I know one of your companions. If you will assemble your people here, I will call my crew together. I think you're going to like this!" He smiled. Brendan gave the big man a puzzled look but nodded. When they had all gathered, Bear addressed them.

"I know one of you, though before this evening, you knew nothing of me. Vander Ray, please step forward." Now it was Vander's turn to give Bear a puzzled look as he stepped toward him. "Allow me to explain," Bear said. "I knew your father. I served with him for many years. We all did." He swept his arm toward his crew. Bear turned to his men and shouted, "First to charge!"

"Last to die!" the men returned in unison. Bear fell in line with his men, facing Vander.

37

"It is with great pleasure that we welcome Commander Zake Ray's son and his companions aboard the *Elite*."

"Welcome!" they called out together as one. They each approached Vander in turn and shook his hand firmly before returning to their duties.

Brendan looked to Drake, who was standing with him and Asten.

"Well, I guess that answers that question. I believe we can safely trust Bear and his men of the Elite First."

"I should think so!" Drake replied.

Asten nodded his head in steadfast agreement. "I've never met the man, but I've heard of Baird Prow. He didn't just serve in the Elite, he's a legend among their ranks."

The *Elite* was every bit as impressive as Bear had indicated, sleeker and larger than normal river barges of the day. Its long cargo deck looked like a sword laid flat, a special part of Bear's design, and was virtually empty except for the few supplies that had been stored toward the stern near the pilothouse. The barge had been designed to accommodate its passengers comfortably, featuring several cabins and a cozy but adequate indoor area for dining, allowing passengers to gather and socialize, even in bad weather. The *Elite* was painted a stormy dark gray that could appear black at a casual glance. Bear's design gave it the look of something built more for battle than cargo and passenger transport.

One of Bear's crewmen, a man by the name of Tay, helped Brendan and Vander get their people settled into their cabins, then showed them around the *Elite*.

Tay was the youngest member of the crew and seemed to be favored by Bear. Tay had been very friendly and extremely helpful while getting Brendan and his people settled into their cabins earlier that evening.

Brendan had found he liked Tay and had taken the time to speak with him and Vander further before retiring for the night.

"I loved your father, Vander. I was very sorry to hear that he'd passed before his time. He took a special interest in me for reasons I cannot explain, but I will never forget his kindness. Bear tells me that Commander Ray made all his men feel special, but that makes it no less personal or special to me. He was a great man and a big influence in my life."

"Thank you for telling me, Tay. I miss that man today as much as I ever have. I serve to honor his memory."

The *Elite* floated through the still night down the Sea River, drifting south on its journey to Inlet Bay. As it did, Brendan was having a restless night contemplating everything that Bear had told him earlier. He'd shared their conversation only with Vander. He'd wished to get his thoughts on the matter and didn't want to burden their companions with limited explanations and speculation.

Vander and he had discussed the information and what they should do about it at length. They'd come to the conclusion that there was nothing they could do except continue to follow the course they were already on. There was no reason to think the enemy could get to Inlet Bay before them. Traveling the river was far faster than going overland. They could not be sure the enemy even knew they'd left on the river, and it would take even more time to discover they had. And their enemy would have to secure a barge of their own if they planned to chase them on the river itself. It was unlikely to happen quickly, and this mysterious enemy would be far behind them with no chance of catching up.

Rising from his bunk, Brendan left the cabin he shared with Drae. Earlier, Drae had applied some more salve to Brendan's shoulder and other wounds he was still healing from, and it had done wonders for the pain. He tested his shoulder gingerly and stretched his back and legs, finding them feeling as well as they had in a very long time.

Brendan strolled out onto the *Elite*'s deck and let his eyes adjust to the dimmer light he found there. It was pleasant and calm on the river, though the night sky was dark with heavy clouds blocking out the stars above him. He was looking over the water, admiring the vast size of the Sea River, when Willow and Aria approached him.

"What are you two doing up?"

"I have something to report to you," Willow said. "I've had a vision. I've seen the enemy that comes for us. Brendan, we will not make it through this night before they find us!"

"Come with me, both of you!" He took them into the dining room, and they each took a seat at a small table. "Quickly now, tell me everything, Willow, and leave nothing out." When Willow finished, Brendan escorted the two young girls back to their cabin and instructed them to wait there. "I'll return as soon as I can," he assured them before leaving to warn the others.

Brendan informed Tay, who was standing watch, that he needed Bear urgently and asked that he meet him on deck. He also requested that Bear have his crew gather and meet his party in the dining room as soon as possible.

Brendan quickly rousted Vander and Starlin, instructing them to get Vander's men, and wake and inform Drake and Drae as well. Brendan retrieved Aria and Willow from their cabin, and they headed to the deck to meet Bear. The three found the big man on deck waiting for them a few moments later.

"I assume we have trouble!" Bear called out as they approached.

"Willow, our seer, has informed me our enemies will be joining us before this night is over. Bear, I have no idea how they could know where we are or how they will approach us. Willow's sight is being blocked for the most part by an unknown force, but her gift is strong, and she still manages to get some visions."

"Perhaps they have a seer as well," Bear mused.

"Vander and I had the same thought. Willow tells me we will be attacked well before sunrise, but not for a good while yet."

"Then they will be coming by air. The river is too wide to attack from land with any accuracy or effect."

"Our thought as well, but not being familiar with this river, or the area along it, we didn't want to assume anything. I don't suppose the *Elite* has any defenses for an aerial attack..." Brendan hesitated at the smile that crossed Bear's face. "Or does it?"

Bear gave him a pat on the shoulder. "Remember, I designed this vessel. We have dealt with river pirates for years. I designed and crewed the *Elite* to deter even the bravest of them. We'll be able to defend ourselves."

"Good! Let's get ready to greet them."

The attack did indeed come before sunrise. Aria, Willow, Starlin, and Drae had all been secured in a cleverly hidden cabin under the pilothouse. They were instructed to lock down, stay put, and not leave the cabin until they were informed it was safe.

The attack came by air, as Bear had predicted, from men flying Zaroes—large birdlike creatures, the deformed products of failed magical experiments. Each Zaroe had two flyers. Both men sat in a special open-air compartment harnessed beneath the winged creature. One flyer controlled the Zaroe, the other the weapons. The creatures no longer had many feathers. Most looked like they'd been pretty well plucked except for the tail feathers and a few strays that stuck out like darts on a well-used board. Huge, thin-skinned wings allowed them to fly.

41

Each wing tip ended in a clawed hand. Zaroes had massive talons and possessed two heads, each with large bright-yellow eyes and a sharp hooked beak. They were hideous creatures subverted by magic for one purpose only: war.

There were at least twenty of them in the attack, though it was hard to tell the exact number as they darted through the dark night sky above the *Elite*. Their attack came fast and without any further warning, but the men aboard the *Elite* were ready, and they put up a ferocious fight in defense of the barge.

The Zaroes were hard to see until nearly the last second. Their weapons were mostly firedrops: heavy glass globes filled with firewash, a thick, highly flammable liquid that would ignite on contact when the globe shattered. Despite the crew's efforts, the firedrops were taking a heavy toll on the barge. Bear had several colorful words for their attackers as he fought alongside the others aboard the *Elite* to control the fires and repel the assault.

The crew of the *Elite* fired battle slings raised from hidden compartments within the deck. But the slings were too slow and were having no success hitting their targets. Brendan desperately loaded all twelve flash pods into one of the slings. The shot, made by a dark-haired man named Olin, brought one of the Zaroes and its flyers crashing to the deck. It slid through a pool of firewash, igniting the firedrops it still carried. The winged creature thrashed and rolled, throwing its two flyers, leaving them sprawled out on the deck screaming as they tried desperately to douse the flames consuming them.

The Zaroe, screeching furiously, tried to take to the air. Vander, who was quickly joined by Brendan, attacked the downed bird before it could rise. The two men, ducking and rolling away often, avoided the thrashing creature and the fires. Brendan, seeing an opening, ran full speed, catapulting himself off one of the thinly skinned wings high into the air. Swinging his sword with great force, he relieved the Zaroe of one of its heads. The great bird, flopping about the deck wildly and flapping its wings futilely, tumbled over the side rail into the river. The two flyers had been nearly consumed by the firewash. Their ghastly remains lay smoldering on the dark deck of the *Elite* beside their Zaroe's severed head.

Unseen until it was too late, one of the Zaroes dipped out of the clouds, grabbed one of Bear's men from the deck, and carried him off into the night. Bear ran desperately, calling out the man's name.

"Tay! Tay!" Bear looked into the dark sky screaming, "Tay!"

To his credit, Tay was still fighting and swinging his sword as he disappeared from sight.

A moment later, a terrifying scream came out of somewhere in the darkness above. Tay fell from the sky, slamming into the front edge of the pilothouse and spinning wildly down onto the deck in a broken heap. Bear ran to him, sliding to his knees beside him. Lifting Tay gently, Bear held him close. Tay, gasping and coughing, sprayed blood and froth from his mouth uncontrollably. His broken body convulsed and seized violently as Bear attempted to comfort him. Tay settled in Bear's arms and his eyes closed. Bear leaned in close to him and spoke in his ear.

"First to charge."

Tay, making every attempt to respond, coughed again, spraying more blood. He opened his eyes and looked into Bear's. He smiled, gasping, "Last to…" Unable to finish the battle cry, Tay lay dead in Bear's arms.

All other attempts to bring the Zaroes down were futile. They were losing the battle and would soon lose the *Elite*. Fires were burning out of control everywhere, and the men could not put them out fast enough. Firedrops continued to rain down, igniting more fires and burning the men as they fought on bravely, even knowing all would soon be lost.

Asten, as he was running across the deck to help fight another of the fires, was hit directly by one of the firedrops and went stumbling over the side into the dark water of the river. Vander ran to the railing but could do nothing as he watched Asten burning alive beneath the water's surface, grasping wildly for a miracle never to come. As Vander watched, Asten slipped away until he was nothing but a dull glow in the river's depths behind the barge.

"We've got to get everybody inside and head for shore!" Bear shouted to Vander as he fought the fire nearest him. Vander sprinted across the deck spreading the word to the battle-worn men. They had no sooner made it inside and secured the door than Willow and Aria came running to Brendan from out of their hiding place.

"Take Aria out on deck now! Do it, or all will be lost!" Willow called out.

Brendan hesitated a moment, then took Aria's hand, opened the door, and stepped out onto the deck with his sister.

The Zaroes and their flyers were wreaking havoc unchecked on the *Elite*. They were swarming much closer now, and one of them noticed the two siblings and came straight for them. Aria, acting before Brendan could pull her to safety, rolled away from her brother and came to her feet in front of the Zaroe. She threw up her hands and turned the Zaroe to stone. The stone Zaroe and its flyers fell toward the river on the far side of the barge. Multiple firedrops ignited as one when they hit the surface, lighting up the night sky.

Aria looked at Brendan and quickly held out her hand, warning him to stay back. She began waving her hands quicker, and the Zaroes started dropping into the river on both sides of the barge. Each one burst into flames that continued to burn on the surface of the water. It was over in mere moments as the last of the Zaroes fell from the sky into the Sea River and were engulfed in fire.

The *Elite* continued to drift with the current away from the slicks of fire lighting up the river channel behind them. Aria turned her attention to the fires still burning on the *Elite*'s deck and created a strong rainstorm over the barge, washing most of the burning liquid off and into the river. Brendan looked at her with his mouth hanging open in awe. Aria, with her red hair flying out behind her, looked a bit like the flames she was fighting as she moved about the deck extinguishing the last of the fires. When she finished, she walked back to the pilothouse, where Brendan was crouching in stunned silence.

Brendan grabbed her and held her tight. "You're amazing, Aria! How did you do that?" he asked, holding her at arm's length, looking for her response. Before she could say anything, the door behind the two siblings flew open, and Willow and the remaining survivors aboard the *Elite* poured out. Bear, along with his four crewmembers, looked around trying to figure out what had just transpired. Unable to do so, they crossed the deck to retrieve Tay's body.

Vander and his men fell in line to show their respect to Tay and his companions. Brendan and the others joined them. All stood silent and waited patiently as Bear and his men carefully placed Tay's broken body on a wooden plank and carried him belowdecks.

Nobody was interested in sleeping now, and Brendan's group sat in the dining room, quietly reflecting on the night's events. Bear stayed belowdecks. His remaining four men had gathered outside the dining room and were talking quietly among themselves before Olin stepped through the door. The man had clearly been shaken by something and struggled to speak as Brendan's group waited patiently for him to find his words.

"I apologize. We do not wish to appear rude. We are unsure if it is our place to say but have decided we should inform you regardless." The man paused, visibly distraught. "Tay was Bear's younger brother."

Chapter 4

Morning on the river came with a slow drizzle and misty gray clouds that blotted out the sun. The gloomy start to the day mirrored the heavy hearts of those aboard the *Elite*. Even in the weak morning light, the damage to the barge was evident. The crew set about their work, doing what they could to make repairs and evaluate any serious safety concerns. Though the barge had sustained heavy fire damage, particularly to the decking, the crew found it had actually held up well enough to safely continue on without stopping to make more serious repairs.

Bear appeared up on deck for the first time since they'd taken Tay's body below, and Brendan approached him immediately.

"My deepest sympathy for your loss," Brendan said— and immediately stepped back in the face of the change washing over Bear as the big man stepped toward him.

"If you knew your sister was capable of defeating them so easily…" He trailed off, choking back tears. He shook his head and leaned in closer. "Why did you jeopardize us! Was my brother's life worth keeping your sister's secret?"

"Bear, I assure you, nobody knew Aria could do that, not even Aria. We knew she had the use of some small magic, but she did not have much control over it. I spoke with Willow and Aria last night after things settled down. While they were locked away in your hidden cabin, Willow had a vision of Aria doing what she did, and how she would be able to. Willow explained this to Aria, and they came running to me. You were there, remember?" he asked, placing his hand on Bear's shoulder. Bear did not speak but nodded.

"Aria turned fourteen years old the morning our group left the palace on our journey here. I gave her a very special gift for her birthday, a pendant that had belonged to our mother. That pendant has somehow unlocked her ability to use and command her magic. Until last night, she had not had a reason to discover this. Willow saw it, or Aria would never have known to try such a thing. Bear, we lost Asten last night as well. I assure you, I would not have put anyone in jeopardy for such a secret."

Bear studied Brendan a moment longer before responding. "I owe you a sincere apology for doubting you. Please forgive me?"

"There's nothing to forgive. We all fought hard last night, and the loss of Asten and Tay weighs heavily on us all, but none more than you. I lost a sister and both my parents to a tragic accident. I was only a child and do not, except for a few foggy memories, really remember them. I cannot imagine how you're feeling. All I can say is that while I did not have the pleasure of knowing Tay long, I was very impressed with him. I liked him very much."

Bear looked Brendan in the eye and nodded before he reached out and shook his hand firmly. He then turned and began to walk away. As he did, he reached up, wiping at his face.

It took three more days to reach Inlet Bay. They were uneventful days, and everyone had a chance to rest and regain their strength. Drae had worked diligently to tend to the wounds of those in need. Most had suffered at least minor burns from the firewash. Cuts and bruises were also widespread among them, along with an array of aches and pains. When the *Elite* finally docked in Inlet Bay, Bear came to Brendan.

"Brendan, I would like to make you a proposal. If you'll pay me what is due and allow me a small bit of time, I will make arrangements to have the *Elite* towed back up the coast, carrying my men and Tay home. I have given this a great deal of thought. I would like to continue on with you and your party."

"It would be our honor, Bear," Brendan replied, a bit surprised. "Though I must warn you, the most dangerous part of our journey may very well lie ahead of us."

"I assumed as much. I have a feeling you'll be running into whoever's responsible for Tay's death before this is over. I'd like to be there when you do."

"Then you are most welcome to join us, so long as you know this: We are in search of the Blue Witch and intend to cross the Dead Bridge into her forbidden land to find her. We seek her help in this matter. But, if it turns out she is behind it all, we'll be walking right into her hands."

"Well, now, that does sound like fun! I'll be going with you."

Brendan paid Bear what was owed to him and gave him his assurance that he would be paid extra for the damage to the *Elite* when their business was concluded. Bear left the docks, promising to return as soon as possible. His men, apparently already informed of his intentions, made further repairs and preparations for their return trip home without their captain.

Brendan sought out Willow and found her and Aria talking with Starlin in the dining room aboard the barge.

"Willow, I would like to speak to you," Brendan announced. The two walked out onto the deck and found an area where they could speak alone. "I would like you to try to see anything that will help us when we get to the Dead Bridge. Even if it does not answer any questions about the witch, we may find something that can help us. We're closer now, and I'm hoping that your sight will be strong enough to see past whatever's been interfering with it."

"I'll give it a try." Willow closed her large hazel eyes and began concentrating. She opened them, then closed them again for a long period of time. *She is so young,* Brendan thought as he watched the girl patiently. When she finally opened her eyes, Willow looked to Brendan.

"I cannot find her. But I did see two of us crossing safely over the Dead Bridge, though I could not see which two. I can see nothing beyond that."

"You've done well, Willow. At least I know you see a crossing. Thank you."

Willow smiled proudly before strolling off. "You're welcome," she called back over her shoulder.

Bear returned as promised and prepared to depart. He'd managed to purchase a rather large horse and saddle that fit him well enough, and he was already packed. Bear spent a few more moments instructing his crew and providing the details of what they were to do with both his brother's body and the *Elite*.

While Brendan was with Willow, Vander had had everyone else prepare to travel, and now they were waiting to depart. All had taken the time to say their goodbyes to the men they were leaving behind before departing the docks of Inlet Bay for the Dead Bridge.

They rode down the coastline along the sea south out of Inlet Bay. It was the first time that Aria and Starlin had ever seen the ocean, and they were each wide-eyed as they rode. Later in the day, they came upon a beautiful sand beach stretching a good distance along the coast, with massive rocks jutting up into the sky from the ocean floor. It was a particularly nice day, with the sun shining brightly above them as they rode. A few large puffy white clouds floated gently overhead, casting shadows down the shore and out to sea.

Aria and Starlin rode down the beach together and through the surf. They'd heard stories of the sea and of beaches, of course, but they paled in comparison to the actual experience of being there. The stories couldn't capture the taste of the salty sea air wafting in over the blue-green water or the majestic sight and sound of the waves as they rose and fell before them. Nor had they evoked the hypnotic rhythm of the foamy surf as it rushed up the sand toward them only to retreat again, over and over, as the sea teased the shore.

Aria and Starlin smiled and laughed like the young teens they were. At sixteen, Starlin was a bit older than Aria. His wavy blond hair and gray-blue eyes gave him much the same look as his older brother. But Vander, being nineteen and having gone through much in his short life, was more rugged in appearance.

Aria stopped and dismounted her horse, pulled her boots off, and quickly tucked them into her saddlebag. She gave Starlin, who'd been watching her closely, a quick smile and a nod, and he followed suit. The two strolled along the beach just out of reach of the surf as they led their horses. Aria found she loved the feel of the warm, wet sand beneath her feet and the way it squeezed between her toes as she walked across it. She breathed the sea air in deeply and could taste for herself the brine within it as she tried to distinguish all the scents it carried.

"Have you ever been to the ocean?" Brendan asked as he rode on the beach alongside Willow.

"I have. A great many times, as a matter of fact." Brendan looked surprised and Willow laughed. "Only in my mind, Brendan, only in my mind."

"Then let's go!" Brendan shouted as he pulled Willow from her horse onto his in front of him. Before she'd stopped giggling, he spurred his horse and they took off down the beach and into the surf. His horse's hooves kicked the frothy seawater high into the air behind them as they raced down the beach, passing Aria and Starlin. Brendan and Willow were laughing and waving as they shot past the two. They turned farther down the beach, then raced back by once again.

All enjoyed the pleasant day's journey south along the coast. They decided to camp on the beach near a roaring river flowing down out of the mountains into the sea. They'd agreed it would be better to cross the Dead Bridge in daylight the next morning, rather than chance it in the dark of night. They also decided they would follow the river canyon farther inland to where they expected to find the Dead Bridge. The group would have to follow it from the ridge above the river, as there was no way to travel upstream along the narrow canyon floor itself.

Two-person watches were set up and switched out several times throughout the night. Morning, however, came without incident. They ate a quick breakfast, consisting mostly of dried fruit and smoked venison and cheese wrapped in thin, flat bread, as they sat listening to the calming sounds of the rushing river. When they'd had their fill, they gathered their things, saddled their horses, and started their journey inland.

It was midmorning when they reached the Dead Bridge. They were on a cliff looking out across the deep ravine the bridge spanned, but they could not see the land on the far side. Nor could they see the bottom of the ravine through the mist and fog drifting about the bridge and blanketing the ravine's floor far below.

The bridge, true to its name, looked like something dead. It appeared very old and rotted, giving anyone thinking of crossing it second thoughts. A growth of black fungus covered it, adding to its ominous appearance. Brendan again took Willow aside.

"I want you to try once more, Willow, but this time, I wish you to touch the bridge as you do. Perhaps the fact that it touches the land on the other side may help in what you are able to see. Do not step onto the bridge, touch it only with your hand."

Nodding her understanding, Willow did as she was asked. She placed her hand on the side railing of the bridge and closed her eyes, and soon she went into a deep trance. A long time passed, and Brendan became increasingly concerned. He reached out to touch her, his growing fear for her safety more than he could bear. But before he reached her, Willow opened her eyes.

"It worked! I've learned several things I believe will be of value to us."

Brendan placed his hand on her shoulder, stopping her. "At this point, we're all risking a great deal. It's time we share everything with those who are in this with us."

Chapter 5

Brendan and Willow waited as their companions gathered around them. Brendan allowed them to settle before speaking.

"Willow has used her gift of sight and has information to share with us," Brendan announced to the group. "I have asked her to tell us all what she's learned, as we're all a part of this and all deserve to know. Go ahead, Willow, what have you've seen."

"The Dead Bridge isn't what it appears."

Brendan looked at the bridge, then back at Willow. "What do you mean?"

"What you see with your eyes is an illusion. The spirit of the bridge is of ancient magic. It serves as a guardian to protect those on the other side from those of this or any other realm. In reality, the bridge is actually very beautiful and looks as new as the day it was brought into this world. It is veiled in magic to disguise its true nature and discourage anyone from trying to cross. Anyone who steps out onto the bridge will be killed. The spirit cannot allow them to cross over."

"How does the Blue Witch travel over it?" Vander asked.

"She possesses a key to its magic that the spirit of the bridge recognizes, one that allows her to travel over the bridge safely," Willow replied. "The Blue Witch has warned that no one is to cross the Dead Bridge. But her warnings have been misunderstood. She was not trying to protect the land on the other side; the spirit of the bridge protects it. She was trying to protect anyone who might attempt to cross it from being killed. The spirit also told me the Blue Witch is currently on the other side."

"Wait, the guardian spirit spoke to you?" Bear asked.

"Yes, in a manner of speaking. I explained what we are doing here and why we need to cross over," Willow answered.

"Will it let us cross?" Vander asked.

"No. Not all of us, anyway. It tells me its creator gave it no ability to change the magic that controls and binds it, and it cannot go against it. However, the spirit wishes to help us. And there are two among us who may cross. It has spoken with the Blue Witch many times and knows her well. It believes, as our king does, that there is danger in the realm of men, and she may be needed here," Willow announced.

"What kind of danger, Willow? And who may cross?" Brendan asked.

"It did not tell me about the danger we face and may not know. The only two who may cross are Aria and myself. Aria possesses magic the spirit recognizes. Are you willing to cross?" Willow asked, looking to Aria.

"Yes. If you're sure it's safe," Aria responded. "But why us?"

"I believe it perfectly safe for the two of us. Why you, I understand; you have the use of magic that the spirit recognizes. It is a mystery to me why I'm allowed.

Brendan, this, I assure you, is the only way. The Blue Witch is on the other side. This is our chance to gain her help. It is what we came here for. But the spirit warns that if anyone else steps on the bridge while we are on it or on the other side, it will have no choice but to destroy them instantly, regardless of their intentions. The spirit assures me Aria and I will be safe in our crossing."

Brendan looked at his sister, then back to Willow, hesitating, before reluctantly nodding. He was not happy with this idea, but what other choice did they have?

The two girls, with everyone watching, approached the bridge. But before they stepped out onto its expanse, Willow grabbed Aria's arm and stopped her.

"It is very important we hold hands tight and do not let go! I can't stress this enough. If we lose contact with each other, I'll be the one who pays the price," Willow cautioned.

"Wait, then," Aria said, pulling a long length of leather lacing from the front of her tunic. The two girls worked to tie their held hands together so they could not accidentally let go. When they'd finished tying themselves together, they turned to face their companions.

"No matter what happens, nobody is to set foot on this bridge!" Willow warned once again as sternly as she could.

Brendan stepped forward and hugged Willow, then his sister. "I don't like this, Aria. Please be careful, though I don't know what meaning those words offer in this situation."

"We will," Aria said as she flashed her mischievous grin. Those watching could not help but be concerned for the two girls. Anything could happen once they stepped out onto the bridge, and there was nothing anyone could do for them if something went wrong. Aria and Willow stepped to the very edge of the bridge and stopped. Aria looked back one last time at Brendan and then squeezed Willow's hand.

"I sure hope you're right about this!" she said as she bent down slightly and kissed Willow on the cheek. Then the two girls stepped together as one onto the bridge.

In the next instant, Willow and Aria were caught up by something unseen and swept screaming in terror off the bridge into the mist. Brendan bolted for the bridge, but Vander caught him and jerked him to a halt.

"We can't help them, Brendan! Stop now!" Vander said, holding Brendan firmly as he fought to free himself. "Remember what Willow said? We are not to step out onto it, or we will be lost! Aria and Willow are dead! There is nothing we can do. It's too late. It's too late!"

Brendan, fighting Vander wildly, was losing control, enveloped in his rage and despair. Vander leaned in close to Brendan's ear as he struggled more desperately to free himself.

"Hold steady now, my friend. I'm sorry. I'm so sorry, but hold now. I'm with you, Brendan, hold now. We have others here under our command. We must do our duty, hold now." Brendan, with tears streaming down his face, finally relaxed enough that Vander could pull him to him, hugging him tightly. "I am truly sorry. That was a cruel trick indeed," Vander said as his own eyes filled with tears.

With Aria and Willow dead, and the bridge clearly impassable to them, the small group found themselves at a loss. Vander called the entire group together, with the exception of Brendan, who wanted time to collect himself and had walked off along the canyon's rim alone.

"The Dead Bridge is a cursed thing claiming the lives of all who step onto it. For all we know, the Blue Witch has never crossed it either. What's known for sure is she has repeatedly warned no one is to attempt crossing it. It's an evil thing! We're at an impasse; it's clear that we cannot cross this bridge. As I said before, we have no way of knowing if the Blue Witch is even on the other side. What Willow was shown and told can no longer be trusted. This whole journey could have been a ruse to lure Brendan and me away from the palace, along with some of my best men, weakening the palace's security. If whoever is behind all of this is powerful enough to bring a Sintin back into this world and block Willow's ability to see clearly, then it could have fed Willow false information through her visions as well."

"Willow did warn us of the Zaroe attack, though, brother," Starlin interjected.

"Yes, she did. But did that information really assist us? Would whoever's doing this really care if a flight of Zaroes was lost, if it helped gain their ultimate advantage? And had Aria not found the ability to control her magic, we may not have walked away from their attack regardless. What if it allowed Willow to see them coming to give us a false sense of security? What if it intended to feed us misinformation through Willow all along? And one more thing: What if, learning of Aria's magic, it drew her and Willow onto the bridge knowing what would happen to them? It seems we have far more questions than answers at this point," Vander said, throwing his hands in the air. The dejected members of the group sat discussing the questions Vander had posed for some time before Brendan returned.

Brendan pulled Vander aside. "I believe our duty requires that we return to the palace. I must report to our king that I have failed him. I want to thank you, Vander. You saved my life. I would have run onto that cursed bridge after Aria and Willow."

"Are you kidding me? I saved myself! If you'd have run out there, I would've run out with you, you crazy fool!"

Brendan managed a weak smile. "C'mon, let's inform the others that we make for the palace," he said, reaching out and shaking Vander's hand.

Brendan explained to the group gathered about him that his plan was to backtrack up the coastline to Inlet Bay without stopping and secure a ship to take them north to Raven's Burg as quickly as possible. He spoke with Bear as they readied to leave, apologizing for what had happened. Bear looked at him with sympathy.

"You won't get rid of me so easily. I'm going to the palace with you. It's been far too long since these eyes have seen the Great Hall. Besides, I still want to be there when we find the one responsible for this. If we're lucky and we hurry, we may be able to sail with the *Elite* back. The *Starlight* does not depart until midday tomorrow. If we ride through the night, we should be there in time." Bear reached out his hand to Brendan; when he took it, Bear pulled him close. "I, too, am sorry for your loss, my friend." The two did not speak again of their losses, preferring not to commiserate. They chose instead to focus their energy on reaching the *Elite* and the *Starlight* in time.

Brendan did his best to manage, but he was haunted by what had happened to Aria and Willow. He was carrying the full weight of his decision, a decision that had allowed the two young girls to be swept off the Dead Bridge to their deaths. It had happened so fast, both Aria and Willow gone in a single terrifying moment, and he could blame only himself. He was hurting, and the pain of wounds unseen was taking a heavy toll on him, though he tried to conceal it.

Not long after the girls were swept off of the bridge, their somber companions left for Inlet Bay. Brendan stopped, looking back one last time at the Dead Bridge, as the others rode on ahead. He stared at the black thing, then gazed across its vast expanse through the mist as far as he could see. He sat there watching the mist swirling about the bridge, unable to pull himself away. With tears streaming down his face, he rode back to the very foot of the bridge. Unable to control his emotions, he began sobbing. He quickly stopped himself, regaining his composure as best he could, wiping furiously at his face with the sleeves of his tunic. He spun about to leave but turned back to the Dead Bridge one last time. "Goodbye, Aria."

Chapter 6

T hey traveled at a fast pace through the night, reaching the port and its docks in plenty of time to be shuttled to the *Elite*. Long, heavy lines secured the barge to the *Starlight*, which would tow it up the coast, as both vessels sat at anchor.

The *Starlight* was a magnificent three-mast vessel and the largest ship currently anchored in the bay. Sailors aboard the vessel could be seen running about the ship making preparations to set sail. The captain of the *Starlight*, a man named Visto Abano, had graciously given Brendan's group permission to join those aboard the *Elite* at no additional charge to what Bear had already agreed to pay. Visto was also kind enough to invite the group from the barge to join him for dinner aboard the *Starlight*, and later that evening sent a large skiff to bring them to the *Elite*.

It was a pleasant, well-prepared meal enjoyed by all. Brendan found he liked Captain Abano very much. He'd shown a real sense of humor, and at one point even made Brendan laugh out loud despite the pain he was in over the loss of Aria and Willow. They all shared stories and enjoyed each other's company, bringing their small group closer together. Brendan found the evening a nice distraction from his disturbing thoughts, and he was happy he hadn't turned down the invitation and stayed aboard the *Elite* as he'd wanted to at first.

It was nearing midnight when Brendan saw Aria and Willow being dragged screaming and kicking off the Dead Bridge. He could see the terrified looks on their faces as he broke away from Vander's grip and ran out onto the Dead Bridge after them. He was able to grab hold of them and pull them back to safety, only to have the two girls begin decaying before his eyes. Aria and Willow, with their hands still bound together, reached out, begging him to help them. He watched, frozen in place and unable to help the two as they withered to rotten skeletons with tattered flesh. He heard Aria's last words ringing in his ears.

"Why, why didn't you save us, Brendan? You could have saved us!"

Brendan woke with a start, sitting straight up in a cold sweat. He swung his legs off the edge of his bunk and placed his feet firmly on the floor. He was still aboard the *Elite*, and he took time to gather himself and his thoughts before standing. He decided to dress and walk off the experience of his nightmare, leaving his cabin for the deck.

Brendan strolled the length of the *Elite*'s deck and stood for a great while at the bow, looking out at the sailing ship towing them up the coast. He listened to the seawater as it rushed by on both the port and starboard sides of the barge, finding the sound soothing.

His thoughts turned to his family, all of them lost to him now; their tragic and untimely deaths weighed heavily on him. He alone had been spared. He felt adrift and unsure of himself, and the weight of it crushed him and tore at the very fiber of his being.

It had been Aria's biggest fear. That something would happen and he would not make it back to her. She had worried every time he'd left her. Each of them was all the other had, and both had been afraid of losing their last family member and being left alone.

The deaths at the mines had been hard on their people, with so many from their small community lost, many crushed so badly they could barely be recognized. Brendan had been very young at the time, but he remembered the funerals. He remembered the graves dug in the ground and watching as his family's tombstones were placed. He remembered some of those who had wished him well and the food they'd brought in the hopes that it would in some way comfort him. Brendan had spent a great deal of time thinking about his mother and how he'd acted toward her on the morning of her death. He felt the shame of it deeply and carried the guilt to this day.

Brendan was so lost in his thoughts, he almost missed the small click of a bootheel on the deck behind him. He dove to one side, rolled to his feet, and drew his sword effortlessly.

"Brendan! Brendan, stop!" Vander shouted. "A little too jumpy there, aren't we, my friend? Are you okay?"

"I was lost in thought and heard a noise."

"Well, I would prefer to keep my head, if you don't mind!" Vander said, sheathing his own sword, which he'd drawn only to protect himself. Vander moved closer and placed his hand on Brendan's shoulder. "You are too—" A massive explosion lit up the night sky, cutting Vander short and knocking the two off their feet, both stunned.

When they rose from the deck, they saw that the *Starlight* was in trouble. As they watched, a second explosion larger than the first nearly tore the *Starlight* in two. Wood and iron mixed with pieces of human flesh rained down on them as once again they were thrown from their feet.

It was Vander who first noticed the man lying on the deck behind them. He ran to him but was unable to do anything for him. The man had been thrown from the *Starlight* all the way to the deck of the *Elite*. He now lay mortally wounded, missing a leg and an arm on one side. Vander turned him over gently as Brendan came to his aid. The man was burned so badly that, at first, the two tending to him didn't recognize him; he reached up, pulling Brendan down close to him with his remaining arm, and tried to speak.

"Traitors!" was all he could manage before his eyes closed for the last time.

Brendan finally recognized the man who lay dead before him. "Visto!" Others were running out onto the deck now, looking to see what was happening. The *Starlight* was listing badly ahead of them, and they were still tethered to her.

The massive sailing ship in front of them was on fire, the flames lighting up the night sky so brilliantly that they could see from Bear's barge the men aboard the *Starlight* struggling unsuccessfully to lower skiffs into the water. Men's voices, screaming and cursing, could be heard carrying back across the water to the barge.

"She's foundering!" Bear yelled out. "Cut those lines now or she'll pull us down with her!"

Brendan and Vander, already close to the bow of the *Elite*, ran to the taut lines, which were nearly stretched beyond their limits, and began cutting through them with quick swings of their swords. The *Starlight* was sinking swiftly and began pulling them faster as water sprayed all about them. Before them, the *Starlight*'s stern rose up out of the water like a dark behemoth from the ocean's depths, drawing the *Elite* to her even faster.

One of the *Starlight*'s three masts, already damaged by the explosions, snapped under the pressure. It swung around the side of the ship before crashing into the water on the port side of the *Elite*, showering those on deck with more of the ocean's salty water. The *Elite* was barreling down on the *Starlight* as the last of the lines were finally severed.

"We're going to hit her!" Bear yelled out. "Brace yourselves!"

Chapter 7

A ria awoke with her hand still tied to Willow's. She sat up yawning and wiped at the corners of her eyes before looking around at the strange new world about her; she had no idea how long she'd been sleeping. She found it was a dark and ugly place, where nothing but scrub trees and rough, dry grass grew from the near-lifeless ground.

"I don't see the bridge," Willow said as she sat up beside her.

"Neither do I," Aria replied as she continued to look about.

"I don't either," a strange voice announced from above them. "What's a bridge?"

The two girls looked toward the voice, then back to each other, then back up again.

"Ick, what is that?" Willow asked. Aria could only shrug her shoulders and kept her eyes on it.

"Who are you?" Willow asked.

"Me. What's a bridge?"

"Where are we?" Aria asked the strange little guy

perched on a large branch above them, ignoring his question. He glanced around, a puzzled look coming over his odd face.

"We're right here!" he said. "What's a bridge?"

"Do you have a name?" Willow asked, taking a step closer.

"I may, I have lots of things. What's a bridge?"

"A bridge is something you use to cross over an obstacle and get from one side of it to the other," Aria said, attempting to answer his question. "Such as crossing over a river."

"Hmm." He paused. "I have one of those. Maybe two. I have lots of things."

"Do you have a name?" The little fellow looked puzzled once again, so Aria tried asking, "What do you call yourself?"

"Me. What's in a name? That which we call a rose by any—"

"It's what somebody calls you when they see you," Willow said.

"Oh…then my name must be Ick What Is That!" the little guy replied. Aria looked at Willow, and they both burst out laughing.

"No, no. What did your mother call you when she first saw you?" Willow tried again as soon as she had caught her breath. "You know, when you were born?"

"'Ew, that's nasty!'" he said, proudly puffing out his chest. "That must be my name. It is a very good name, I think! What is your name?" the little guy asked.

"Willow," she replied.

"That's a stupid name. Mine is much better! What is yours?" he asked Aria.

"My name is Aria, Aria Pandane."

"Well, Aria, Aria Pandane, that is a better name than Willow; hers is a stupid name. My name is better than yours, too, though, I think."

"I'm happy that you like it." Aria laughed. "May I call you Ew for short?"

He thought a moment and then replied, "If I may call you Aria for short."

Aria smiled at Willow before responding, "You may indeed, Ew."

"I will just call this one Willow. It is a stupid name, though...poor thing."

Ew jumped down out of the tree and stood in front of the two girls. The little guy only came up to Willow's waist. He was so ugly that he was cute, the two girls agreed. He had wild curly black hair growing in splotches all over his light-brown skin. He had an oversize head and very large hands and feet, and was a bit stocky. Ew's facial features were oversized, including his ears, and all were just a bit off-kilter. He had large, crooked square teeth too big for his mouth and was a bit cross-eyed. Ew wore nothing but a short pair of beige pants made of some kind of heavy cloth that did not quite reach his knobby knees and was secured only with a drawstring.

"Ew, what can you tell us about this land?" Aria asked.

"Everything. It's mine, it is one of the things I own."

"Oh, that's nice," Aria continued, not at all convinced it was true. "Does anyone live here with you?"

"There are others." Ew shrugged his shoulders. "Some good, some bad."

"Do you know the Blue Witch?" Aria asked.

"I know someone who's blue. She told me once some call her the Blue Witch. That's probably her. She's my friend. I do not own her, though. She says I cannot."

The two girls looked at each other, excited. "Will you help us find her?" Willow asked.

"Ew already knows where she is!" he said. "She sleeps in the glass house. I own it. I own lots of things."

"Will you take us to her, Ew? We must speak to her right away," Aria said.

"You can see her, but you can't speak to her. She sleeps in the glass house. Will you be my friends if I take you to her?"

"Yes, of course we will," Aria said.

Ew looked at the two girls holding hands, noticing for the first time that they were still tied together. As he turned and began to lead the way, Ew held his hand in the air without looking back at them and waited. Aria smiled at Willow as she took Ew's hand with her free one and the three walked on together.

"How far is it to the glass house?" Aria asked as they were walking through a large field of wildflowers later that night. Flowers of all different sizes and shapes surrounded them, but all with only dull, pale, colorless petals. None were pretty or looked familiar. They stretched out as far as they could see before them, and to both sides as they passed through them. There were trees scattered randomly in the field and beyond, all of a kind neither of the two girls had ever seen before either. They wondered if all of them were dead since they were bereft of leaves—and any other signs of life, for that matter.

"It's pretty far. We will be there in time, though, I think," Ew answered.

When they finally reached the far end of the field, Ew took them to a path that entered a patch of woods and led away from the field of wildflowers. It was not long before the three came to a small lake. Ew led them around the edge of the lake, walking along a stretch of rocky shoreline until they reached a small creek that fed into the lake. Ew let go of Aria's hand and reached down, cupping water in his hands and drinking. Willow and Aria did the same, finding that the water was cool and possessed a pleasant-enough taste. As they drank, Ew started hopping back and forth from one foot to the other.

"We must hide!" he hissed. The girls didn't know what was happening, but in this strange world, they were not about to take any chances. Ew reached up and grabbed Aria's hand. "Hurry! We must hide, he's coming!"

Ew led them off the shoreline just inside the woods and pulled the two girls down behind a thick clump of bushes.

"He can't see you. He'll take you if he does! And he'll hurt me...he always hurts me! I don't own him," Ew said in a hushed voice.

"Where are you, you nasty little thing?" a rough-sounding voice called out. "I know you are here!" Aria and Willow could not yet see who was speaking. "If you continue to hide, I will hurt you even more when I find you. Come out now!" the voice demanded. Ew looked at the two hiding with him with tears in his eyes.

"I must go. He can't find you. It would be bad for you. He is very mean. He takes my things and hurts me. I would not want to own him."

"Wait," Aria whispered, "stay with us!"

"No! I must go, or he will take you both." With that, Ew leapt out from his hiding place to face his tormentor. "I'm here," he announced.

"Come here now!" the voice demanded. Ew did as he was ordered, and his tormentor pushed him to the ground. The two girls moved just enough, and very quietly, so that they could see who was taunting Ew. It was another of his kind, whatever that was. Only this guy was much bigger and stronger and was far better looking than poor little Ew. He kicked Ew as he lay on the ground and then stepped on him. Ew's tormentor yanked hard on a tuft of Ew's hair, pulling a large handful out as Ew began to cry, begging the bigger creature to stop.

The two girls, still in hiding, looked at each other and nodded, both thinking the same thing. They stood and quietly slipped up behind the tough guy picking on Ew.

"Hey! Who do you think you are, hurting our friend?" Willow shouted.

The bully nearly jumped out of his skin. "Who are you?"

"Us," Willow said sharply. Aria looked at Willow and burst out laughing.

"What are you laughing at? Are you laughing at Brog?" the bully demanded, approaching Aria and bumping into her thigh with his chest. "Huh, are you laughing at Brog?" he repeated, bumping his chest into Aria's thigh once again.

"Who is Frog?" Aria asked. Willow snorted as she started to laugh, and Aria soon joined her.

"I am Brog, not Frog!" he yelled. "And you should fear me!"

"Why?" Aria asked nonchalantly as she kicked at a small stone at her feet.

"I will hurt you if you don't do what I say. I will steal you both. I have stolen lots of things. So, you will do what I say, or you'll be sorry!"

"I don't think so, Frog," Aria said. "I'm getting bored with you already, you arrogant bully. You need to hop along now, Frog—we have someplace to be and you have delayed us long enough."

Little Ew was sitting on the ground not too far away, grinning from one big ear to the other watching the scene. Brog was furious and started hopping from foot to foot.

"You know what? I don't like you two. I'll just wait until you leave, then I'll deal with this ugly little thing!" he said, pointing at Ew. "Oh, I'm going to hurt you bad for this!"

Aria was furious. She raised her free hand and made a couple quick gestures, and Brog shrank to half the size he'd been only a moment before; he was now far smaller than Ew. With another gesture from Aria, Brog became hideous to look at, like a rotting frog carcass. Aria reached down and snatched Brog up by one arm and dragged him to the edge of the lake.

"Take a look at yourself, Frog!" she said, pointing to his moonlit reflection in the water. "That's the real you. You see, Frog, picking on someone weaker than yourself doesn't prove you're strong, or even brave. But it does make you a pathetic coward. And nobody will mistake you for anything else from now on. Now, hop away, little bully frog, before I really get mad!"

Brog took off running down the shoreline, yelling as he did, "I…don't…like…you!" He was soon gone from sight. Ew got up and walked over to Aria and Willow. He looked up at Willow and smiled.

"I like your name much better now." He hugged Willow's leg, then turned and hugged Aria's. "You are both very young to be so brave. My daughter was very brave once too."

"You have a daughter, Ew?" Willow asked.

"I did. She was murdered a long time ago. My daughter was very special to me. I was betrayed by one of my own family, and she was taken from me," he said, his eyes watering. "You remind me of her. Come! We must go," he said, and turned to lead the way. He stopped and, without looking back, held his hand in the air.

Chapter 8

The *Elite*, now free of its towlines, tore through the heavily damaged hull of the *Starlight*. It was a final unneeded death blow to the great sailing ship, which splintered into sections falling and splashing into the water to either side of the barge, all of which were destined to rest at the bottom of the ocean in mere moments. The barge's momentum had slowed but managed to carry it just clear of the doomed remains of the *Starlight*. Those aboard the *Elite* watched as the last of the *Starlight* slipped beneath the water's surface on its way to the ocean floor.

The *Elite*, with no way to power itself, was now adrift at sea. Bear ordered all lanterns lit and a distress flag raised. He wanted any survivors lost in the dark waters to have a beacon to make toward, and to be sure the *Elite* would be visible to any other vessels near them.

"We can do nothing else to help those who may be out there," Bear said to Brendan and Vander as the two stood with him on the deck looking out over the water around them. "They will have to come to us if they can."

By morning, only one of the *Starlight*'s crew, a man named Junto, had been rescued. He told them someone had sabotaged all of the winches that lowered the lifeboats, rendering them useless, and the men had been struggling to cut them free. Two of their crew had been seen going overboard and rowing away from the ship. This was being reported to their captain when the first explosion happened. Junto explained that he had seen a large two-headed birdlike creature scoop the two from the sea and fly off with them moments before the second explosion. The second one had thrown him off the ship and into the water.

"Brendan, I would like a word with you and Vander in private," Bear said as they sat in the dining area later in the day. Bear led them to his private cabin, where the three sat at a small table in the corner of the sparsely decorated room.

"We're adrift and essentially defenseless out here. I think we can safely say the two men who left the ship early were the traitors Captain Abano tried to tell you of. They must have been paid by somebody very well to turn on their own like they did. I'm surprised, to be honest, that a Zaroe was sent to get them. It would have been rather easy to tell them one would, only to leave them adrift at sea after the deed was done," Bear said.

"We have a rather limited supply of rations, including fresh water, so I will instruct the crew we will be limiting all rations to emergency levels out of an abundance of caution. We only had enough for ten days for half the amount of those now on board, and we've already gone through two days' worth of those. I do not know how long it may take for another ship to spot us, but we better hope that it's within the next few days or we'll be in real trouble."

"Do many ships pass this way?" Vander asked.

"Yes. We're in luck there," Bear replied. "The current here will push us back southeast, keeping us in the shipping lanes, and ships travel up and down the coast here regularly. There is a good chance we'll be spotted in the next day or two by a ship large enough to help us, but we can't assume we will. I know we need to get to the palace as soon as possible, but I think we can agree there's nothing we can do at this point but hope we're spotted sooner rather than later."

"I would agree. Bear, I'm concerned a second attack has been waged on us. At this point, I am more confident than ever that whoever's behind all of this has the gift of sight or a seer in their service. It's the only reasonable conclusion I can come up with. If I'm right, making it back to the palace is not a sure thing. Do you have any thoughts on how we might proceed?"

"We don't know who the enemy is or where to find them, so I think we keep our lookouts watching for another ship. We get ourselves towed to the nearest port and make for the palace. We can develop a new plan from there."

"I agree. Do you think we could—" Brendan started to ask, but he was interrupted by a lookout's call.

"Ship! There's a ship to our port side and afar back, heading toward!" the man called out. The three men seated in Bear's cabin rose and filed out onto the deck. The watch pointed, calling out, "There, Captain!" Bear and the others looked back across the water, searching for the ship. It took them a moment to spot it, but it was there.

Later that day, they were in the port of Calday, not quite halfway up the coast. Bear made arrangements for his crew and the *Elite* to be towed on up the coast and home to Ravens Burg. With their supplies replenished, Brendan's group, along with Bear, headed northeast out of Calday.

They camped that night at the base of the Shale Mountains. They planned on a very early start, and a long ride through the mountains, and beyond, the next day.

Vlix and Trite took the first watch of the night and sat together on a knoll where they could easily keep an eye on the camp.

"Vlix, do you think Commander Ray is right?" Trite asked.

"About what?"

"That our enemy can see what we're doing."

"If they're a seer, or have one in their service, they could, I should think. Why?"

"I've been feeling as though we've been watched ever since we left the palace. I didn't want to bring this up, but I think whoever's watching is close to us, not some seer from afar. I think it might be someone among us. I've said nothing, because there are none of us who warrant any such doubt. And I've found nothing yet to confirm my feelings."

"Trite, my young friend, these are strange days to be sure. Keep your eyes open, as will I, for anything out of place. Never doubt your own instincts, and they will serve you well."

Brendan and Bear relieved Trite and Vlix on the next watch. The air was cool and crisp at the base of the mountains but not yet cold. The two sat for some time enjoying the stillness of the night as they both sorted through their thoughts. They avoided conversation as time passed beneath a clear sky filled with an impossible number of stars, and they sat scanning their surroundings for any sign of movement.

"I think we've been outsmarted and outmaneuvered from the start of all of this," Brendan said, breaking the silence they'd shared as they watched the camp from the knoll. The knoll gave them excellent visibility in all directions. Any trouble would be seen coming from a good distance on a night such as this.

"It would seem so," Bear replied. "We're hampered by an enemy we know nothing about, and it makes things difficult. We have no way to know what they want, where they've come from, or how many there are. We do know they have the ability to see our moves and can attack at any time if they wish, or so it would seem. I do believe one thing, though, Brendan," Bear said, turning to face him. "You're their main target."

Brendan looked at him, stunned. "Me? What makes you think that?"

"Think about it; it's either you or Vander. I think it's you. I thought at first it was because you killed the Sintin and stopped Zantan, but I don't think that's it. Your family possesses some form of magic, perhaps stronger than you even know. Forgive me for saying this, my friend, but your sister is gone. If she was the target, why sink the *Starlight*? I think they planned to sink the *Elite*, but the two hired found no opportunity to get aboard my barge. So, they did the next best thing: send the *Starlight* to the bottom of the ocean, intending for her to pull us down too," he said, cocking an eyebrow at Brendan and waiting for his response. "It's the only way I can really make any sense of it. After Aria displayed stronger abilities than she knew she had, she was manipulated onto the Dead Bridge along with our seer, thus eliminating both in what may very well have been one well-executed maneuver."

Brendan looked at him for a long moment before he replied. "Something has been eating at me for a while now, Bear. I have not spoken to anyone, not even Vander, about it. The fact you're seeing things as you do makes me think maybe I've been right about the way I've been feeling. I've replayed the assassin's attack in the gardens over and over in my mind. I assumed that his target was the king. But something bothered me about it. Bear, this was a highly trained man in excellent condition. He fought me well until Vander put his sword through the man's throat. As I said, I've replayed that attack over and over many times." Brendan paused a moment longer, examining the event one more time before speaking again. "Bear, I don't think Zantan was trying to kill the king. I think he was trying to kill me."

Bear did not look all that surprised. "That makes sense. It was a piece I was struggling with myself. Why was somebody interested in killing King Tennington? He's been a good king; we are not at war and have not been for a very long time. And more important, if the king was the target, why delay until you had a chance to return? But what makes you think you were the target?"

"The angle of the assassin's attack was all wrong, if his target was the king. However, it was perfect, perfect, Bear, if it was intended for me. Had I not been very aware of him and only pretending not to be, I might very well be dead. If the Sintin was meant to kill me and failed, Zantan could easily have been dispatched to Andavar to ensure the deed was done."

"It would explain why he didn't make an attempt on Tennington's life while you were away. He was waiting for news of your death, or for your return. It would've appeared as if someone had attempted to kill the king and you died defending him," Bear said, stroking his beard. "Hmm. Now, my friend, the question is…why you?"

Chapter 9

A ria turned to Ew and swallowed. She wiped her mouth and smiled.

"Tell us more about the glass house, Ew," She said as the three companions ate a late meal Ew had gathered and prepared consisting of strange but edible root vegetables.

"It's not a house you would want to live in. It's a place of death," Ew said reverently.

"A place of death! Is the Blue Witch dead?" Aria asked, pausing between bites.

Ew laughed and shook his head. "No, no, she is there for other reasons. She sleeps there because no one else can enter the glass house and she can rest in peace. She knows some of the spirits and wishes to be near them."

"You said we could see her but not speak to her. I don't understand; why not?" Willow asked.

"It is where many of the dead's spirits can be seen. When she comes, she will be on the other side. She will not speak to you from the other side, and you may not speak to her. You can see her, though. If she wishes to speak to you, she will cross over to our side. You'll see. We will be there in time. We have plenty of time."

"Are you sure she is there now?" Aria asked.

"Yes, yes, she is there. I own the glass house. I own lots of things."

After finishing their meal, they continued on their way through the dark. It was not long before the two girls came to a sudden halt, pulling little Ew to one side with them. They froze where they were, watching two enormous gray creatures speaking in a guttural language they did not understand. The creatures were as tall as most of the larger trees and thicker, with heavy muscles.

"Ew, what are they?" Willow asked in a hushed voice.

"The Brothers," Ew replied. "They will not bother us. They can't see us. They are blind now."

"But what are they?" Aria asked.

"They are the last of the great sea trolls of Aland. There are other trolls, smaller ones, but none left like these. They are very old. They are the last of their kind and soon will be gone as well. I own them; I own lots of things." The three moved closer to get a better look before continuing on.

"They're amazing!" Willow said.

"Come, we must go." Ew urged them on.

It was much later when the three came to what Ew called the glass house.

"We can't enter," Ew said. "We can only stand before this window and wait on the spirits of the dead. If we wait, you will see your Blue Witch is with them. Wait. Do not speak to the spirits," he said.

Willow closed her eyes briefly. When she opened them again, she looked to Aria, who was already looking at her. "Step no closer, Aria. To touch this water is death."

The three were standing in front of a small waterfall cascading in a thin sheet from a pool above a rectangular stone. The large stone, which jutted from beneath the hillside pool above the mouth of a dark cave's entrance, was adorned with carved symbols and script. The markings could be seen through the water flowing over it on its exposed face. But none of it was recognizable to the two girls.

The stone overhung slightly the opening of the cave. The water had the look of shimmering glass as it flowed over it, and they could peer through it into the dark on the other side. The water fell to a depression that sloped away, causing it to drain back into the mouth of the cave, allowing them to come directly up to the cascading water yet still be standing on dry ground.

"Watch, and you will see them," Ew said in a hushed voice. Aria and Willow stood with Ew, watching. At first, nothing happened, and Aria grew more and more impatient.

"What are we doing, Ew?" she asked. "Watching this water or looking for bats?"

"Watch, you will see them, they will come, they always come. Some call my glass house the Window of Souls. We can see them, and they can see us. We will see your Blue Witch too, I think. Watch, watch!"

They did watch, and they could see small lights floating in the darkness beyond the water far back in the cave. The darkness of the cave began to give way as the number of spirits grew and came ever closer. They would stop, looking out through the water at the two girls on the other side, studying them, and then, in turn, would move on. Two spirits, however, soon came and lingered, unwilling to leave. A young couple, looking at Willow. When the others beyond the water saw that the couple would not leave, they gathered to see why. Willow closed her eyes for a moment and could see them with her as a much younger child. When she opened her eyes again, they were filled with tears, and the two spirits pulled back, waving to her, and were gone.

"They were my parents," Willow said as tears began to run down her young face. "And I couldn't even speak to them." Aria pulled her close and held her.

"She's here!" Ew announced. The young girls turned and looked into the Window of Souls. A young girl, not much older than Aria in appearance, approached the window. Her skin was light blue, and she had long silver-blue hair and blue eyes that sparkled enchantingly. She did not stop, as the spirits had. She stepped out from the cave through the cascading water, remaining perfectly dry, and stood directly in front of the three. She reached out to Aria, and Aria took a step back despite herself.

"Do not be afraid. I mean you no harm, Aria."

"You…you know my name?"

"I have known you since the day you were born. In fact, I was the one who chose your name."

"How…how can that be?" Aria asked, confused. "Are you…are you my mother?"

The Blue Witch smiled warmly and shook her head slowly in response. "No, I am not your mother, Aria, though I knew her and your father well before their deaths."

"Then you must know Brendan, my brother. And you would have known my sister, Brielle."

"I have known Brendan his whole life, as I have you, Aria. I knew your sister, Brielle, too. As it happens, I was there when she was born as well. I knew your family very well and was saddened deeply when they were taken from us." Again, the Blue Witch reached out to her, but this time, Aria did not move. The Blue Witch examined the pendant she wore around her neck closely and smiled warmly.

"It was my mother's. Brendan gave it to me on my fourteenth birthday," Aria explained. "You may have seen her wearing it."

"I did. Your mother wore it from time to time, though it actually belonged to your father. Why have you crossed the Dead Bridge in search of me?"

"Brendan was sent to find you by special request of King Tennington. The king wishes to speak with you about recent events in our realm, if you would be willing to do so. Brendan is waiting on the other side of the bridge for us."

"If your king wishes to speak with me, I will go with you. I must say, Aria, I was surprised to see you here with that pendant around your neck and not Brendan. But his having given it to you as a gift does explain that. Aria, no one waits on the other side of the bridge for us. Those who were with you have left to return to the palace. You see, time here is a bit different than in your world. We'll join them there when the time is right."

"Do they think us dead?"

"Yes. I have warned against attempting to cross the Dead Bridge many times. They assumed you were killed by the spirit of the bridge," the witch answered. Aria was lost in thought for a moment, thinking of Brendan and of how he must have felt, believing he had lost her.

"Please tell me how you know my family," Aria said.

"When the time is right, I will tell both you and Brendan everything I know about your family, Aria. Willow," she said, turning her attention to the little girl and smiling before bending down closer to her. "We shall speak of your family and the secrets kept from you as well."

Willow smiled back, and then reached out and hugged her.

"We are needed in the realm of men, and we'll leave here soon enough, but I must ask you something now that you are here at the Window of Souls, Aria. Would you like to see your parents before we leave? I'm certain they would like to see you."

Aria, stunned by the question, could only nod. The Blue Witch stepped back through the water and moments later returned with a man and woman. They looked out through the water at Aria with such sadness and regret it broke her heart. They were young and beautiful, shaded before their time. They were there but a brief moment and then they were gone.

"Wait! I want to spend more time with them. I want to see my sister, Brielle!" She stopped herself as the Blue Witch stepped back through the window and stood before her once again.

"Another time, perhaps," she said, looking to Ew. Ew ever so slightly nodded.

Chapter 10

B ear and Brendan sat atop the knoll looking over their camp as they spoke of their situation.

"Something has changed in our world, Brendan—a shift, if you will," Bear mused. "Can you think of anything you would've been involved in prior to your encounter with the Sintin and run-in with the assassin? Anything that could have set these things in motion?"

"Maybe. We have spoken about my family's being killed when I was young and Aria only a baby. Aria now wears our mother's pendant. I gave it to her as her birthday gift. I believe it must have something to do with that. After obtaining it, I wore it for safekeeping until I gave it to Aria. That is only important if, as I'm now thinking, it is the pendant they've wanted all along," Brendan responded. "Here's the thing, Bear. As I said, it was stolen from our mother's body. I spotted a large man, one every bit as large as you, wearing it in a very dangerous tavern I'd been in on other business of the king's. It was a tavern called the Red Rooster. Perhaps you've heard of it, or of the Rooster Massacre?"

"I've heard of the Red Cock, and everyone's heard of the Rooster Massacre."

"I was there that night. It was the night I came upon the man wearing the pendant. I commented on the pendant's beauty and inquired after its origin. Had the man purchased it from the thief or come by it honestly, I would have paid whatever it took to purchase it from him. He had had a few too many drinks, though, and bragged about taking it off a beautiful red-haired woman trapped under some rubble after an explosion in a mine. He claimed that he'd been there at the time of the explosion in search of a man he intended to kill. Though he had been in the mine, he had not been hurt. He told me he could have saved the trapped woman, but he had other ideas. The woman begged the man to help her. She told him she had three young children, and one only a baby less than a year old. He bragged to me of how scared she was, and how she kept saying she didn't want to die, didn't want to leave her babies."

Brendan paused a moment, taking a deep breath, and then exhaled slowly before continuing. "He admitted to me that he'd laughed at her and spit on her as she pleaded. He boasted about how he'd laid his hands all over her while she lay helpless to stop him. He told me of how he tore her blouse open. And how it was then he discovered the pendant and took it from her. He told me about how he'd pulled out his knife and showed it to her, taunting her, before cutting her neck so she would slowly bleed out. And how he'd watched her die."

Brendan shook his head in disgust. He could see him still as he bragged of the deed; Brendan had been stunned by the man's arrogance as he spoke so openly of his crimes without fear of consequence.

"I explained to the man that the woman he spoke of was my mother and told him I was going to kill him and take her pendant from his corpse. Naturally, being such a large man, he laughed at me and tried to attack me first. I killed him and did as I promised, taking the pendant. He must have been a man of some importance in the area, because several men tried to come to his aid. I do not know how many I killed that night, but there were a great many. I was so angry and so out of control by the time I left that tavern, I was soaked in blood from head to toe, and bodies were strewn from one end of the place to the other. There was not one left living among them. I vowed that night Aria would never know of my part in the Rooster Massacre. It was nasty business, and I was forced to kill many more fighting my way out of that town. I seriously doubt any powerful being would have cared enough for that lot to seek revenge, but what if my putting the pendant on somehow triggered something that our enemy could sense? What if some magic had lain dormant in it with the thief, only to reveal itself when I put it on?"

"The idea does seem to have some merit," Bear replied, mulling it over. "News of the Rooster Massacre reached my ears in Ravens Burg. From what I was told, you thinned out a real den of thieves and murderers that night. So, Brendan, do you possess some form of magic?"

"None I'm aware of," Brendan answered. "I did have the pendant on when I caught up to the Sintin, though…" He thought for a moment. "My sword felt different to me. And its touch pained the Sintin greatly. Perhaps the pendant helped me to defeat the demon in some way I'm not aware of."

"That idea, too, has merit," Bear said. "Perhaps we are on to something here. It may have helped you the night of the Rooster Massacre as well. Not with the first man, but the others."

"I hadn't thought of it. But looking back on it now, I'm almost certain it did."

"Problem is, the pendant's lost to us."

"It is. I think Vander and my duty still calls us to the palace to report to King Tennington on what has—" At that very moment, something moved on the far side of the camp. It was subtle, but both of them caught it. It was Starlin, they realized a moment later. He slipped quietly from the woods back to where it had appeared he was still lying asleep and had been all along. It looked to the two as if he'd slipped back into his own body.

"Did you see that?" Brendan asked in a hushed voice.

"Yes!" Bear hissed.

The two watched the form closely for a while longer. They witnessed Vander stir, roll over, and then sit up, yawning and stretching his arms over his head before wiping the sleep from his eyes. Vander looked up, scanning the sky, then rose and stepped over to Starlin, shaking him gently. Starlin rose as if he'd been soundly sleeping. A moment later, the two brothers were heading toward the knoll for their turn on watch.

"Say nothing," Brendan mouthed to Bear, and Bear gave him a nod. When Vander and Starlin finally reached them, Brendan yawned before greeting the two.

"It's been quiet to say the least. I was looking forward to some sleep, but then I realized something. We are facing a very dangerous situation here, Vander. I want you to listen carefully and keep your eyes open." Brendan gave Vander a subtle glance, making eye contact.

Vander knew instantly that Brendan was telling him something was seriously wrong. And so he remained silent, giving Brendan a nonchalant nod of acknowledgment.

"Starlin, do you have the smoked fish, the ones we bought in Calday? They're in your cousin's pack, I think. I'd like some before I turn in," Brendan said, knowing full well they had purchased no such thing in Calday.

Vander looked to his brother for his reply. Starlin nodded and pointed back toward the camp wordlessly.

Then, seeing the look on Vander's face, the creature knew it had been discovered.

The thing leapt out of its host's body, growing far larger than Starlin, who collapsed to the ground with a gasp and did not move. It faced off against the three men, who'd leapt to fighting stances at the sight of it without hesitation or fear. The large aberration was nearly featureless and looked like a wraith, moving and drifting in front of them like an inky black mist.

"Anybody ever run across one of these things before?" Bear asked.

"Never even heard of one!" Brendan answered, attacking. He struck out at the thing with a quick series of blows, spinning his blade in his hand and rotating his body as he did so. His sword, flashing through the night, found nothing but mist and air. The black mist re-formed for a split second and struck Brendan, sending him sprawling across the ground.

Vander attacked with an impressive display of his own skill with a sword, but this time, the thing was still in solid form, and he sliced into it. The creature howled in dismay and washed over Vander, attempting to smother the life out of him. The black creature tore at Vander's chest and shoulders, trying to get to his head. But Brendan was back on the attack.

Brendan's sword found it a solid being and wounded it badly enough that it could no longer become mist. It remained a solid nightmare, screaming and howling at its attackers. It was tall and thin, wearing nothing to cover itself. It looked like a large man who'd been burned severely, its skin hanging off it, with raw flesh and even bone exposed in ragged sections.

Bear, in awe of Brendan's and Vander's attacks, was on the move as well. He circled behind it, and seeing his opening, he attacked. He slid down under a wild last-second swipe from his enemy and took off one of its legs above the knee with a clean sweep of his sword. The dark creature toppled to the ground and tried to come to its remaining knee, howling and grasping desperately for Bear.

Brendan's and Vander's swords struck simultaneous blows that should have finished the thing off, but it lashed out, catching Vander. It sent him flying into Bear, and the two crashed to the ground. Brendan, reacting with blinding speed, spun and swung his sword a final time, and the creature's head toppled to the ground and tumbled several feet away. Its headless body reached and grasped wildly at the air around it before finally falling over and lying still. They dragged its body into a clearing, covered it in a mound of sticks and branches, and set it on fire.

Bear picked up Starlin, and the four of them left the knoll and went down into the camp. They woke Drae, and the healer began tending to Starlin, who finally regained consciousness. Drae then checked over the other three for injuries. He found that Starlin, dazed and a bit confused, had no recollection of what had happened to him but was in good health otherwise.

The other three, while bumped and bruised, were also in good condition, except for some deep scratches that Vander had received. Drae applied some of his special balm, taking Vander's pain away almost instantly. No watch was sent back to the knoll. It was decided they would continue on their journey; with all that had just taken place, nobody would be getting much sleep anyway. After the last embers of the fire were extinguished and the ashes scattered, the group mounted their horses and rode into the night.

Chapter 11

With the Blue Witch leading the way, the girls and Ew headed for the Dead Bridge. They had not walked far before Aria turned to her with another question.

"Will you tell me about my father's pendant? When I put it on, it helped to unlock stronger magic within me, and helped with my control of it."

"It is part of a story that I will not enjoy telling, Aria, and I think it should wait until Brendan can hear it at the same time. I will not want to tell it twice. It is part of your family's history and you deserve to know, but it will have to wait for now," the witch said with a kind smile. "How did you happen to come across these two girls, my little friend?" she asked Ew, changing the subject.

"I found them looking for a bridge underneath me. They call me Ew," he said with a big toothy smile. The witch looked at him, a bit puzzled. But Ew smiled once again. "I think it is a great name!" he said with an emphatic nod. "And it suits me just fine."

"Ew it is, then."

"Have you always been blue?" Willow blurted out, no longer able to bear wondering about it in silence.

"No, Willow. Not always," she responded. Aria gave her a quick glance, her head full of questions she wanted to ask, but knew she had to wait.

"Let me ask the two of you a question," the witch said as they continued walking. "Why are your hands tied together like that?"

"That's easy. When I spoke to the spirit of the Dead Bridge, I was told that Aria has protection on this side of the bridge because of her magic. And if we were to become separated, I would die," Willow answered. The Blue Witch glanced at Ew, and Ew gave her a quick, barely perceptible nod that only she could detect.

"I assure you, Willow, as long as you are with me, you need not be tied together any longer." She reached out and gently untied the two girls' hands. For the first time since they had prepared to step on the bridge, the two separated.

When they arrived where the bridge was supposed to be, it was not there. At least, the bridge could not be seen. The witch raised her hand, and the bridge appeared, responding to her silent request. It was not the black, dead-looking bridge, however, but rather the beautiful one Willow had told the others about before they crossed.

It was white, with towering arches and flowering vines covering a great deal of it. The brightly colored flowers and their leafy green vines starkly contrasted the bone white of the bridge. Its design was clearly elven in nature, with intricate carvings and detailed inlaid pearl and silver.

The Blue Witch walked up to it and placed her hand on the side of it. She spent a long moment with her eyes closed, communing with the spirit. When she was done, she looked to Ew. He smiled and nodded.

"Aria, Willow, this is where we must leave Ew. He will not be going across with us."

"No! You must stay with us, Ew. Wouldn't you rather go with us?" Willow asked.

"Please come with us. We don't want you to be hurt when we leave," Aria said, kneeling down in front of him. "You simply must come with us, Ew."

"I cannot come with you, my young friends," Ew said, his voice changing along with his appearance. Ew transformed before their eyes into a very handsome silver-haired elf in long dark-green robes, carrying a tall walking staff of burled wood with an emerald-green stone affixed to its top. "This is how most think an elven king should look," he said. "This is my realm. I protect it, and all the creatures that live here, from your world and the troubles that have long plagued it. I have done so since the beginning of its time. My name is Andentine. Behold my kingdom!"

Andentine held out his hands, and the world changed around them. It was beautiful beyond anything the two girls could have ever imagined. Incredible gardens of green grass, bright flowers, and trees of all sorts and colors lay before them. The land was filled with lakes and streams as far as the eye could see. Towering waterfalls poured down from snowcapped mountains reaching high into a sky of brilliant blue that appeared without end. The stale air they had been breathing for days was now fresh and smelled sweet to the two girls as they breathed it in. Their senses were heightened to levels they had never known could be achieved as they attempted to fully absorb the world about them.

The land and waters were filled with all manner of magnificent creatures of old, many that were thought to no longer exist in any realm. Faeries of all kinds flittered about, and one landed on Willow's shoulder. She waved to Willow, then bowed to all of them before flying off again.

Trolls and elves could be seen at peace with gnomes and dwarves. The two girls were shown in the air before them vast cities and small villages alike, all appearing as if they'd been built that very day. No flaw could be found in this world, and the two stood in awe of what they were being shown.

Each new scene presented something wondrous. Dragons soared in the sky above them, along with an array of birds and other flying creatures too numerous to count. Aria and Willow stood in stunned silence, trying not to miss a thing.

Andentine showed them large forests full of wildlife the two could not have imagined. Some were massive beasts, others as small as insects. He showed them an entire community of people that were as small as the fingers on their hands, and then giants who towered over them.

Andentine then showed them a castle perched on an overhanging cliff looking out over a great azure sea. It was an astonishing structure of vast size and beauty. A large keep could be seen at its center. A sprawling curtain wall was surrounded by a deep river-fed moat stretching from one edge of the cliff around the castle grounds to the other, creating twin waterfalls spilling several hundred feet to the sea below. The two girls could smell the sea air and feel its cool breeze washing over them as if they were there.

Large battlements dotted the castle walls, but none were manned. Instead, large draping vines with brightly colored blooms poured over them and down the white walls. The massive drawbridge was lowered, welcoming an array of visitors of all types and sizes coming and going from the castle. Massive white stones carved into the shapes of great tall trees ringed the castle from one side of the cliff to the other. The stone trees reached high into the sky, with the curtain wall around the castle stretching between them. The castle would be virtually impossible to breach if ever attacked, but it was the magnificence of its size and beauty that held the girls' attention.

"This is my home," Andentine announced. "I call it Elveshenge." The Blue Witch and Andentine watched the two girls, admiring their amazement at everything they were being shown. Time had stood still as Andentine showed his guests his kingdom through his magic.

"I have enjoyed your company, my young friends, and would ask that you come back and visit me whenever you wish. The bridge's spirit will never harm you or those with you when you do. I must say farewell for now, for you are needed and it is almost time," he said as he began to transform into little Ew once again. Aria and Willow knelt down and each gave him a hug. Both wiped away tears as they rose to leave.

"We will come see you again," Willow promised. Ew smiled, then turned and walked away whistling a soft, calming tune.

The three watched him a moment longer, then turned away and crossed over the bridge. When they reached the land on the far side, they stopped and looked back at the rotting black structure known as the Dead Bridge.

"I will take us to see King Tennington, but we have other business first," the Blue Witch declared. "There may be danger from here on out. Aria, should anything happen, do not attempt to help me. Your magic is powerful, but it does not come close to that of my own, and I do not want you harmed thinking you would be helping me. Willow, I have some ability as a seer, but it is not the gift that you have. We may need your sight before this is all over, so stay alert."

"Something or someone has been attempting to block my sight," Willow said.

"He is an ancient being known as Vantrill. He wishes to control and rule over your lands as he once fought to do. Andentine banished him and his demon minions to a dark realm after they became jealous and attempted to take over his lands as well. Andentine told me Vantrill invaded your kingdom with an army of demons hundreds of years ago and claimed it for his own. This caused a war, forever changing this world. He does not yet know how they came to your world. But Andentine no longer has the power he once did in your realm, or any other but his own, and cannot help us here, as he would wish to."

The Blue Witch transformed into a large, strong man who gave the impression he was nobody to be trifled with. The two girls leapt back from her as one.

"Oh, I'm sorry, I change my appearance whenever needed so I won't be recognized."

"That's why you're never seen here, unless you choose to reveal yourself!" Aria exclaimed.

"That's correct, Aria. In my natural state, I could not go unnoticed, and I would draw far too much attention if we were seen before I'm ready. We need to get to Andavar and help the king prepare for the assault on the palace and army. It is going to come like a storm soon.

"I'm going to take us just outside of the city walls of Andavar; we are needed there first. You will not feel a thing and we will not be seen as we first arrive. When I know there is nobody around to see us as we appear, we will do so. Hold my hands now." The two girls looked at each other with trepidation but did as they were asked. The three stood holding hands for only a brief moment, and then they vanished.

They materialized far outside the city walls but within sight of them, to the west of the palace. The Blue Witch, still in the form of a large man, looked around closely while cloaked in invisibility. Finding they were alone, she removed the magic that hid them.

"We need to wait here," Willow said. "Brendan and the others will be coming up the road at any moment."

"Please tell me you're sure, Willow!" Aria said, putting her hands on the young girl's shoulders and turning her to face her.

"They're coming, Aria! And they're in trouble! They're being hunted, and those chasing them are trying to stop them from reaching the city."

"She's right, Aria. That's why I brought us here instead of the palace. They're coming!" the Blue Witch hissed. "I will help them—hide now!"

Aria and Willow ran and hid behind a stone wall that meandered along the road. The witch returned to her normal form and then disappeared from sight altogether.

"Aria, do as the Blue Witch said. Do not attempt to use your magic on what is coming." Willow looked frightened. "You cannot stand against these things, and they will seize on your magic the moment they sense you have it. You must stay hidden."

Aria nodded, and in the next moment, Brendan and his group, riding as fast as they could on tired horses, broke into view. Demons were clinging to both their backs and those of their horses. The demons were tearing and biting at the riders and their wild-eyed mounts. Two of the horses went down, along with their riders—Drae and Starlin, the two girls realized.

Brendan and Vander, shaking off the demons, rode toward their fallen friends and scooped them up without slowing. More demons were coming up the road from behind the group and were closing in on them. Some rode great black cats that darted and cut in around the fleeing horses while avoiding their pounding hooves. Others were aboard flying insects that looked like giant red hornets. They were trying to cut off the horses by flying directly in front of them. The demons atop them were reaching out to grab the reins from the riders' hands. The buzzing of the insects' wings mingling with the screams of the demons aboard them was surreal.

The Blue Witch appeared on the road before them. She attacked the demons with thick bolts of blue fire shooting out from both hands, scattering them and freeing the riders and their horses from their tormentors, and destroying the wasps and the demons riding them in great flashes and explosions. Brendan's riders rode past her, then turned back to watch the horrific battle. The Blue Witch stood alone against the demon horde. They came for her now, forgetting their original prey. *Too many*, Brendan thought, *they'll overwhelm her*. She disappeared, only to reappear in a better position to attack.

Aria, seeing the array coming for the blue girl, fought the urge to help her. Willow clung to her arm; all they could do was watch. Brendan and those with him found themselves in the same position. The battle raged on before them as the Blue Witch drove the demons back and killed them one by one.

The witch was being attacked on all sides as the demons abandoned their unified frontal attack. The great black cats and their riders were circling her, sensing a chance to take advantage. She quickly dispelled the thought, incinerating the first to attack. The ground around her was littered with the bodies of the dead and dying. The demons had taken heavy losses, but they still had the advantage of numbers and did not let up their attack.

The Blue Witch, fighting hard, was beginning to show some signs of slowing. The demons, sensing this, renewed their onslaught. She fought on, killing those that came closest in the next rush, and then she went down for the first time, overrun. A spectacular flash of blue flames threw those around her back, screaming and burning.

A second rush overran her again, but this time she had help. Brendan, along with Vander and Bear, unable to simply watch any longer, charged in, attacking the demons. Vlix and Trite, seeing them charge, were right on their heels. They tore through the demons, giving the witch a chance to gather herself and launch a new attack of her own. The demons and their mounted creatures alike were reeling from the new attack, and the Blue Witch was now dispatching them with renewed energy.

Trite took a charge from the last big cat and its rider as he stumbled backward over a dead demon's remains. The big cat was on him immediately, ripping him to shreds as he fought beneath the beast. Bear and Vander, already running to assist Trite, attacked the big cat and its rider. The cat lunged for Bear, and Vander put his sword through its exposed chest, killing it before it hit the ground. Its rider was thrown sprawling at Bear's feet, and Bear reached down and nonchalantly broke the rider's neck.

Vander knelt down beside Trite, but he could see the damage was too much. Trite opened his eyes and tried to speak but could not form the words.

Vander spoke close to his ear. "I know what to tell your mother. She will always be taken care of. You have my solemn word." Trite nodded and closed his eyes. He would not open them again. His chest heaved up and down with his last gasps, and then he was gone.

Brendan was locked in a ferocious battle with a demon much larger than the others. The demon wielded a sword as well and showed great skill with it. Neither combatant was able to gain an advantage over the other.

Brendan could not think of the last time he had been truly challenged. Even as good as Vander was, he was still no match for Brendan's uncanny skill with a blade.

When the demon grew impatient and advanced recklessly, Brendan saw the opening he'd been looking for. He slid under the advancing demon and drove his sword up deep into its gut. It groaned and toppled to the ground facedown behind Brendan, who was lying on his back between the fallen demon's legs. He had closed his eyes, shielding them from his victim's spraying blood, and had yet to reopen them when he heard Vander's voice.

"So! You thought it a good idea to lie down in the middle of a fight and take a nap? You know, you're getting pretty arrogant these days!" He laughed and reached down, taking Brendan's hand and pulling him to his feet. "We lost Trite," he said, turning deadly serious.

Brendan could only nod. There was nothing he could say. Two of the three men Vander had selected were now gone, and Trite within sight of his home.

"Is everyone okay here?" Drae asked as he ran up.

"We're good, check on the others," Brendan answered.

"That's a big boy," Vander said, looking down at the demon Brendan had just killed. "Do you think that was it?"

"Do you?"

"Nope. I think they were testing us. I think it's going to get a lot worse when their full forces are unleashed," Vander said.

"That's my thinking."

"Brendan!" Aria yelled as she ran to him and jumped into his arms.

Brendan lifted her in the air, swinging her around. "I thought I'd lost you forever when you were taken off that

100

bridge!" he said, hugging her tightly before setting her down.

"The spirit of the bridge did as it promised; it took us to the other side. It scared Willow and me nearly to death, taking us as it did; we were not expecting that. I have lots to tell you, though, when we have the time. Brendan, the Blue Witch knows us! She has information about our family that she's going to share with us."

"Then I shall look forward to speaking with you both. I'm so happy to have you back, Aria!" he said, hugging her again. "Willow! It is good to have you back as well!" he said as she approached. He bent down and gave the child a warm hug and kissed her on the cheek.

"I saw what happened to Trite, it was awful."

"I'm truly sorry that you had to see that. Trite will be sorely missed."

Even with the loss of Trite, there were many happy faces and long embraces as the group welcomed Aria and Willow back. The longest and warmest embrace, however, was that shared by the Blue Witch and Brendan. The Blue Witch had held him tight, which had surprised him.

"Thank you for helping us. You are truly amazing!" Brendan said.

"I am happy to help, Brendan. But know this: there is a war for control of these lands coming, and there is much we must do to prepare for it. I must speak with King Tennington as soon as possible."

Chapter 12

B rendan found Vander with Willow and overheard him as he was asking about his brother.

"Why did you insist that Starlin go with us?"

"Though I could not see everything as I should have, I knew, as Brendan did, that something was wrong at the palace. Brendan felt it in the Great Hall, as I did elsewhere in the palace that same night. Neither of us could be sure of what it was, but we were both troubled by it. I tried to use my sight after I was asked to go on this journey. I was able to see a version of the future. In it, Starlin and Aria were brutally murdered. They were torn to pieces in the Great Hall, and what was left of them was lying scattered on the steps to the throne. I could not see what form of evil had done such a thing, but I knew we could not leave them to such a fate."

"You were right, Willow," Vander said. "Starlin's body had been taken over by some kind of demon, a kind none of us had ever seen before. Brendan, along with Bear and I, was able to destroy it after discovering its presence. We burned its remains to ensure it never rises again."

"Vander, I am sorry to interrupt, but the witch and I want to speak with King Tennington right away," Brendan said.

"I'm ready. Please excuse me, Willow. And thank you for insisting they go; you clearly saved their lives."

Willow nodded, and Brendan and Vander left to join the witch. The three of them rode on ahead of the others to the palace. They soon found themselves seated in a private room off the king's chambers, awaiting Tennington. The king arrived moments later, and upon seeing the Blue Witch, he approached her and welcomed her before addressing them all.

"We have been suffering attacks throughout the surrounding villages, and even within the city walls, since the day after your party left," he began. "Demon attacks on men, women, children, even animals. The losses have been heavy, the attacks so random we have been unable to defend our people. Most stay in their homes and do not dare venture out. The city markets are abandoned, and travel has all but ceased. Vander, we have lost over thirty of the Watch in these attacks, and now some have left it to be with their families to ensure their protection."

Tennington noticed the look on Vander's face and quickly addressed his concern. "They did so with my blessing, Vander. I ordered in reserves, but only those men and women who are single were called upon. I have placed the army on full alert. That is the way of it here," he concluded. Brendan and Vander followed with a full accounting of what had taken place since their departure, up to and including the loss of Trite. When they were finished, the Blue Witch addressed Tennington.

"Great king, I have been traveling between this realm and that on the far side of the Dead Bridge for some time now. In that realm lives the elven king, Andentine. He has been that realm's keeper and defender for as long as it has existed. Over four hundred years ago, this world was cast into a savage war. A being known only as Vantrill attempted to take over this realm and nearly succeeded. Vantrill considers this world his, though he and his demons were defeated by the first king of men and later banished to a dark realm for all eternity by Andentine," she explained.

"He has somehow broken his bonds and returned. Vantrill and his demons intend to have their kingdom back. He will kill anyone who opposes him or refuses to submit to his will and will enslave any who do submit."

"Will Andentine help us? Can he banish Vantrill and his demons again?"

"No. Andentine can no longer wield such power beyond the borders of his own realm. Andentine has, however, given us hope. He has given us three weapons to use against Vantrill and his demons. I am not prepared to reveal the nature and use of these weapons just yet, but I will when the appropriate time comes."

"What do you mean you will not reveal them? If these weapons are to be used, we need to have the knowledge of them now! I command it of you, witch!" Tennington was showing signs of the stress and burden of protecting his people. He had spoken without thinking, and now it was too late to take his harsh words back. He stood defiantly before those gathered with him. The Blue Witch calmly walked over to him and reached up, whispering in his ear for several moments. The beleaguered king looked at her in utter shock when she was through, then nodded without saying a word.

Plans for defending the city were discussed and gone over once again, and they decided to bring as many woman and children, along with the elderly and disabled, inside the city gates as possible. Every detail had been addressed and seen to. The kingdom of men was made ready for a war unlike any it had fought in over four hundred years. Messengers were sent out to even the farthest of outposts, recalling all men and women posted there back to the city. They would make their stand there at the heart of the kingdom. They would have preferred some distant battlefield or a fortress far from the capital city of Andavar, but that would not be the nature of this war. The Blue Witch had made it clear this would be a concentrated attack on the capital, the army, and those defending the realm of men there. She informed them that their enemy was intent on possessing and ruling the realm of men, not destroying it. Their citizens were alerted to the impending war and ordered to take all precautions to protect themselves and their families.

Beyond the great walls and heavy gates, Andavar's location itself was a natural defense. The city was built on a mountainous peninsula in the Crystal Lake. The lake was enormous and surrounded the city on three sides, making an attack of any size from those sides all but impossible. An outer defensive wall mirrored the inner city wall, with large courtyards and walkways that stretched across the peninsula between them. A deep spring-fed creek ran the full length of the area between the walls, serving as a natural moat. Small footbridges crossed the creek here and there but were much too small to allow an advancing army to use them effectively. A larger road and bridge connected the two walls and provided the only ways in and out of the city.

It was late evening when the Blue Witch called on Brendan and Aria to join her for a walk in the palace gardens. As the three strolled and enjoyed the warm evening air, a clear night sky filled with bright stars shone above them. The gardens were quiet, and the smell of the fresh flowers was pleasantly pungent this time of year. They found they had the gardens all to themselves.

Brendan was stiff and sore from his earlier battle and moved a bit gingerly, though Drae had once again done an excellent job of taking care of him.

"I have many things to share with you two. Most of which will be very difficult for me to talk about. And much of it just as difficult for you to hear," the Blue Witch said. "Brendan, I have already shared with Aria that I knew your parents, and that I've known you both all of your lives. I also told Aria I was asked to choose her name by your mother." Brendan gave Aria a confused look before the Blue Witch continued.

"I know you believe your mother had the use of magic but refused to use it. That is not true. Your mother did not have the use of magic. Though she wore your father's pendant often, she hated magic, and she feared it. Your magic comes from your father's side, not your mother's. Your father did not possess it himself, but your sister, Brielle, did have the use of magic, much to your mother's displeasure. When your sister turned fifteen years old, your father unknowingly gave her a gift that unlocked her magic. A pendant identical to the one you now wear, Aria, except that it had a stone of another color. Neither your mother nor your father was aware of its power." The witch stopped, lost for a moment in thought. She continued walking to a small table near a fountain and indicated they should sit. The witch hesitated for some time, watching the fountain's water rise and fall, before continuing.

"Your sister went to the mine the day you were left orphans, as you know. She entered the old section of the mine, which was considered safe for those visiting their family members. Picnics were often held in the cool shade at the mouth of that section, and on special occasions, celebrations would also be held there. As your sister waited for your parents to meet her for lunch, she decided she would quickly explore a closed vein of the mine. It was a crystal mine, as you may know, and she wished to see if she could find a small one for herself. She wandered too far and too deep into the old section of the mine as she searched. But there, quite by accident, Brielle discovered a fantastic crystal, one of a color she found mesmerizing."

"How do you know all of this?" Brendan asked.

"I have the gift of sight, Brendan, and many other abilities, for that matter. I have watched this scenario play out many times since that day. You see, I knew many members of your community and struggled with the loss of those who died that day. I wished to better understand what took place, and to know who or what may have been to blame for their deaths." The witch, again lost in a moment of thought, broke out of it and continued.

"Brielle wanted the crystal for her own and attempted to free it but struggled to do so. She became frustrated at first, and then angry, wanting it desperately and knowing she had to return quickly before it was discovered she was down there. She continued her attempt to free the crystal, becoming even angrier, until finally, unable to free her newly found prize, she screamed in frustration, grasping and pulling on the beautiful crystal as she did. In a flash, a massive explosion rocked the mine. The explosion that trapped and killed all of those poor people, and your parents."

"Brielle caused the explosion!" Brendan gasped. He was devastated at the thought, and the ramifications of it. "If you know that much…then you know what took place with our mother afterward, and how her pendant was taken from her…don't you?" he asked as tears filled his eyes.

The Blue Witch withered as tears welled up in her own eyes. She looked away, a child lost, and ashamedly so. She hesitated several moments before answering, "Yes."

Chapter 13

Early the next morning, Brendan found himself wandering the Great Hall alone, except for the men and women of the King's Watch, of course; they were always at their posts. He had struggled with a restless night, unable to find the sleep he so desperately needed. His mind had been racing, poring over all the Blue Witch had revealed to Aria and him the evening before. He wanted to hear more—a great deal more, in fact—of what the witch could share. But she had said they would speak again soon, before rising and walking off through the courtyards alone.

Aria and Willow were still sleeping, as far as he knew. At one point, as he wandered aimlessly through the palace, he noticed that Vander, too, was up early, doing his duty, preparing for what was to come. The others of his group were enjoying their beds and extra rest as they healed from the demon attack they had suffered the day before. Drae had insisted on remaining personally in charge of their care, though, in truth, they were in good hands with the healers of the palace and none had been seriously injured regardless. It gave Drae a purpose and kept him from feeling out of place at the palace.

Starlin continued to show no ill effects from the demon who'd inhabited his body. He'd reported to Drae and Vander that he could not remember a thing regarding it. They believed that the demon had hidden within him to spy on first the palace and then the group who'd left to find the Blue Witch.

Brendan, seeing Bear enter the room as he paced, changed his course to meet him. "This hall is a marvel, to be sure," Bear said as Brendan neared him.

Brendan looked about quickly and nodded. "Were you able to get some rest?"

"The best I've had in some time. I think Drae made sure of it." Bear laughed. "I saw Aria and Willow a moment ago; they were eating in the dining hall, if you would like to join them. I've already eaten."

"Thank you, Bear, I will. What're your plans today?"

"I believe we'll be at war in the next day or two, so I'm going to spend a bit of time here in the Great Hall before seeking out a few men I know who are still serving in the Elite First. I'll be ready when needed."

Brendan put his hand on the big man's shoulder. "Thank you, my friend, for everything you've done for us." Bear smiled and nodded but said nothing more as he turned his attention back to the Great Hall.

Brendan left for the dining hall and found Aria and Willow still there, now joined by the Blue Witch.

"Good morning, ladies," he said. "May I join you?"

"Please do, Brendan," the witch replied. "I still have much to tell, and I feel I must tell you now." Willow started to rise, and the witch put her hand on her arm. "Please stay with us, Willow, some of what I must say will concern you. But let's do leave here."

The four of them left the large dining hall for the palace gardens. Surrounded by the peace and tranquility of the gardens, they each took a seat at a small table. They settled and the Blue Witch began to speak to them once again of the tragedy at the mine.

"Your sister did cause the explosion that killed your parents," she began, addressing Brendan and Aria. "Brielle's pendant's effect on her magic was still unknown to her. Her magic, responding to her anger and frustration, caused the explosion. It was sudden and it was incredibly powerful. Her new magic, acting to protect her, shielded her from the blast, but not before the crystal she'd been trying to obtain was freed and in her hand. The crystal absorbed and then intensified the magic before disintegrating into a cloud of crystalline dust enveloped in the magic that surrounded her. She absorbed it all into her body as the magic was drawn back within her. The blue crystalline dust fused with her body and her magic, turning her blue…" Tears fell from her eyes as Brendan and Aria looked at her in astonishment. "I am Brielle, your sister, and I alone killed our parents and all of those innocent people that day," the Blue Witch said, unable to look at her two siblings. "Can you ever forgive me?"

Brendan was stunned and hesitated before answering. "You carry a heavy burden that needs to be laid down, Brielle. But do not sit there and expect Aria or me to ever forgive you for what you did." Brielle sat in silence and did not look up, believing herself undeserving of any forgiveness. "You killed our parents, and all of those poor people…but it was a terrible accident. You did nothing wrong. You were an innocent teenage girl. You didn't mean for it to happen, and it wasn't a mistake on your part. Brielle, look at me now," Brendan demanded.

Brielle raised her head to face him, and Brendan could see the tears flowing down her blue face.

"We will never forgive you. You must understand this. Never will we forgive you for killing our parents. For to do so would indicate in some way we could find blame in you, and we cannot. Do you agree, Aria?"

Brielle and Brendan looked to Aria for her response. Aria looked to the two and smiled through her tears. "With all my heart."

Brendan stood and stepped before the Blue Witch. Aria scooted her chair back, giving them more room, as Brendan stood looking at the Blue Witch, his sister Brielle, for several moments. She did not look up at him as her tears continued to fall. Brendan offered her his hand, and she hesitated a brief moment before taking it. Brendan brought her to her feet and then to him, hugging her for a long time before releasing her. He looked at her differently now, through tear-filled eyes of his own. "Welcome home, Brielle."

They seated themselves back at the table with Willow, who had sat quietly watching the reunion of the three siblings. The abandoned child with no family of her own had been crying along with them.

"Willow, I know you have questions as well. Questions about your family and why you were found on the palace grounds alone. I'm sure you've tried to use your gift of sight to discover these answers for yourself, have you not?" Brielle asked, looking at the little girl sitting with her. Willow nodded. "You have not been able to, and for good reason: I did not allow it." Brielle paused a moment as Willow wiped her eyes.

"You briefly saw two shades you thought were your parents at the Window of Souls, but you did not find anything out about them or yourself. I will tell you now, Willow, they were not your parents. They were your guardians, and they'd raised you from a baby. They were good friends of our family, and we loved them dearly.

They were kind enough to take you in and take care of you, but they had not been raising you as their own. They took care of you until you turned four years old. It was not long after your fourth birthday that they were murdered by a man known to Brendan and me." Brendan, who had been listening closely along with Aria, looked at Brielle, utterly confused.

"I will explain, Brendan," Brielle said, continuing. "Though I will not divulge the nature of this completely, so do not be alarmed. You had a rather notorious encounter with a large man in a tavern some time back, if you will recall. A man whose name is of no importance to us here," she said, giving Brendan a knowing look. "That man murdered Willow's guardians. I was across the Dead Bridge in Andentine's realm at the time and had been there for some time, recovering from injuries I had received. It was my intention to hunt the man down and dispatch him myself before Willow's guardians were murdered. But somehow, he was always hidden from me, protected in some way by a very strong magic. Had I been able to do so, Willow's guardians would still be alive. Your chance encounter with him, Brendan, could not have come at a better time. It had not been easy and had taken far too long, but I'd finally found the source of the magic protecting him and had destroyed it. I was on my way to pay him his last visit when you ran into him in the tavern."

Brendan was stunned. "So, had you not just destroyed his source of protection…?" he mused.

"You most likely would not be sitting here today. I'm sure the man showed no fear of you," Brielle said.

"No. He was a large man and quite sure of himself."

"And he had every right to be. He was an important minion of one of Vantrill's most prized assets, a very powerful sorcerer named Agathon. And under that sorcerer's full protection, that man had murdered, raped, and robbed without consequence for far too long. I fought Agathon and eventually destroyed him, ending the man's protection and power."

Brielle turned back to Willow. "Here is what you must know, Willow: you do have family." She took a long pause before speaking again. "And they are sitting here with you now." Brielle paused for a brief moment as the three sat staring at her, stunned. Then they looked to each other for any sign of recognition as to what they were hearing but found none in the others' faces.

"Willow...precious child," Brielle said, barely able to speak the words as tears filled her eyes. Willow stood and came to her, searching her face cautiously.

Willow was strangely drawn to the young blue girl before her. She was filled with emotions she could not control or yet fully understand. Willow anxiously anticipated what the Blue Witch's next words might finally reveal to her of the mystery that had been her life.

Brielle looked at Willow, tears falling freely from her eyes as she struggled with the words. "I am your mother."

Chapter 14

Bear strolled through one of the eight long barracks of the Elite First as an honored guest. He was present for their inspection in preparation for the impending war. The unit was flawless, and Bear would have expected nothing less. The Elite First, as its name implied, was the best of the best. The unit accepted less than one in ten of those skilled and brave enough to apply. Their ranks now consisted of eight hundred intensely trained men and women.

Their commander, a man named Shray Stinson, had known Bear since he had first come to the Elite near the end of Bear's service. Commander Stinson was pleased to see Bear and took great pride in escorting him personally. The Elite was in full force and prepared, under Stinson's leadership, to be deployed at a moment's notice.

Vander had seen to every detail he could think of in preparing the palace and the King's Watch. The King's Watch was on full alert as well. He'd altered their normal posts, putting them on short watches with quick rotations to keep their minds fresh and their eyes sharp. The palace had been stocked with a variety of extra provisions and medical supplies. All secondary doors had been barred and locked down.

The army stood ready: six thousand men and women were camped surrounding the outer defensive wall of the city, and an additional two thousand in reserve were camped between the outer and inner walls, on the far side of the creek channel from the palace. King Tennington was in his war room with his closest advisors, receiving and reviewing reports from a multitude of different runners updating him on every aspect of the preparations. They were satisfied that they were as prepared as they could be but worried it would not be enough.

King Tennington requested the Blue Witch and Willow be brought to him. When they arrived, he ordered the room cleared.

"I would like to know if either of you can see when our enemy will attack," he said. "It would be of great benefit to myself and all those in command, if you're able to tell me."

"The time has yet to be determined, Your Highness," Brielle responded. "I believe our enemy is waiting. Vantrill's forces are just as prepared as ours. He knows we are waiting, so he toys with us. The longer he waits, the greater the advantage he perceives himself to have. His forces do not have to stand on high alert while they wait for an attack to come to them. He waits because he can, knowing our forces will eventually begin to weaken mentally and physically. And when they do, that is when he plans to attack."

"What do you recommend we do then, and how should I address you? I know you only as the Blue Witch. Do you have a name?"

She smiled at Willow and then looked back to King Tennington. "My name is Brielle Pandane, Your

115

Highness. Willow is my daughter. I am Brendan and Aria's sister."

The king looked completely stunned. He looked at Willow, and she bobbed her head to one side and then the other before shrugging.

"How long have they known this?" he asked.

"They learned of it just this very morning, my lord. I told you that Andentine provided us with three weapons to use against Vantrill and his army of demons. Brendan, Aria, and I are those weapons. We will help you fight this enemy, but I would ask that as we do so, you keep my daughter with you at all times and ensure her safety."

"Of course, but what will the three of you do against such a force?"

"With a little help from the army and a few surprises, we will completely destroy them," she said. "Please order your men to stay behind the three of us. They are free to use what weapons they wish from there, so long as it helps and is not directed anywhere close to us. But let no man charge to the front, not even those of the Elite First, as they are accustomed to doing. The time for them to charge with honor will come, but it will not be now. We will not wait on Vantrill as he would like; I will see to that. When you're fully prepared, I will force his hand."

"I will see that it is done, if you're sure about this."

"I am," she said confidently over her shoulder as she turned and walked out of the room.

"The Blue Witch is your mother?" the king said, scrunching up his face.

Willow shrugged her shoulders, then sighed, exasperated, as she shook her head. "It's a long story."

Chapter 15

B rielle left the king's war room, soon followed by Willow, who quickly caught up to her. They met with Aria and Brendan and took them to a small, secluded meadow outside the city, far from any watchful eyes. As her companions waited, Brielle put herself in a trance.

She searched for and found the enemy army. She measured their strength and quickly looked for any sign of Vantrill. She could see the darkness of him in a large room in a keep. He was in an abandoned castle that had crumbled away to almost nothing but scattered stones. Few rooms remained, surrounded by bits and pieces of an old stone wall. Dry weeds blew about the rubble at the bottom of the moat. A broken and rotting drawbridge lay open across it. A couple of tall towers were left standing, but very little of the castle itself was still serviceable. She did not recognize it or its surroundings, but that mattered little to her. Brielle brought herself out of the trance, satisfied that they likely would not be disturbed.

"I informed King Tennington that Andentine provided him with three very powerful weapons with which to defeat Vantrill and his demons," she began. "We are those weapons."

Brendan glanced to Aria, only to find her looking at him, just as confused. He then turned his attention back to Brielle. "I do not think you mean my sword or Aria's magic. How, then, are we these weapons?"

Brielle reached into her robes and produced a pendant much like Aria's, but with a dark green stone at its center. She handed it to Brendan, who examined it closely. "Brendan, you have a powerful magic within you as well, my brother. This pendant will unlock it, as Aria's unlocked hers. Do not put it on yet. I will assist you in controlling your magic. There are three of these pendants that I am aware of, and they have been in our family for as long as anyone can remember. I have been told their history and why we possess them," she said, pulling out the one she wore from the neck of her robe. It was the same as the others but with a dark-blue stone.

"Our magic is as old as time itself. It comes from the faerie world. It was a special gift to our family. Our family has been the guardian of this magic since the elves left this realm, taking with them their magic and all that of the faerie world, long ago. It was Vantrill who drove them out. He broke through to this realm from another and claimed it as his own. The elves lost over a third of their people, including Andentine's younger brother, fighting him and his demons. Andentine then made the decision to escape this realm. The first king of men begged Andentine not to abandon them. Andentine, sick of war and heartbroken at the loss of life, especially that of his brother, refused to stay. But he gave our ancestors these three pendants and the gift of a powerful magic. Our family blood has carried that magic ever since. The magic was given to our family alone, but not all will have the use of it. For those of us who do, it is already within us. The pendants are the keys to unlocking its full potential and serve to magnify its power," she explained.

"Our ancestors finally defeated Vantrill, in a manner of speaking. Vantrill ruled over this realm for his benefit alone. It was a very dark time for our people. With the help of these three pendants and our family's new magic, we were able to regain control and drive Vantrill and his demons from this world. Vantrill had always been jealous of Andentine and the new kingdom he had created for the elven people with the help of those of faerie. Vantrill fled this realm for Andentine's and attempted to overthrow him but failed to do so and was banished. Now he has returned to reclaim what he believes is his, and he thinks he has grown more powerful than ever before. He is mistaken in this, and I intend to capitalize on it."

"Why was this gift given to our ancestors? Why our family?" Brendan asked.

"Because we are the direct descendants of the first king of men, Ethan Pandane. The magic was given to him and his two children to save this world if they could. Andentine pleaded with Ethan to bring his people with him to the new realm, but the king of men refused to do so. This was so long ago it has all but been forgotten in the history of men. It was Andentine's plan to take everyone with him and then seal off this realm, trapping Vantrill and his demons. Ethan was proud, though, and refused to lose his kingdom to a thief. His mind was bent on killing Vantrill and his demons, down to the last one. Ethan's hardened heart kept the race of men in this realm. After Vantrill's attempted invasion, Andentine and those of faerie created the Dead Bridge and its spirit guardian to protect their new home. Ethan and the world of men found themselves alone and cut off from the elves and all those of faerie. We are the only weapons that can defeat Vantrill, so it falls on us to end his threat. I will spend as much time as possible training and teaching you in the use of your magic in order to prepare you for what we must do, but we haven't much time. Shall we begin?" Brendan and Aria, whose heads were still spinning, mindlessly nodded their agreement.

"Aria has used her magic some, but I never knew of mine. I have no idea how it will make me feel or how to control it," Brendan said as they began.

"I will use my skill with magic to keep you under control as you learn. I want you to put your pendant on now, Brendan. You will not feel anything, just as you did not when wearing Aria's," Brielle said.

Brendan put the silver chain around his neck, and after looking momentarily at the pendant, he let it rest against his chest. Brielle was right; he felt nothing, no change washed over him, and he did not sense any magic presence within him.

"Brendan, I want you to turn that stone into a rabbit. You need only tell your magic what you want; it will do everything else."

Brendan stepped closer to the stone that Brielle had pointed to. He felt foolish not knowing what to do and was uncomfortable with the feeling.

"Don't overthink it," Brielle said calmly.

Brendan looked at the stone and thought about its being a rabbit. That didn't work. He then asked it to turn into a rabbit in his mind, and that did not work either. He tried staring at the stone and picturing it as a rabbit, and again nothing. Finally, he was told to stand back and let Aria try. She stepped up near the stone, raised her hand, and it became a rabbit and hopped off.

"What am I doing wrong?" Brendan asked the two.

"You are either wishing or asking the stone to change itself. The stone has no power to do so. Let your magic do it. Once you use it a few times, you will see what I mean. Don't try to overpower it. You must wield your magic with ease. Do not think about it; let what you desire happen through the use of your magic. Choose another stone and try again."

Brendan tried again and nothing happened. He grabbed his pendant and looked at it closely. "I think mine's broken," he said. The three girls laughed, and he along with them.

"Let me try this again," he said. He cleared his mind and raised his hand at a stone, willing the magic to act and expecting it to obey him, and this time, it did. A rabbit the size of a mouse was now in the stone's place.

"Oh, how cute! Is that all you've got, Brendan?" Aria taunted, then giggled and winked at Brielle. Brielle smiled but said nothing. "I guess it's better than nothing, but what are you going to do with one that size? Maybe you could keep it in your pocket for luck?" Aria said, giggling again, and then broke into outright laughter at Brendan's expense.

"All right, Aria, that's enough," Brendan said as he turned and raised his hand. This time, the rabbit became the size of a horse. Brendan gave Aria a smug look over his shoulder. "Size, huh?"

Brielle quickly turned the giant rabbit back into a stone. "Keep going," Brielle said, and he did. He started changing many things small and large, and then changed them back again. Within a short amount of time, he was getting very comfortable in controlling his magic.

"Okay, now you need to really feel the power of it. Destroy a tree!" Brielle commanded. Brendan turned and without thinking shot a bolt of wicked-looking green fire slamming into the tree nearest them, destroying it instantly.

"Aria, it's your turn. Destroy one of those over there," Brielle again demanded, and pointed.

Aria did as she was told, sending a burst of red fire slamming into a tree a bit farther away. The tree was completely destroyed by the effort.

Brielle worked with both of them for a very long time, making their challenges more and more difficult, until both Brendan and Aria could follow her commands without hesitation or mistake. Next, the two learned how to disappear and reappear in another place. It was challenging for both at first, but they soon became quite adept at it.

"Now for defense," Brielle announced. "What I do now will hurt a bit, and you won't like it, but it will not injure you, I promise," she announced as she walked over and seated herself with Willow at a small table nearby. "Defend yourselves!" she shouted. With that, she waved her hands and stinging blue bursts of electricity danced and crackled in the air. The blue charges attacked the two in short bursts, chasing and shocking them repeatedly. At first, they ducked and rolled, trying to avoid them using their physical training. They were completely unsuccessful at outmaneuvering the relentless bursts. Brendan said a few choice words as he tried again to avoid them, while Aria was having a bit more fun as she ran about. She would scream and then laugh each time she was shocked.

Brielle looked at Willow, who was having a great time watching the two. She was laughing and clapping as she taunted her aunt and uncle.

"You can run but you can't hide!" Willow shouted at the two. "Use your magic!"

Brielle could not help herself; she loved the fact that her daughter finally knew of her and, more important, had accepted her. She wished things could have been different for the two of them, and perhaps in hindsight, they could have, she thought. It was a thought that affected her deeply, one she found hard to reconcile with her conscience.

Brendan and Aria were having fits as the stinging bits of electricity chased them down. They continued to rely on their physical speed and agility to avoid them, but were slowing as they tired and simply could not escape the relentless stinging charges.

"You must use your magic!" Willow called out again. Something changed within Brendan first, and then Aria. They stopped running and stood their ground. Each began to weaken the electrical charges and then simply block them altogether.

"Excellent!" Brielle applauded. "Now it really gets fun!" Four demons appeared, all shooting the shocking charges as they surrounded them. This time, the siblings stood their ground, blocked the charges, and destroyed the demons while working together.

"Continue!" Brielle shouted. Now there were a dozen demons using various weapons to attack them. The two destroyed them with ease.

"It gets harder now!" Brielle shouted at the two, not giving them a break. A dozen demons and a pack of moon wolves ten strong surrounded them. Moon wolves were half-man, half-wolf beasts that had once roamed the woods of the Shale Mountains. They were descendants of the dark creatures in Vantrill's old army. Nobody had seen one in years, and only Brielle knew the real reason why.

Aria and Brendan were facing impossible odds. They were breathing hard, bent forward with their hands on their knees. Aria looked to Brendan. "I've got an idea. Follow me!" she said, and disappeared, with Brendan doing the same a split second later.

Willow applauded and laughed as they did. The two reappeared several paces behind Willow and her mother. Aria raised her hands, and a barrel of water appeared over the two. As the water poured out, Brielle blocked it instantly without looking and diverted the water back over Brendan and Aria. Her two siblings stood soaking wet and disgusted as the last of the water poured over them. She stopped the training exercise, and the demons and moon wolves disappeared.

"You were smart to abandon your position," Brielle said as she took Willow by the hand and walked off with her toward the palace. The two soaked siblings looked at each other, dumbfounded.

"Our sister, the Blue Witch, is very good, isn't she?" Brendan said.

"Yes, yes, she is," Aria answered, wringing the water out of her hair.

Their training continued later that day. This time, Brielle sat them down for a talk before starting.

"You are both capable of using your magic and controlling it. Now I want to tell you what you are truly capable of, and what your limitations are, so that you are prepared for what is to come."

"Forgive me, Brielle, but it seems as though our magic has no limits," Brendan said.

"Do not be fooled, either of you. Magic has its limitations. As strong and as powerful as our family's magic is, it will not make you smarter, faster, or stronger. It will not in itself increase any skill that you possess, for that is not the nature of our magic. Our magic is primarily meant to be a weapon and defense for us. There are other benefits and uses of it, of course, but they are more limited. Those uses are by-products of the magic's origin," she explained.

"Magic can be either a blessing or a curse to you," she continued. "But it must never be taken for granted. It is your mind and your will that must control and wield it, not your emotions. Emotions can be fickle, and therefore dangerous to you when you use your magic. Control your emotions, and you will have control of your magic. But I warn you both, if you lose control of your emotions, you could lose control of your magic. It may not work, or it may not work in the way you intend. In the extreme, it could even harm you, or others you do not intend to harm."

"Harm us!" Aria exclaimed.

"Yes. Do not misunderstand me, Aria, it will not turn against you. But if you are out of control when using your magic, you are inviting disaster. Magic is not a toy. It is nothing to be trifled with. And remember this, both of you: magic demands a price."

"What do you mean? What kind of price?" Brendan asked.

Brielle looked away, silent, for several moments. When she looked back, she gazed intently at each of the two. "It will change you."

Brendan and Aria looked to each other, but neither could bring themselves to ask how.

"Will our magic lose its strength if we use too much at one time?" Aria asked instead.

"Your strength will fail, not your magic's. Your magic resides within you, but it does not draw its strength from you. Your magic draws its power from the world around you. Be aware of this. Should your strength fail, it will not be your magic's power that fails you, it will be your ability to call upon it and wield it effectively."

Returning to their training, Brielle taught the two what she could in the time they had to work with. She was patient with them when needed but pressed them to excel quickly, demanding perfection in their execution of her instructions. While she knew they still had much to learn, it was clear that they were both powerful, dangerous, and capable of defending themselves. One fact remained painfully evident to Brielle: Brendan and Aria still had nowhere near her capabilities, and it would be a very long time, if ever, before they did.

Chapter 16

W hen she had finished her training with Aria and Brendan for the day, Brielle took Willow by the hand and they walked the palace gardens together. They enjoyed the pleasant evening air as they strolled the stone paths that meandered through the vast, lush gardens. Brielle and Willow could once again smell the sweet, welcoming array of scents of the garden's offerings as they made their way along. Neither spoke, the two very much enjoying the quiet connection with one another that had long eluded them.

"Willow, I will tell you more about yourself if you will allow me," Brielle said in a hushed and hesitant voice.

"I would like to know much more actually," Willow replied. "I would like to know who my father is, and why I was left to be raised by others. I would like to know why you look so young, when you must be many years older than you appear."

"Then let's sit for a bit as we talk," Brielle said, and pointed ahead to a bench along the walk. The bench sat on the edge of one of the garden's large ponds. Lily pads lined the banks and their large blooms were on full display. Several brightly colored dragonflies flittered about them. A small fish broke through the surface, seeking what was beyond its reach, before splashing down into its familiar world once again.

Brielle hesitated for some time as she sat staring out over the pond, gathering her thoughts. *How do I tell my child everything I must?* She struggled with her words and what she should say first, before finally gathering her will and beginning.

"When the accident I caused happened, I was devastated. My magic had protected me from injury, but I had been turned instantaneously blue. The magic, acting to protect me, took me outside the mine, well clear of the scene, to a spot just inside the woods near the mouth of the mine. From there, I watched as some made it out but quickly realized my actions had trapped and most likely killed many innocent people. I hid there, scared and alone. I watched as people screamed for help, but few could come to their aid. It was a horrific scene of frustration and utter devastation. I did not fully understand at the time what had happened or why, but I was certain that I was to blame. I could not use the magic to help, as I had no understanding of it or its potential. I was fifteen years old, afraid and alone. I was blue from head to toe and ashamed of myself, so I stayed hidden. I stayed there in the woods until it was dark. I watched and knew that few had made it out of the mine alive. I watched on through the night as workers brought body after body out of the mine and laid them on the ground. Many were crushed and sickly twisted forms, and I became ill at the sight of them, retching several times as I waited to see if my parents were alive or dead. As the dawn of the new day broke, it became all too clear my parents were among those lying dead on the ground. I cried and wanted to scream out but knew that I could not. So, I held myself, rocking back and forth, crying, until something of who I'd been was lost to me."

Brielle fell silent again. Willow squeezed her hand gently and waited for her to speak.

"I watched the next three days as the bodies were removed from the site and all further rescue attempts eventually forsaken. I didn't know what to do, so I watched during the days and lay on the ground there in the woods and cried myself to sleep each night. When I awoke on my last day there, it was still dark, and I was both thirsty and famished. I slipped down to the mouth of the now-abandoned mine and scavenged water and food left behind by the rescuers, and the families who'd gathered hoping for better news of their loved ones." Brielle glanced at Willow, who was listening intently, and then quickly looked away.

"I became a creature of the night then. I would stay hidden during the day, afraid to show myself. I traveled by night, scavenging for food and water as best I could. I hated the magic within me and refused to use it for a long time. I replayed the events at the mine over and over in my mind. As I did so, I became angrier and even more frustrated with my magic. One night I decided that I was going to master it. I was not only going to use the magic for good, but I was going to gain complete control over it, so I would never accidentally do any harm again. I made my way deep into the Shale Mountains, where I would be able to work on my skills undisturbed. There, I camped along a stream where I was able to easily catch fish to eat. I ate what berries and plants I was able to scavenge as well." Brielle stood and looked down lovingly at Willow.

"I spent a great deal of time training myself in those mountains. Many hours a day, day in and day out, I trained. I trained in the use of my magic for many months, which became years. One night, as I finished washing in the stream, I stepped out of the water to find that I was being watched—hunted, even. The moon wolves had found me. I had only heard rumor of them. That there was one pack that remained in those mountains, the spawn of those in a demon's army of old. I was surrounded and had no choice but to stand my ground and fight. Running was not an option. I was naked and had no weapon other than my magic to defend myself. I fought, Willow, using my magic. I found it far too easy to kill. I'd trained so much that the magic was simply a part of me. I killed them one after the other. I did not allow even one of them to escape my wrath that night. The hunters became the hunted, as they'd found a creature far more loathsome than themselves," Brielle said, seating herself again before continuing.

Brielle shook her head, fighting back tears. "It was that night that I decided I would no longer hide away in those mountains. I needed to change form to go unnoticed, and my magic allowed me to do so. I changed my appearance so that I looked like an ordinary young woman, my former self, but at my actual age of nineteen. I descended the mountains on the west side and came upon a small village. I managed to find work there in a little candle shop and tried for a brief time to live a normal life. I'd spent almost four years in those mountains alone and wanted to start living again. While living in the village, I met your father. A young man named Adon. We spent a great deal of time together and fell deeply in love with each other. He was a kind and handsome young man, and I was very much smitten with him. We planned to marry and were soon finalizing the plans for our special day. It was the best time of my life." She stopped, becoming lost in her memories.

"Something happened to my father, though, didn't it?" Willow asked. Brielle looked at her with tears in her eyes and nodded. She moved away from the bench to the edge of the pond. Willow left the bench and went to her, and they held each other for several moments.

"I was working in the candle shop one day when a crowd started to gather out front," Brielle continued. "The owner went outside to see what was happening. I was in the back and did not know anything was taking place out front. The owner ran back to me and told me there'd been an accident and to hurry. There was a wagon in the street out in front of the store, with a crowd gathered around it. The store's owner pulled me through those gathered until I was right beside the wagon. In the wagon, Adon lay badly injured. I screamed out and jumped up into it, kissing his face." She paused once again as she relived the moment.

"I learned he'd been working that day helping his father cut down trees to clear a section of land on their farm. A wheel on the wagon they were using to haul the wood became damaged and was failing. Adon had jumped down off the wagon to see what he could do to fix the wheel. As he was checking it, their horse was spooked by a snake crossing the ground in front of it and reared back. The wheel collapsed and the wagon fell across Adon's chest. His distraught father was eventually able to get the wagon off him and brought him into town to the doctor's office next door to the candle shop. His father believed nothing could be done for Adon, but not knowing what else to do, he had brought him there hoping against all reason he was wrong. Adon looked up at me and tried to speak but couldn't. I did not yet know of any power I had to heal, so I kissed his cheek again and held his hand as he died. Had I thought it possible to heal through my magic, I may have been able to save him," she said as she glanced at Willow. "I could not bear my great sorrow in the days that followed. I left and did not attend Adon's funeral. I was devastated once again by tragedy and death, and sought solitude once more."

Brielle took Willow by the hand. "Come, let's walk for a bit." The two set off down the garden path together once again.

"When I left the village, I did not wish to live. I wandered for days south along the coast, finding myself drawn to the Dead Bridge. I knew the story of it but no longer cared what would happen to me as I stood before its black expanse. I screamed in frustration and ran onto the bridge, assuming I would be killed. Instead, I found Andentine waiting for me. He welcomed me to his realm, and we spent a great deal of time speaking with each other.

"It was then that he told me of our family's history. He explained that the spirit of the bridge recognized my magic and accepted it, and this was the reason I'd not been killed crossing. Andentine told me that while I was welcome to visit any time I wished, I could not stay in his realm permanently, though I desperately wanted to. Andentine insisted I find my place in this world." Brielle looked at Willow, studying her for a moment, before continuing.

"Before I left Andentine and his realm, he told me something I had not yet discovered myself. He told me I was with child—you, Willow." She stopped, reaching to Willow, and took both of her hands in her own.

"I want you to know you saved my life, Willow. Knowing I had a part of Adon still with me, and our child to look forward to, gave me a reason to live. You gave me hope, Willow." She pulled her daughter to her and hugged her tight. "I love you so much." When Brielle finally released her and stepped back, Willow looked to the ground, then back to her.

"Then why did you leave me for others to raise? Why did you abandon me?" Willow began crying, her pent-up emotions unleashed. "I was alone too, you know! I had nobody! I've been living for as long as I can remember wondering who I am and why I was found in front of this place alone. I cried myself to sleep in the dark of night too! I wondered why my parents didn't love me. I couldn't understand what I'd done to make them cast me out. Why did you leave me?" Willow sobbed as tears flowed down her face. She pulled her hands away from Brielle and turned away from her.

"I left you because I loved you too much to put you through what being with me would have done to you. I wanted you to have a better life. One I could never have given you. After I had you, I realized life with me would not be fair to you. I knew, Willow, I could not provide you a normal life and a steady home. A place where you could grow up with your friends and be safe from the danger I would surely put you in if you remained with me. It is because I love you, Willow, not because I don't, that I gave you up. You did nothing wrong. I wanted the best for you. I've made a lot of mistakes and been wrong about a great many things. But I was determined to do the right thing for you, regardless of what that meant for me," Brielle said.

"I came for you when I learned of your caretakers' murders. When I found that you were at the palace under King Tennington's care, I wanted to take you with me desperately, but I knew you would have a far better life here than I could provide for you. So, I left you here in the king's care. I will always think of him fondly for the kindness he has shown you."

"I would've rather been with you, no matter how bad it was or how we had to live. I hated not knowing who I was!" Willow said, a bit less angry than before but clearly still upset.

"I want to share something with you, Willow." Brielle looked down, her emotions getting the better of her once again as she fought to maintain control of herself. She looked up at the sky, her blue eyes filling with tears. "You were not alone, Willow. I spent as much time with you as I possibly could. I—"

"You did not! I never saw you until we were at the Window of Souls! Don't lie to make me feel better!"

"That is not exactly true, Willow; let me explain. When you were a baby, I would use my magic to transform myself into one of your caregivers. I would hold you for long periods of time in my arms, watching you sleep. As you grew and began to play with others, I would transform myself into a child, and we would play together. I spent as much time with you as I could, Willow, though never as myself. I loved our time together and cherished it immensely, but I could not be seen as myself. Being with you was such a pleasure to me but was also so very cruel. I had to leave you over and over again, when I wanted nothing more than to stay with you. A great many times, I left crying, barely able to pull myself away from you. It crushed me to leave you. I thought I was the only one suffering. But I realize now how unfair it was to you. And for that, I am truly sorry."

Willow looked at her mother and began crying again. "So, you do love me?"

Brielle, full of regret and thinking of what could have been, could only nod, unable to speak. Willow embraced her, and they held each other close as they wept.

Willow lay awake in her bed that night trying to use her gift of sight to see her father when he was alive, but found her sight was still being blocked. Only now, it was worse, and she could not see anything at all when she tried to use it. She lay there, lost in her thoughts but a bit more at peace with her life.

Chapter 17

T he following morning, Brielle came to Willow's room to take her down for breakfast. She knocked politely and waited for a response from within, but none came. She tried once more with the same result. She smiled as she opened the door.

"Wake up, sleepyhead, let's go—" Brielle stopped midsentence. Her daughter's bed was empty and unmade. She started to walk out of the room, thinking Willow must have gone down to the dining room without her, but stopped herself. She could feel it. Something was wrong. She went back to the bed and placed her hand on it, closing her eyes as she did. Her eyes snapped open and she bolted from the room.

Brendan and Aria were seated at a table in the dining hall preparing to have breakfast with Bear and Vander.

Starlin, Drae, and Drake walked in and pulled up chairs at the long table. They were soon joined by Vlix. Each member of Brendan's group had been invited to stay at the palace, and all had accepted the invitation to do so. Vlix had no sooner sat down than Brielle ran in.

"Willow has been taken!" she blurted out. The group came to their feet as one.

"What's happened? How do you know she's gone?" Brendan asked.

"I went to get her for breakfast, but her room was empty. I felt something was wrong and placed my hands on her bed. There is no doubt in my mind. Vantrill has taken her! I must go. I have to save her."

"We'll help you." He glanced at Aria and she nodded. "What's your plan?"

"No. You will stay here and help the army. I will go after Willow alone."

"We must come with you!" Aria insisted.

"No. I have taught you what I could in a very short time, but your abilities are still nowhere near mine. I will be better off going alone. You must stay here. Vantrill has obviously altered his plans. He expects us to come after Willow, and that's when he'll have his army attack. If I go alone, you'll be able to give support to the army just as we planned. Please inform our king that I will return with Willow as soon as possible." She noticed the dejected look on Vander's face. "Vander, you and your men could in no way have prevented this. But you must inform Tennington that the attack is going to come this day. I must leave, but I will return as quickly as I can."

She was there one instant and gone the next. Vander was off and running at full speed to inform Tennington without a word to the others. Brendan turned to Bear.

"Aria and I must take up our positions. Where do you plan to be?"

"I will be with the Elite, of course," Bear answered with a devilish grin.

"Starlin, I have already spoken to Vander about this. I do not know what he has told you, but you will assist Drae. You are not to leave the palace and the protection of Vander and the King's Watch. Do you understand?"

"Yes, Vander told me. Drae's aware as well."

"Very well. Good luck to you all this day, and be safe."

Bear grabbed Brendan's shoulders firmly. "I expect to see you and Aria when this is all over, so you two be careful." He released Brendan and turned to Aria. He stood looking at the girl, then smiled and bent down, hugging her. "Take care of him out there; you know how he gets."

Aria hugged him back. "I will, Bear. I promise."

They all knew what was expected of them, and they left for their respective destinations. Vander and Vlix would take their places with the King's Watch. They would stand with the Watch as the last line of defense closest to the palace, though neither liked being at the rear of the action. Drake went to scout ahead. Starlin and Drae made their way to the care center that had been set up for the expected wounded.

Brendan and Aria left to take up their forward positions. They were each going to be outside the outer wall, out in front of the Elite's forward position. Behind them would be a third of the army, with two-thirds in reserve between the curtain walls and manning the battlements. There had been much debate about keeping a full two-thirds of the army in reserve, but Brielle had convinced King Tennington it would be the best strategy on this day.

As the army stood ready to march off to war, a lone rider in light armor rode through the outer gates of the city to join them. Cheers rose up from the assembled men and women as he passed them by. It was King Tennington himself. Tennington felt there was no other place he should be than out front with his troops.

"And what exactly do you think you're doing out here?" Commander Stinson asked.

"I'm exactly where a good king should be on a day such as this, Commander!" Tennington responded emphatically.

Stinson nodded. "Will you at least agree to stay with me, Your Highness? The Blue Witch and I have a few tricks planned and I would feel better if you did."

Tennington looked at his commander and nodded. "Very well, Commander, I would be honored to join you."

"My lord." Stinson bowed from atop his mount.

All was now ready. If the Blue Witch was right, Tennington thought, the attack would be starting very soon. He was worried for Willow, and his thoughts drifted to the child. The Blue Witch's daughter; who would have ever thought it? He glanced over at Stinson and found the man looking at him intently. He nodded to signal that he was ready, and Stinson returned the gesture.

Bear was at the rear of the Elite and just in front of Stinson and their king. He felt young again as he waited. Being on the battlefield before the start of war took him back to his youth. He thought of Tay, taken too soon from the world of the living, and all that had happened since Brendan Pandane had walked into his life. Life often had a way of deciding on its own path, regardless of the plans fretted over by those living it, he thought, smiling and shaking his head.

Brendan and Aria were in their positions at the very front, a good distance apart, though still within sight of each other. They had each taken up a position beyond the stone fences lining the main road leading to the palace. Brendan was on one side of the road and Aria on the other. While they were both well out front, they could still see the front lines of the Elite forces if they looked back for them.

Commander Stinson rode forward and came alongside Bear. "I would like your help, Bear, as both an advisor to me and a protector of the king. It would be a great honor to us both if you would join us."

"It would be my honor and privilege," Bear replied. The two immediately returned to the side of their king.

"Your Highness," Stinson said to Tennington. "May I present Baird Prow? Baird is the most decorated veteran the Elite First has ever been privileged to have among its ranks."

"We have met, Commander. Thank you for joining us, Bear. I assume Commander Stinson would like a little extra protection for his aging king," he replied, cocking a knowing eyebrow at Stinson. "I'm not that old, you know."

"As you say, but I would like to see you grow much older, my lord."

A moment later, it began. Waves of Zaroes and their flyers flew in from the rear over the lake. They began unleashing their firedrops on the assembled army, who were now cursing and scrambling to avoid the firewash as best they could. Many were unsuccessful and were badly burned.

The Zaroes and their flyers were clearly targeting the army and not the palace or the city. Brendan and Aria, from their forward positions, began knocking the Zaroes out of the sky, sending them crashing to the ground, where their firedrops exploded on contact in great blazing flashes. Their burning carcasses began to litter the grounds around the palace, both inside and outside the walls. They came in great numbers, but Brendan and Aria cut them down one by one. The Zaroes that could retreat did so, to the cheers of the men and women on the ground.

Brendan and Aria's attention was diverted back down the wide road that led to the palace. They could hear drums pounding and the heavy footfalls of the enemy army marching ever closer. Two young giants bound in huge chains came into view. Brendan thought them at least thirty feet tall. The two towered over the demons who controlled them. Aria and Brendan looked across the road at each other and then focused again on the giants. They left their hiding places, leapt over the walls, and met in the middle of the road before the two.

"We call to you, good giants!" Brendan yelled ahead to them. "Do not fight us this day, for we are not your enemy! Andentine offers you both a place in his realm forever if you join our cause!"

The two giants looked at each other, grinning. They had been kept in chains and under spells, forced to serve their captors for far too long. They turned and pulled the demons holding their chains flying into the air as they broke free. They swatted their captors like flies as they flew toward them, and the demons about them scattered as pieces of their brethren rained down on them. The two giants gathered their chains and began thrashing the demons nearest them, ripping them apart. The demons panicked and tried to flee but were either beaten with the chains or stomped upon. Brendan and Aria ran to the giants' sides and began destroying as many of the demon horde as they could.

The demons were a hideous mix of men and beasts of all kinds. Some of them were larger, others smaller. Some walked upright, some on all fours, and yet others slithered along the ground. There were even those who were winged and could fly for short distances. They were bits and pieces of flesh and bone strung together with muscle and sinew, dark things that were rotten and decaying, many missing parts of themselves. Most carried a weapon of one kind or another. Clubs, spears, maces, and pikes were most common, while some did carry swords. Although, in truth, their vast numbers were their real weapon.

The king's army did as they had been ordered and held back, while those at the vanguard of the demon army were in complete panic. The two giants, with Brendan's and Aria's help, were driving the demons back and littering the road with their dead. The demon troops left standing went into full retreat and fled from sight. Again, the men and women of Tennington's army cheered. The two giants faced Brendan and Aria once again.

"I am Tanton, and this is my brother, Tiden," one of the giants said.

"This is my sister Aria, and I am Brendan. Thank you for joining us!"

"We wish to go to Andentine's realm. It has been our dream for as long as we can remember. Is the offer you made honestly from him? Is it true?" Tiden asked.

"It is indeed. I give you my word on it," Aria assured them.

"Then my brother and I are at your service," Tanton replied as he and Tiden towered over Brendan and Aria.

"We have been held as slaves for far too long," Tiden told them. "They thought they could hold us in these chains and force us to fight for them. A blue girl appeared before us and told us a young man and woman with red hair would stand here on this road and offer us a haven in Andentine's realm if we turned against the demons. She freed us of the spell that held us prisoners. She warned us not to harm you or any with you when we came, and to join you if we wished to enter Andentine's realm. We could only hope that it would be true."

"That was our sister, Brielle. She's known here as a very powerful witch. She is called the Blue Witch, for obvious reasons," Brendan replied. "If you would please join our king, King Tennington, they will be expecting you. The Blue Witch asked you be positioned there, with him, Commander Stinson, and a large man—by our standards—known as Bear." The giants nodded and left to take up their new positions in the rear with the king.

"So far, so good," Brendan said to Aria. "Are you ready for what comes next?"

"Of course I am!" she said, flashing her mischievous grin.

Chapter 18

Brielle, cloaked in invisibility, searched the old dungeons of the castle she knew to be Vantrill's. Though she was not familiar with its location in the realm, she was able to take herself there using her magic. She was concentrating on her search, staying focused and alert to any possible danger. She had seen Willow being held in a cage somewhere in the castle's dungeons but still had to find exactly where. Vantrill would almost certainly be able to sense her presence, so she hurried to find Willow and get them both out of there as quickly as she could.

She drifted through the dungeons searching for her daughter, knowing full well she was walking into a trap and Willow was the bait. She was also certain Vantrill's army would have started their attack by now. She hoped some of her surprises for them were working out as she'd planned.

Suddenly, she heard a loathsome voice in her head. "Blue creature of magic, welcome! I've been expecting you."

"Where's the girl?" she demanded, speaking the words in her mind.

"She's having some fun here with me. Would you care to join us?"

"Let's make this easy on both of us, Vantrill. I'm taking her back."

"We shall see, blue one. I may even allow her to be taken, if I get what I want."

"What do you want?"

"Why, I want that pendant you wear around your neck, of course."

"That's not going to happen."

"Oh, I think it will. I think you'll give it to me gladly to see your daughter safely returned to you. Particularly when you see how we've been playing while we've waited for you."

Brielle could hear Willow screaming from somewhere ahead. "There's no reason to hurt the girl," Brielle said calmly. "She'll be leaving this place with me. Whether you're still drawing breath when we do is up to you."

"You are very brave to talk to me that way. But I sense the fear you have for your young daughter's life. It's beginning to overwhelm you. You reek of it."

"I do indeed fear for her life. She is afraid and defenseless. I, however, am neither, nor do I fear for my life. Know this, Vantrill: should you actually harm her, you will not live to see the end of this day."

"Oh, blue one, you are so confident in your skills, or at least you wish me to believe you are. You have the use of magic, girl, but your powers pale in comparison to mine. I will do what I wish with your young daughter. Things you could not possibly imagine another capable of, if you do not hand over that pendant."

"If you're so powerful, why do you want my pendant?"

"That's a fair question indeed," Vantrill hissed. "Because your pendant is capable of magnifying the power of magic to levels far greater than the bearer's own ability. Andentine designed them to do so. It was a very clever way for him to help your ancestors force me to abandon my realm. But then, I was much weaker in those days. It won't happen again, not with the power I now possess." Vantrill paused before continuing.

"Once I have the pendant, I will return your daughter to you unharmed. My demons and I will leave this realm forever and finish what we started long ago. I will have the extra power I need to exact my revenge on Andentine, and I will have his world for my own."

"So, let me understand this. You ruined and subverted this realm in the past with your greed and lack of empathy for its people. You lost what you falsely claimed to be yours after taking it by force. And now you wish to grow even more powerful so you can invade another realm and make the same mistakes all over again," Brielle spat back.

"Do not lecture me, girl!" Vantrill hissed. "I'm through with your foolish attempts to frighten me with your meaningless threats. Bring the pendant to me now or your daughter dies!" A door at the far end of a long corridor to her right opened. "Now!"

"Don't harm her! I'm coming." Brielle made her way to the doorway and stepped through. A form of Vantrill's magic immediately attacked her. She easily walked through the trap without slowing. She crossed the room to where Vantrill's dark form was seated and sat in the chair across from him.

"Did you really think that pathetic attempt would work on me?" she scoffed.

"No. But I thought you'd be disappointed if I did not throw a little something your way," Vantrill said, still hidden in the shadows of the darkened room.

"Where is my daughter, Vantrill?"

"She's safe…for now. I only sought to bring you here so we could speak of a peace between us."

"Peace? As we speak your army of demons is attacking my people."

"We've not yet agreed on peace. But peace is what I wish for, for you and me. My anger is no longer directed at your world. It is a means to an end. My hatred and wrath are aimed at Andentine and his kingdom for all he's cost me."

"You take no blame for your part?"

"I certainly do not! This is my home! My realm to rule over as I see fit! Andentine and his miserable elven magic cost me dearly!" Vantrill insisted, raising his voice for the first time.

Brielle was sure she had hit a major nerve. "For what it's worth, it does seem unfair that he deserted this world but left magic behind to torment you. Even if I now possess that magic."

Vantrill leaned forward in his chair but still lay within the shadows. "It was unfair. If he did not like what was happening here, he should have taken his elves and left. Had he done so, I would have no hatred of him. And he could have simply banished me back to this realm, my home, when I invaded his realm seeking my revenge the first time. I had all but won the war for this realm before his little magic trick."

Vantrill paused for a long moment before continuing. "The world he banished me to was a horrible place, so dark and loathsome," he said. "I'll make Andentine pay for sending me there. Do you see now why I must have the pendant? It is the key to my continued freedom, and my revenge."

"Hmm, I see. But how could I be sure you wouldn't turn on us after defeating Andentine and come back here to wipe us all out?"

"Why, I would have no reason to do so. I would have exacted my revenge on Andentine and captured a truly magical realm of my own. You would have my solemn word on the matter. And I know there are two other pendants around your siblings' necks."

She looked at him, trying not to show her surprise. "True, they would be a significant deterrent."

"They would indeed. Do you have something against Andentine as well? It appears to me you do."

"I've crossed the Dead Bridge many times seeking Andentine's permission to look into the Window of Souls. I want to see and speak to my parents, who were killed when I was a young girl. He refuses to allow me that small favor. It is unfair and cruel."

"Andentine pretends to be fair, but he is cruel, isn't he?"

"He has been to me, even if he doesn't realize it," she said with her head hung low.

"Do you take me for a fool! Did you think I would fall for this childish ploy?"

"No, but I thought you'd be disappointed if I didn't throw a little something your way."

"I do admire your confidence, even your arrogance. I know you think you're more than a match for me, girl, but I assure you, you are not!"

Chapter 19

Commander Stinson looked out over the men and women under his command and then to his king sitting astride his mount beside him.

"Are you ready for one of those surprises I told you about, Your Highness?"

King Tennington glanced at the two giants and then back to Stinson. "I thought these two were a pretty big surprise. You have more?"

"I do. Those two are the Blue Witch's doing." He laughed. "Watch this!" He gave a signal, and a moment later, dozens of round projectiles flew from somewhere behind them. They landed far out into the demon army's ranks, each one exploding with violent force and ripping hundreds of the enemy apart.

"Shade me! Impressive, Commander! How did we come by such weapons?"

"I've been working with an armorer in Ravens Burg who owns a shop called the Raven's Sword. He's very talented and has made a few trips to see me lately to deliver them and train us in the usage of them. They are far larger versions of a weapon he calls a flash pod."

"Ah yes, I believe I've seen the smaller version up close. Well done, Commander!"

Aria and Brendan had watched the projectiles flying overhead and exploding well beyond their positions. They were part of the plan and the siblings had been expecting them. The two stepped back out onto the road and began to advance. The vanguard of the Elite First kept its distance but advanced with them.

Aria and Brendan were destroying the enemy with blast after blast of green and red fire. They did not slow as they continued their advance. They cut through the enemy lines, decimating the nearest demons. The Elite First, and the army behind them, closed their ranks behind the two siblings. They were now only a short distance away as they all marched forward, continuing to destroy their enemies. Then Brendan and Aria stopped. Each launched a bolt of their fire high into the sky above them before disappearing from the road.

The legendary battle cry of the Elite First rang out: "First to charge…last to die!" The Elite charged down the road, past where Aria and Brendan had just been, and cut into the enemy forces with an intensity that was shocking. The enemy scattered but was ridden down by the men and women of the Elite. The Elite force chased the enemy over a steep hill before them. Moments later, they came roaring back over the hill, spurring their mounts furiously, followed by more demons than could be counted. They turned and formed ranks, still well out in front of Aria and

Brendan, who had reappeared farther back on the road, and the rest of the king's army behind them.

Stinson quickly gave another signal, and a new round of projectiles flew overhead into the ranks of the demons at the crest of the hill, tearing through those in pursuit of the Elite First. The Elite charged, cutting through the enemy again, driving them back and finishing off any remaining wounded from the blasts. They were again forced back by sheer numbers, but this time, they did not stop and rode past Aria and Brendan's new positions. Aria and Brendan attacked again and again, killing hundreds of the demons. The demon bodies piled up so high, they were blocking their own forces from trying to counter and advance. The war raged on like this through most of the day before the demons, having taken such heavy losses, came no more.

Two members of the Elite, a young woman and man, rode to Aria and Brendan and carried them back to the king's side. Cheers rose up from the Elite and the army as they rode past.

"Well done!" Tennington said to them. "It has been a long day and it has been ours. We shall return within our walls and regroup. Commander Stinson, I would ask that you join us in the Great Hall when we get back," he said before turning his attention to the two giants.

"My friends, I have an area that can accommodate your size in the palace; it is known as the Great Hall. There are large doors I believe you will be able to pass through with ease. Please join us as well." The two brothers nodded. "Bear, I would ask that you stay by my side."

Bear bowed and rode beside him as he returned through the gates. They were greeted with loud cheers from the reserve troops as they rode past. Vander stood waiting to greet them as they entered the Great Hall.

"Captain Ray, join us!" Tennington called to him. When they had gathered together in the Great Hall, Tennington gestured for Aria to join him. "Do you think you could use your magic to help us accommodate our large friends here?"

Aria smiled and raised her hands, making a couple of gestures, and two giant-sized chairs appeared for the brothers. She made a couple more gestures, and a large, raised table appeared at the far end of the council table where the giants' two chairs sat. She looked around the Great Hall and again gestured, and there were suddenly two beds with matching bedding and pillows. Aria looked up at the giants, gauging their reaction.

"Please let me know if I may provide you with anything else for your comfort."

The two looked at each other and began whispering. They then looked back to Aria. "Um…perhaps something for the night urges?" Tanton asked, cocking his head toward the two beds.

"But of course, gentlemen." Aria giggled, adding an appropriately sized chamber pot by each bed.

"Thank you, my lady," Tiden responded.

"I don't think it could have gone much better today. I'm proud of each and every one of you," Tennington began. "We know this is by no means over, but we'll eat and rest as we can. Enjoy your food and wait here for my return. I wish to visit the wounded before we talk further. We have much to discuss." Then he left those gathered, with Bear and Vander at his side.

Tanton and Tiden rose from their new chairs and gazed at the stained-glass ceiling above them in awe.

"Have you ever seen such a place, brother?" Tiden asked. Tanton could only shake his head, speechless. They examined closely the carved beasts that were holding up the ceiling of the hall. They were impressed at the size of them; each was larger than even they were. They then turned their attention to the colorful mist dancing and swirling just above the white marble floor. They looked at each other and grinned, clasping each other's shoulders.

Food and drinks were soon brought in by servers and placed on the council table. The servers looked at the two giants sitting at the end of the table and stopped short.

"We've been preparing for the two of you since early this morning," the head server announced. "The Blue Witch told us to be expecting you." Tray after heaping tray of meat, potatoes, vegetables, and bread was brought in and placed on their part of the table by several servers using steps provided by Aria. Several barrels of ale soon arrived for each of the giants as well. Aria looked over and noticed the problem first. She raised her hand, and two sets of silverware and napkins appeared, along with plates and glasses of appropriate size. Tanton and Tiden waved, thanking her.

King Tennington, Bear, and Vander made their way to the makeshift infirmary. There, they found Drae and Starlin working with those injured in the initial Zaroe attacks. They were nearly all burn victims. Some had been burned severely and were barely hanging on. Drae and Starlin had fallen into a good rhythm together. Starlin had found he had an interest in healing as well as a knack for it. There were other healers working and tending to the wounded, but Drae and Starlin were working exclusively with each other.

"How goes it?" Tennington asked as he entered the room.

"I believe most will live, Your Highness. But there are some who are beyond our skill," Drae responded. "Some of those we expect to live are burned so badly they will carry the scars the rest of their lives. We'll get them fixed up as best we can. Won't we, Starlin?"

"Yes, we will," Starlin agreed.

"So, we have not lost anyone yet today?" Tennington asked.

"None that have made it here, my lord, and I'm told there are no other wounded."

"Well done. Keep up the good work and do all you can for their comfort." With that, the king visited with those who were up to it and whispered words of encouragement to the others. Some of the wounded either tried to stand or would attempt to sit up at his approach, but Tennington would quickly stop them, telling them to stay put and rest. When he was through and had been assured he had seen everyone, King Tennington left the room with Bear and Vander by his side once again.

Chapter 20

Brielle was confident as she faced her enemy in the darkness of the room about her.

"Vantrill, there is no need for us to bicker back and forth any longer. As I said, I am leaving here with my daughter. You've achieved a small part of your goal by getting me to come here. But now I'm leaving. If you attempt to harm my family again, you will see what kind of match I am for you," she said. Brielle continued sitting calmly in front of Vantrill, staring him down without flinching, until she faded away, leaving only the empty chair.

Brielle, speaking through the image of herself she had created, had used the time to search the dungeon chambers and locate Willow. It had taken longer than expected, but she had found the girl unconscious on the floor of a cell at the back of a lower level of the castle's dungeons.

Brielle had silently dispatched four guards and freed Willow. They were safely away from the castle well before she ended her conversation with Vantrill and her image vanished. Brielle and Willow appeared in the Great Hall near the council table just as the evening's meal was being finished.

Brendan and Aria immediately rushed to them.

"Are you okay?" Brendan asked.

Aria, not waiting for a reply, grabbed Willow and hugged her tight. "I am so happy you're safe."

"We're fine," Brielle replied. Willow nodded. "Vantrill took Willow to force me to him. He wants one of our pendants desperately, but he couldn't have taken one of us in such a way. I tricked him in order to rescue her, and he's going to be furious, to say the least."

"Our tricks worked here as well. Better than we could have hoped for!" Tennington said as he welcomed her back. "While some were seriously injured, we did not lose a single man or woman. At least not yet; I am told some are beyond our healers' abilities and will not live through the night."

"It will be much more difficult from here on out. Vantrill underestimated us, as we expected he would. He will not make the same mistake twice."

"What suggestions do you have for us moving forward, Brielle?" Tennington asked.

"Pull all of your men inside the outer wall this night. Leave no one exposed beyond it. I will put up warding magic. It will alert me of any movement by our enemies. Willow and Aria will stay with me for their protection. Extra security should be placed with Brendan as well. We do not know what surprises Vantrill will bring us this night, so we must be extremely cautious. I will stand with Brendan and Aria at the front tomorrow. As I said, Vantrill wants one of our pendants. If he obtains one, he will surely come for the others. We could leave this realm for Andentine's, ensuring he could not obtain one, but it would mean abandoning our people. Our family will never cede this realm to Vantrill. Willow and I will attempt to see his plans in advance if we can, but he will be trying to block us at every turn now. If you will pardon me, my king, I will go and do what I can for the wounded."

"Very well. Thank you, Brielle. Captain Ray, see to those extra security measures. Commander Stinson, pull all your men inside the outer walls. Set a strong watch on the wall and within, but no one is to be outside of it. See that no more strong drink of any kind is allowed this night," Tennington ordered.

Brielle made her way to the infirmary and was met there by Drae and Starlin.

"I would like to help those who are injured," she said. "Though, in truth, healing anyone, even myself, has not been a strength of mine, but I've been working on that of late."

"Anything that will ease their pain or help in these soldiers' recovery would be most appreciated," Drae said.

Brielle stepped back and motioned for those attending the wounded, including Starlin and Drae, to move behind her. She raised her hands, and a sparkling blue mist began to form at her fingertips. The blue mist continued to grow and drift out into the room. From one end of the room to the other, it swirled around the wounded, seeking out their injuries.

Burns were healed and ruined flesh renewed as the mist continued to envelop the wounded. The patients began to rise from their beds, looking at themselves and touching new, healthy skin where only melted flesh covered in greasy salves had been moments before.

They were looking about bewildered, trying to figure out if they had died and this was some part of their afterlife. They could see their friends and companions surrounded by the blue mist as they scanned the room, confusing them even further.

As the mist began to recede and things became clearer in the large room, they could see they were each healed, even those previously thought beyond any hope of surviving. Cheers went up from the men and women. They began hugging and congratulating each other. Some were even jumping up and down on what would certainly have been their deathbeds as they celebrated.

"Well, now, I have to be honest," Brielle said, turning to her two companions. "That went far better than I'd hoped."

Drae and Starlin looked at each other, awestruck. "I don't know why I even try." Drae laughed. "Now, that's how you heal the wounded!"

That night, Tanton and Tiden lay awake in their beds. They were looking at the vast glass ceiling of the Great Hall, which was darker now but still magnificent in its beauty. They spoke about Andentine's kingdom and the elves. And they spoke as well of those of faerie and the majesty of the land that the Blue Witch had described to them.

"She did say there were others like us there. I wonder how many," Tiden mused.

"All our kin, and a great deal more, I should think," Tanton managed to say in a rather groggy voice before yawning.

"Then there must be at least some young women among them. We may be able to find wives and have children. Real families...and homes...of our..." Tiden's dream of how wonderful their lives in Andentine's realm would be carried him off to sleep. Tanton, lost in his own, was already there.

Chapter 21

T he creature flew with the stars shining brightly above him, his blood-red scales shimmering in the moonlight, great wings propelling his long, muscular body with ease as he skimmed along the cloud cover below. He kept his clawed feet and legs folded up beneath him as he flew, his long tail serving as rudder.

The red dragon dipped down below the clouds, checking his bearings as he thought about his orders and how much he was going to enjoy the execution of them.

The palace was peaceful, and many of the weary were getting much-needed sleep. Brielle had done as she'd planned and put up a warding barrier around the palace, giving those within its walls a great deal of extra comfort. Men stood watch on the walls and within, but no one was beyond the outer wall.

Vander's men were posted throughout the palace, but his best were guarding the rooms of King Tennington and his guests. Vander had made it clear that his men were not to attempt to question anyone in the palace who did not belong there. They were under strict orders to sound the alarm and attack on first sight without warning. Those within the rooms had been informed of these extra measures. They were all introduced to their guards and told that there would be no changing of them this night. Those guests and their guards were the only ones allowed in those rooms and halls. Brielle then sealed those areas of the palace with magic to protect them all even further.

The red dragon climbed higher in the sky as he neared the palace and those sleeping within. He banked into a sharp dive, slicing through the thick clouds that had moved in during the night. The red nightmare crashed through the glass ceiling of the Great Hall and hovered above the beds of the two giants. Shards of colored glass rained down around him, falling onto the beds and the hall's floor. The dragon drew in a great breath and spewed out his fire, incinerating the beds and the giant forms under the covers in them.

Alarms were raised, and the closest members of the King's Watch arrived in the hall a moment later. They could see the red dragon flapping his wings above what was left of the two beds and the charred forms. Then they saw the two giants making their move from out of their hiding places.

"Hello, Dazmare! Did you really think you could sneak up on us! We can sense your kind from miles away," Tanton yelled out as he ran, then leapt into the air, grabbing ahold of the dragon and pulling it down to the floor with him. Tiden latched on to one of the dragon's large wings, breaking several bones in it, before he was thrown across the room. He crashed hard into one of the pillars of the hall, his impact shattering the great carved beast.

Tanton was wrestling with the dragon as the beast sprayed fire, attempting to free himself from the giant. Tanton had to abandon his attack to avoid being burned further. As the beast finally got free of Tanton, Tiden dove headlong into him, bringing the dragon and himself crashing into another of the carved pillars.

"Dazmare, you filthy lizard, why have you come here!" Tiden called out.

"You and your brother have disappointed our lord. I've been sent to ensure you're punished for your treachery!" Dazmare hissed.

Tiden began hammering the beast with hard punches as fast as he could throw them. "Vantrill was never our lord, worm, he was our captor!" Tiden spat.

The dragon roared his displeasure, spewing fire and snapping his mighty jaws. Pools of fire burned across the hall's floor, their flames licking at the air hungrily. "You will be punished nonetheless!"

Tanton, avoiding the pools of fire, picked up a large section of an arm that had broken off one of the carved stone pillars and struck the dragon hard across its back. Dazmare reared up, lifting Tiden high in the air as he did. Tiden held on around the dragon's neck just below his jaws, squeezing his arms around the dragon's throat, attempting to keep him from breathing and spewing his fire. Tiden's powerful arms were having the desired effect until the dragon rolled violently and began shuddering his entire body, throwing Tiden free.

Tanton swung the great stone arm, turning himself completely around, and landed a crushing blow to the dragon's head. It broke the beast's jaw, sending many of its jagged teeth flying across the hall. The dragon stumbled, reeling. But as he did, he whipped his long tail out, catching Tanton and sending him crashing into another of the stone pillars. An ear-shattering crack in the roof's framework could be heard above the fray, sending those of the King's Watch who were observing the fight in the outer alcoves running for their lives.

Tiden again rushed the dragon. The wounded beast, attempting to spit his vile fire, could no longer open his broken jaw fully, and liquid fire spilled out without fully projecting. The burning liquid splashed over Tiden as it washed down the front of the dragon. Dazmare was unaffected by the fire, but Tiden was engulfed in flames and screamed as he ran across the hall before crashing to his knees and falling facedown. His great body landed heavily across the stairs leading up to the king's throne. Tiden's head, falling hard, came to rest on the king's great chair of power, and he lay still.

Tanton attacked with a vengeful fury at the sight, swinging the stone arm again and again at the dragon. Dazmare attempted to take flight, spreading his great wings and flapping them as hard and as fast as he could, lifting his wounded body off the floor.

Before the dragon could make good his escape, Tanton caught him with a powerful swing of the stone arm and sent him crashing to the floor and sliding on his side through another of the hall's pillars. An entire section of the Great Hall's roof shattered with a thunderous roar and collapsed. Tanton was able to jump clear just in time as it and one of the great pillars came crashing down on the dragon. The red dragon known as Dazmare twitched once and was no more.

Tanton rushed to Tiden's aid. His brother's breaths were short and shallow as his body fought for each one.

"Hold on, my brother, we finally have something to live for," Tanton said soothingly, close to Tiden. Tiden was burned so badly, Tanton was unable to recognize him. "We have wives and children to look forward to, Tiden; do not leave this world now, not now. We will be living in Andentine's realm soon."

"Do not forget me, my brother. Think of me often when you are there."

"No, Tiden, I beg of you, don't let go. Do not leave me now, not now." Tanton clung to his brother, holding him close, but his desperate pleas went unheard by Tiden, who was already gone.

Chapter 22

Vantrill sat alone in the same dark room he had been in when he spoke to Brielle. He knew he had lost the dragon Dazmare in the fight with the two giants. He cared nothing for the fact that Dazmare had been killed. He was, however, extremely disappointed in the dragon for not taking both of the giants with him out of this life.

His anger and frustration at the losses he had taken already because of the Blue Witch turned to rage as he sat thinking of his next move. He had lost a great many of his demons, but that was to be expected; they were nothing more than fodder. Losing both of his giants and his dragon was one thing; they were expendable as well. But losing the Blue Witch and her daughter to a simple trick was another. He had been too confident, he thought. He had been so sure he was the one in control of the conversation and the circumstances that he was blind to what was actually happening.

The door to the room opened, and two demons stepped in. One carried a covered tray of food, the other a pitcher of strong ale and a tall glass. They could sense their master's ill mood and wished nothing more than to set the trays before him and exit the room quietly. But that was not to be. The one carrying the tray of food made a slight clinking noise as he set the tray down.

Vantrill's thoughts were disturbed, and already in a foul mood, he seized the two, lifting them both up by their necks over his head, one in each hand. He had moved so fast from his seated position that they had no chance to escape. Vantrill looked at the two terrified creatures struggling to free themselves from his grip with complete disdain. He began squeezing their necks until their eyes squirted from their sockets and dangled down their deformed faces by the nerves. He then threw the two, one and then the other; they crashed into the wall near the door they had entered through only moments before.

Two more demons ran into the room and looked at the two crumpled bodies at their feet, then to Vantrill, whose back was now to them. They quickly looked at one another, and both shrugged their shoulders before turning their attention back to the two bodies. They each took one of the dead by the wrist and dragged the bodies from the room. Ever so quietly, they closed the door behind them.

Vantrill's mood was no better for having killed the two demons, but he returned to his thoughts. He sat for some time before rising with a smile on his face and exiting the room. He walked down the long corridor with a new sense of purpose, a new plan developing in his mind. He was content; he now understood why he had failed in obtaining the real object of his desire, the thing he needed and wanted most.

Demons of all sizes and forms made sure they were well out of his way as he moved through the ruins of his temporary lair. They scattered and scurried around like insects before him. It gave him great pleasure to know that these nightmarish things feared him as they did.

Vantrill descended a great many steps winding down into the lower cells of the dungeons. He followed a corridor that descended even farther and then went down another set of stairs that were narrow and steep, taking him deep into the bowels of the castle.

It was moist, and the air foul this far belowground. No light penetrated the pitch black but that of his own making. As he walked, his form glowed, radiating a soft light about him. When he reached the bottom, he was facing a single cell door. He unlocked it without a key and stepped into a corridor with three small cells cut back into solid stone on his right. Heavy bars faced the corridor, but there were no doors within them to the three cells.

"I have need of you, if you wish to redeem yourself with me," he announced.

"How long have I been here?" a voice coming from the back of the cell nearest to him asked.

"It's been a little over four hundred years by my count."

"Four hundred years, you say?" a voice from within another of the cells mused. "Has much changed?"

"Not as much as you would think," Vantrill answered. "I have need of you. If you do as I wish, I will release you forever."

"What do you ask of me, Vantrill?" a voice in a different cell asked.

"I want you to bring me the three pendants of Andentine. Three descendants of Ethan Pandane wear them now."

"You ask too much, Vantrill!" another voice quickly responded. "That could be my undoing!"

"It is much to ask," Vantrill agreed. "But it would be worth the risk to earn your freedom, would you not agree?"

"I don't know that I do," a voice in another cell spat back.

"Then I will depart for now. Perhaps I will have need of you again in another four or five hundred years," Vantrill said as he turned to leave.

"Wait!" the three voices said in unison. "I will do as you wish, if you free me fully."

"And I have your word on this?"

"You have my word," a voice from the far cell answered.

Vantrill said nothing as he stepped closer and unlocked the magic of the three cells, freeing his prisoner.

Chapter 23

Tanton held his brother as he openly wept. Wisps of smoke drifted toward the Great Hall's ruined ceiling from Tiden's burned body as Tanton clung to him.

"Tiden, how could you leave me?" Tanton cried out. He looked at his brother and shook his head. "You fought well, Tiden. You will be honored by our kin when they learn of your bravery and sacrifice."

As Tanton held his brother, a blue mist began to form around him, engulfing his massive form. The blue mist swirled and churned as it covered him completely. Tanton fell back, unsure of what was happening.

"It is beyond my ability to bring him back, Tanton," Brielle said. "I am truly sorry."

"Is there nothing you can do?" Tanton pleaded. "Anything, anything to help him. I beg you, do something, witch!"

"Tiden is beyond my help. There is only one who can help him now. Stand back!" she ordered. "If I do this, Tanton, Tiden will not be able to return."

"Will you take him to Andentine's realm?" he asked, looking at her hopefully. Brielle nodded. "Then I would not want him to return here. I will miss him terribly, but I will be full of joy knowing that he is in such a wondrous place and waiting for me there."

"Tell the others that I will return soon." With that, she took hold of Tiden and they were gone.

When Brielle and Tiden appeared in Andentine's realm, Andentine was already waiting. Andentine looked over Tiden carefully. He began to grow in stature, becoming every bit as large as Tiden. He carefully bent down and gently opened Tiden's mouth. Andentine drew in a deep breath and slowly released it into Tiden's mouth and down into his lungs. Brielle watched closely as Andentine breathed his magic into Tiden. It was a sight she would not forget. Andentine stood in his spirit-like form and looked to Brielle.

"You know, Tiden is of the faerie world and belongs in this realm. I will keep him here with his family and those of his kind. You must know that because he is such, I have the power to restore his life, but I do not have that power with the men and women of your realm. You must be the one to save them. Vantrill has been keeping a most dangerous weapon hidden away but has now released it. Even he is not guaranteed to defeat it should it turn on him.

"Tiden will recover soon enough," he said, looking again at the giant. "Stay with me here until he does. Let me help you understand your enemies better while we wait, so you will have a better chance of defeating them." Brielle nodded and watched a moment as Tiden began to heal before her eyes.

"Vantrill wants one of my pendants," Andentine began, now back to his usual form. "You know this already. But you do not know this: he has a spirit he captured and imprisoned many centuries ago. It is a very dangerous thing even for you with all of the powers I have given you. You will need to keep Aria and Brendan away from it. They cannot stand against it, not even together. Know this, Brielle: it is pure evil and does whatever pleases it in the moment. Vantrill was once a very powerful being, as you know, but he is weaker now than he's ever been and is just now realizing it. Do not underestimate him. Now that he is back from the dark realm, his power grows by leaps and bounds. He knows this to be true as well."

"How can you help me, Andentine? You must know that he wants the pendants so that he can attack you here."

"Yes, I know of his desires. I assure you, Brielle, he wants far more than that," he said, looking her over. "He is foolish to think he can come here and succeed in his plans, but that will not stop him from destroying your realm trying to gain what he desires. You may already possess what you need to prevail, but I will give you more. I warn you, Brielle: you must become what you have hated most in yourself to succeed against Vantrill. His desires, I fear, run far deeper than you realize."

"I fear that part of myself more than anything, as you well know, Andentine," Brielle said reluctantly. "But I will do what I must."

"Hand me your pendant," he said. Brielle did as he'd requested. "It is beautiful, is it not? So powerful, and yet so light to the touch." He cupped it between his hands. Andentine closed his eyes, and Brielle watched as his hands began to glow. Rays of light began to break free from between his fingers and palms, and Andentine pulled the light back with his voice.

"Now, now," he chided the light. "Do not run off, you are needed here." His hands opened, no longer glowing. In the palm of his hand was her pendant, but the stone in its center was changed.

169

"Brielle, once I place this back around your neck, it will forever become a part of you. You will not be able to remove it ever again." Brielle nodded. "This will be quite painful, so open your blouse and brace yourself, child." She did as he instructed.

Andentine gently placed the pendant around her neck. As it fell to her bare chest and the chain settled around her neck, she jolted violently and screamed out long and shrill. She fell to her knees, tearing at the pendant, but could not pull it free as it began melting into her flesh, burning her terribly as it did.

She began to twist and turn, fighting the intrusion into her flesh and soul. She was sweating and panting as if possessed, and her eyes rolled back in her head. Andentine placed his hand on the young girl's head and she calmed. When she looked again, she could see that only the surface of the pendant remained showing above her skin. She reached for the chain and found that it, too, was fused with her.

"What have you done?" she screamed from her knees, fumbling with her buttons.

"I have ensured your realm will have a true chance to survive," Andentine said sternly. "You are to be its High Protector. I have given you great power and infused you with both the knowledge and the skill to defeat your enemies. I charge you with the protection of both this realm and the realm of men. I wish you to defend the realm of men and protect it. Make it better, Brielle; heal the land and serve its people. Become their High Protector if Tennington will agree to it. If not, act of your own accord, as you have in the past."

Brielle continued to touch the pendant's surface and run her fingers over the chain, absorbing and contemplating Andentine's words as she rose to her feet.

"That was far more than painful, Andentine," she spat. "But I will, as always, do as you ask of me. Thank you for this great gift and honor," she said with a deep bow. As she rose up to face him, she found she was now facing Ew, and he flashed his big, toothy grin at her.

"Very well, Brielle, you have everything you came here for." With that, little Ew touched the giant lying next to him and Tiden awoke and got to his feet. "Tiden, my large friend, follow me and I will take you to Andentine." Ew turned and winked at Brielle, then spun about and strolled off whistling. He stopped a short distance away and turned back. "Until next time, child."

Tiden looked about, amazed and in awe of the vast beauty of Andentine's realm. He could see other giants, many of whom he recognized, approaching ahead of him. Tiden turned back to Brielle, wiping away tears from his eyes, struggling to speak.

"Please tell my brother…" He paused, choking back his tears. He looked about once again at the magnificence and impossible beauty of the world around him, then he turned away from her. He was unable to fully dry his eyes before turning back to Brielle once again. "Tell Tanton…tell him I am home, and I will see him again one day."

Chapter 24

Brendan and Aria had continued training with each other in the early-morning hours. They worked on new uses for their magic and improving their understanding of it. They had learned of the fight in the Great Hall and were surprised they'd not heard any of the commotion. Apparently, Brielle had been the only one to do so in their part of the palace. Their rooms being so far from the hall, they'd slept without waking. Willow, who'd joined them for breakfast, had not heard anything either. Aria and Willow were just as surprised they hadn't stirred when Brielle left their room.

They learned from Tanton of Brielle and Tiden's departure, and they offered him kind words of encouragement. He was battered himself but had refused treatment, remaining mostly silent during breakfast, until he broke down in tears and left to be alone.

A bit later that morning, Tanton sat outside on a special bench Aria had provided to accommodate his great size, with Willow sitting high upon it with him. Willow was giving the orders, and Aria and Brendan were responding as they continued their training. Willow was once again enjoying the experience and did her best to trip up Aria and Brendan but found she could not.

The morning was troubling for the King's Watch as well as the army units, all of which were under Stinson's command. Stinson himself was the most troubled. The Great Hall had been heavily damaged. Most of the men and women serving had found time during the night or early that morning to get a look at the damage, and the dead dragon. Repairs to the hall were to be delayed by order of King Tennington. He felt it better to wait until this conflict was resolved before undertaking such an extensive repair. Tennington, however, had finally asked Brendan and Aria if one of them would use their magic to remove the dragon's remains, and Aria had done so before leaving to train.

Later in the morning, as Brendan and Aria's training was wrapping up, Bear and Vander joined them. They quietly watched without comment as Willow put challenge after challenge to the two trainees. They'd done very well adapting to her different commands. There was no doubt their skills were much improved, even in such a short amount of time.

Brielle appeared near the bench where Tanton and Willow were seated, arriving unseen. While all were paying close attention to the training, she threw an added twist into the mix, remaining out of sight.

As Brendan and Aria were following Willow's commands, they were attacked once again by blue bits of electricity. Not one bolt got through their defenses as they fended them off, and then looked for Brielle. Upon finding her, they welcomed her back.

Tanton looked at her, and she could see in his eyes his longing for some news of his brother. Brielle held out her hand to Tanton, and he stood, then gently picked her up and walked off with her. Tanton stopped and held his hand open before him, allowing Brielle to stand in his palm so she could speak to him easily.

Brielle was able to look directly into his eyes as they spoke. The others could see from a distance but not hear what Brielle was saying. When she finished speaking, Tanton ever so carefully brought her close and gently kissed her on the cheek.

Later that day, Tennington called the group to him in the gardens. He waited until they were all present before he began to speak.

"Brielle, we have followed your lead and advice to this point, and it has proved sound," he began. "The loss of Tiden and the damage to the Great Hall have been heartbreaking, to say the least, but these are the results of this war. We know this was only the beginning. Brielle, I would ask you to provide any information that you can to help us succeed further," he finished, looking to her for her response.

"Vantrill has unleashed his most dangerous weapon yet. He sends it to gain one of the three pendants. As you know, I returned earlier from Andentine's realm. Andentine has provided me with his counsel and given me what assistance he could. Many will not like what I have to say, especially Brendan and Aria," she said, looking directly at the two.

"You will turn your pendants over to me for a short while. It is too dangerous for you two to face the creature that comes for us. I will take the pendants and face it alone. It cannot obtain even one of them to take back to Vantrill or the realms of men and elves will be lost. You will both retain your magic. However, it will be greatly reduced without your pendants."

"I hate to say this, Brielle, but what if you should fall against this thing? It will have all three pendants," Brendan said.

Aria was nodding with the same concern. "We could help you," Aria added.

"No, Aria, you can't," Brielle said firmly. "I know you two have been learning to use your magic, but your abilities are still a great many years behind mine. Andentine has given me additional knowledge and extra powers and abilities to help our cause. He has tasked me with defeating Vantrill and his new weapon, as well as defending both his realm and this one. My king, Andentine has given me much with which to assist your realm. I am to be your realm's High Protector, if you are willing to accept me as such. This is at the direct request of Andentine. But as he stated, and I fully understand, it is your decision to accept this."

"Very well, Brielle, you shall from this moment on carry the title of High Protector; you have most assuredly earned it," Tennington decreed, needing no time to think it over.

Those in attendance at the impromptu garden meeting congratulated her. Brendan and Aria handed their pendants to her, and she placed them both around her neck.

"I will return them to you as soon as possible," Brielle promised.

"You never told me why you appear so young when clearly you are older by many years," Willow said as she approached her mother. She stopped before Brielle, looking her up and down. "I would like to know."

"You're right, Willow, we didn't get to that part, did we? Let us find a quiet place where we can enjoy some privacy," she said, taking her hand. They walked along the garden paths, not speaking as they did, to an area where they could talk in private. There, the two took a seat on one of the many benches along the walk. Brielle hesitated several moments before speaking.

"My appearance—the one I allow others to see—is myself at the age I was when I lost myself as a young woman, except for the color of my skin, of course. Perhaps it brings me some comfort to hold on to a part of my youth in that way. I have continued to hide my true appearance since the loss of your father, though I do not hide my blue color. I have learned to accept it as being—"

"I wish to see you as you really are," Willow interrupted. "You're my mother, but you look like my sister. You hide yourself in your black robes and magic for your own reasons, but I want to know the real you. Will you show me the true version of yourself?"

Brielle sat silently for some time before answering the young girl staring at her so intently. "No. I'm afraid if I do, Willow, you will never want to see me again."

"I've waited my whole life to know my mother. I wish to know the real you, not this false image you offer to others. You must allow me more than mere strangers."

"You do not know what you ask, Willow!" she said a bit more sharply than she would have liked. "I will not be what you've imagined or wished for in a mother."

"But it will be you. That's what I wish for now."

"I have not shown my true self to anyone since the tragedy at the mine. Not even Andentine. And I have changed much since that time. Do not ask this of me, Willow."

"I wish to see you, the real you. I want to see my mother. You must show her to me!"

"I can't! It is more than I could bear."

"You must. You simply must. I deserve to know you as you really are!" Brielle sat for some time without responding. "Please show me. You have hidden your true appearance from me my entire life. It's not fair you continue to do so now," Willow pleaded.

"I would ask, if I do this, Willow, for you to forgive me for having done so."

Willow looked at her now, concerned at what she might see. "Of course I will," she answered, already beginning to regret her request but refusing to change her mind.

Brielle stood and waved her hand in a circular motion around the two of them, creating a barrier blocking anyone who might approach from seeing or disturbing them. She removed her robes, laying them neatly on the bench. Beneath her robes she wore a tight pair of black leather pants, soft black boots, and a white long-sleeve blouse. Brielle's hands trembled as she began to unbutton her blouse. Tears flooded her eyes as she removed it and laid it carefully atop her robes. She glanced at Willow and then quickly turned away. Brielle, standing before Willow with her back to her, gathered her long hair over her shoulder, fully exposing her back. As tears streamed down her face and fell to the ground at her feet, she allowed her magic to transform her.

"Oh, Mother!" Willow gasped. Immediately, she regretted asking Brielle to accept this indignity. "I'm sorry. I'm so sorry. I didn't know."

Before her stood a fully grown woman not yet thirty years of age. Her upper body was ravaged by gruesome scars. Something unimaginable had rent and disfigured her.

Bite marks could clearly be seen littering her back and arms. Brielle turned, throwing her hair back over her shoulder, and Willow could see that around her neck were the three pendants of Andentine. The one with the blue stone was burned deeply into her flesh. Her skin was still blue, as she stood exposed above her waist. Brielle raised her head, and Willow for the first time was able to look upon her mother's face. Brielle was scarred horribly there as well. But Willow could see that beyond the ruined flesh, her mother was still a beautiful woman.

Brielle returned to the young woman of fifteen years old she'd been before and awkwardly rushed to put her blouse and robes back on.

"Do you see now why I wish to hide my true appearance, Willow?" she asked.

"Yes," Willow said, unable to hold back the tears that traced her young face. "The moon wolves?"

"Yes. Among many other vile creatures over the years. I told you I'd found my magic easy to use after so much training, and of how I used it to kill all the moon wolves. That is all true. What I did not tell you, Willow, is I paid a terrible price as well."

Chapter 25

Vantrill stood at the doors of the cells, which were now open. A form stepped out of the far cell, then another to his right, and yet another directly in front of him. The three forms came together and combined into one directly before him.

"I've waited all these years, thinking I would kill you when you dared to show yourself again. You have given me something far more challenging and more interesting to do. I've given you my word, and I will keep it."

Vantrill, believing that he was the more dangerous of the two, showed no fear or concern. "Killing me would be far more challenging and interesting than you think, spirit."

Three voices laughed from all around him, as the spirit was again in three forms and had him surrounded. "No, Vantrill, it wouldn't."

Vantrill for the first time felt fear wash over him. A cold chill ran up his spine, as he now understood the spirit had only been toying with him over the years. "Well, we won't have to worry about that," he said, trying to sound a bit more confident than he really was. Only a moment before, Vantrill had been certain he could best the spirit if needed; now he was not so sure he would want to face it. "I shall expect to see you soon with at least one of Andentine's pendants." Vantrill turned and left the sprit creature standing in the dark as he made his way back from the cells, taking with him the glow of his form. The spirit creature waited in the dark but a moment longer before he vanished from the castle's dungeons.

The old man with flowing gray hair and a short, neatly trimmed beard to match was dressed in a fine suit of dark clothes as he walked along. He was in no hurry this day, and as others passed him on the road, he greeted them cheerfully. He stopped to exchange pleasantries with one young couple and their small boy before continuing on his way.

The old man carried a short walking stick of highly polished black glass featuring an intricate inlay of three silver horses running down its length, from the silver carved ball grip at its top to just above its bright tip at the far end. The old man twirled it from time to time as he whistled a lighthearted tune.

As daylight slowly faded into night, the man came ever closer to the outer walls of Andavar and the palace beyond. It occurred to him, as he made his way, that he was the only one on the road and had been for some time. He assumed it must be the time of day, but could it be something else keeping people off of the road?

Perhaps the fear of another attack, he thought as he continued on toward the palace. Then he stopped, knowing at once he had made a mistake. He felt the magic barrier he'd just passed through. *Too late now*, he thought. He continued on, waiting for the owner of the magic to challenge him. He did not have to wait long and did not get much further, as a young blue girl in long black robes appeared on the road before him a short distance ahead.

"Why do you approach? All have been given orders not to."

"Forgive me, my lady, I meant no harm. I am merely traveling through this part of the realm and wish to see the Great Hall with my own eyes, if I may do so before I die."

"You may not. Nor may you take any of the pendants of Andentine back to Vantrill."

"It would be better for you, little witch, if you simply gave them to me."

"I will not, demon spirit, and I never will. Be gone and spare yourself!"

"Oh, I think I'll stay long enough to obtain what I came for, Blue Witch. Yes, I know of you. I know the truth of who and what you really are. I know you're Andentine's little creature. And you should know, I have no fear of you."

"Then you should know you're a fool," the Blue Witch spat back.

"Perhaps I am. Perhaps I'm not. But I will leave here with your pendant, Princess," he said, his voice razor sharp. "Hmm...it seems I know things about you that you do not yet know yourself. It's fascinating. I know you far better than you know yourself, Princess! I know the truth of who and what you really are."

"I am no princess, and I know myself all too well. You should be smart enough to know that I will end your miserable existence before you leave here this day," she spat with an icy glare.

The spirit laughed hauntingly. "Do you know nothing of your past, girl? Nothing of who you really are? Oh, how I would love to be there when you discover the truth!"

"Save your games, spirit. I know exactly who and what I am. I know I'm a scion of the first king of men and of his royal blood. Call me princess if you wish, but let's delay this encounter with words no longer."

"Is that what you think?" He laughed wickedly. "Let us begin, then!" he said, transforming into the dark spirit and splitting into his three forms. The three spirits moved about attempting to surround her. The Blue Witch stood calmly, not responding to the threat.

"This is your last chance to leave here with whatever you call your life, spirit."

The spirit attacked, rushing at Brielle with blinding speed from in front of her. The witch blocked its efforts and spun to face the attacker approaching from behind her. She threw it back with such force it went sprawling out across the ground. The Blue Witch found herself under full attack by the three separate forms of one spirit, turning back and forth, bringing up her magic to defend herself, before striking out with blue bolts of fire as she attacked them in turn.

The creatures were shrieking, enraged at the blue girl as they were thrown back again and again by the bursts of thick, heavy flames. One of the dark forms managed to latch on to Brielle's arm. Before she could free herself, another of the spirit's forms grabbed her and pulled her to the ground. Brielle blasted them with an enormous burst of her fire. The force of it threw all three of the spirit's forms away from her. She came to her feet immediately, spinning and throwing fire in all directions.

The spirit continued to voice its displeasure at her fire as it circled her. It renewed its efforts, darting in and out from three different positions, ripping and tearing at her robes and flesh, as their battle raged on back and forth on the dark road. Neither combatant was able to gain an advantage, nor were they willing to concede anything to the other as they fought on.

"Give me what I desire, girl, and I will leave you in peace!" one of them hissed at her.

"Yes! Give it to me now!" another demanded.

"What do you think I've been doing since I first found you here? I've been measuring your strengths and weaknesses. I've been learning what you are. And now I'm through with you. You will not have what you seek, evil spirit, but you will have the eternal peace and freedom of a final death for your efforts this day."

"You do not have the power to end me, Princess!" the third spirit spat. Those were the last words he would ever speak. The Blue Witch vanished from her position amid the tripartite spirit. She began to appear and disappear, rapidly changing her position, each time firing enormous bursts of blue fire into the creatures. They began to break apart, screaming and hissing in frustration and anger. Finally, having absorbed extraordinary damage, the three came together as one.

He smashed his walking stick to the ground. It shattered into a black mist. Three haunting silver steeds of the dead rose from out of the mist, rearing up and whinnying shrilly before pounding their hooves back to the ground. The spirit tried to make his escape, mounting the nearest of them.

The Blue Witch latched on to him with her magic and pulled him from the horse's back to the ground. She wrapped the demon spirit in a binding magic, in the form of a large, wicked-looking blue constrictor snake. The three spirit steeds were rearing up, whinnying and stomping their hooves repeatedly at the sight of the snake.

The Blue Witch

The snake coiled around the demon, squeezing him tighter and tighter as it positioned itself to swallow its prey. It opened its mouth, unhinging its jaw to envelop the demon spirit as he lay helpless and wide-eyed in its coils. The snake slowly worked its mouth, positioning its prey to be taken headfirst. The spirit's eyes focused on the Blue Witch until they were soon covered. The snake continued to work the spirit creature's body through its mouth and down its length. When the snake finished swallowing its prey, it lay with the sprit's large form outlined within its swollen body, flicking its forked tongue in and out of its mouth.

The Blue Witch and the three spirit horses watched as the spirit attempted to free itself from within the snake's body. The spirit pressed upward from within the snake until his face was clearly visible through the reptile's thinly stretched skin, screaming helplessly. When the spirit stopped struggling and lay still, the Blue Witch recalled her magic, and the snake and spirit within were gone.

The Blue Witch stood there but a moment longer, staring at the three spirit horses as they stared back at her. She stepped toward them, raising her hands; the blue fire came to her hands, crackling and sizzling as it danced around her fingertips. "You are free! Unless you'd rather stay and fight me as well." The spirit horses looked back and forth to each other, then turned as one and bolted from her, disappearing into the night.

Chapter 26

Arriving back at the palace, Brielle found Brendan and Aria seated at the council table with Tanton and Bear in the remains of the Great Hall. Willow, Starlin, and King Tennington, seated nearby, were preparing to eat a fine-looking meal. A variety of his most favorite dishes had been ordered by Tennington and was just now being served.

"Brielle!" Brendan exclaimed, rushing to her side. "Are you okay?"

They could see Brielle's robes were damaged and loose, her clothes beneath torn and stained with blood, her hair matted to her head with sweat and dirt. She did not answer Brendan. She removed the pendant with the red stone from around her neck and placed it around Aria's neck. Aria looked to Brendan and then back to Brielle. Brielle removed Brendan's pendant and, holding it out to him, collapsed. Brendan deftly caught her, scooping her into his arms.

When she woke, Brielle found she was in bed, with Willow sitting in a chair at her side.

"Good morning," Willow said. She got up from her chair and crawled in beside her mother and hugged her.

"What happened? How did I get here?"

"You passed out after you returned. Brendan carried you here. Drae came to check on you, but he couldn't find anything but a few bad scratches. How do you feel?"

Brielle checked herself over, then snuggled closer to Willow. "I feel amazing, like nothing happened," she said, smiling and touching her finger to Willow's nose.

Willow giggled. "Drae said you'd be fine, but I didn't want to leave you. You didn't get any dinner last night, and it's late morning. Do you want breakfast?"

"Yes, I'm starving!"

"Do you want it brought up here, or do you feel like going down?"

"Down, I think," she said, smiling. Brielle washed up, and then discovered that her clothes had been mended and cleaned while she'd slept and were left folded and ready for her use. She found her clothes felt soft and fresh once again, and they smelled wonderful to her, like fresh sweet flowers. She picked up her black robes, examining them.

"Brendan wouldn't let anyone touch your robes," Willow informed her.

"I will have to thank him for his concern," she said as she held her robes before her. They were still dirty and damaged from her encounter with the spirit creature. She waved her hand over them, and the pattern within them glowed with a soft blue light in response. As she held them before her, she shook them out once. To Willow's amazement, they now looked as good as new.

The two made their way down to the dining hall and ate their breakfast alone but for each other. When they finished their meal, they went to the Great Hall to see who was about. They found that most everyone was there, including Tanton. They all enjoyed each other's company, laughing and joking with each other, trying their best to forget much of what had happened, and not wishing to think about what was to come.

King Tennington soon joined them. He, too, enjoyed the light mood and sprit of the group of friends. But he, as well as the others gathered, needed to focus on what was to come, and he began by addressing Brielle.

"Brielle, will you tell us what you suggest based on the latest developments?"

"Yesterday, I left here suddenly because the barrier I'd placed around the palace was breached. As I expected, it was the creature Andentine had warned me about. The creature sent to acquire Andentine's pendants. I was able to best the spirit creature and dispatch it. Vantrill will soon realize this. He has lost at every turn so far, and I believe he'll throw everything he has at us in one final attempt to gain control of this realm. It will be a fight such as none of us have ever known. We will, with your blessing, my king, use a similar plan of defense with a few minor adjustments and tricks thrown in." She glanced at Tennington, and he alone knew the meaning of her look.

"I will be in the center with Brendan and Aria to either side of me. We will spread out and do all of the damage we can. I would ask that you, Tanton, join us up front with the Elite First backing us up, followed by the full force of the army, my lord. Bear, you have been asked to stay with our king once again, and I would ask that you continue to do so. I would also ask that nobody move forward of my position until I give the signal."

Brielle stopped, looking directly to Tennington before continuing. "Your Highness, I have no military training. I do not know nearly what you and Commander Stinson do about war. It is the information and guidance provided to me by Andentine I have relied upon to advise you thusly. I can only tell you that my brother, along with my sister and I, should be out front to slow Vantrill's army down and reduce its numbers."

"I appreciate your candor, Brielle," Tennington responded. "I believe your thoughts and Andentine's guidance have proven correct; we will continue to listen to and follow both. As I said before, you have served us well in your assessment of the enemy and how to defeat them. Have you seen the timing of Vantrill's next attack?"

"Yes, my lord, he is coming himself this time, and with his full force. I expect them here by dusk this evening. I know that you and Commander Stinson have our forces ready to mobilize and we will be prepared to meet Vantrill and his army when they arrive."

"Yes, we're ready," Commander Stinson confirmed, coming to his feet.

"Commander, I would suggest you hold off and keep your men relaxed until later today. Vantrill wishes this battle to take place at night. He feels the darkness will give his forces an edge. It will not. But we will let his forces march all day while we rest ours. We will be fresher and stronger for having done so," Brielle said. Commander Stinson nodded and took his seat once again.

"Very well, then, we are agreed. We keep our forces back for now and assemble them before Vantrill and his army arrive this evening," Tennington said, standing to signal the discussion was over.

"My king, we should speak in private," Brielle said. Tennington nodded, and the two walked out of the Great Hall to an adjacent area.

"I have made all of the arrangements needed for what is to come this day, Brielle. I know it was difficult for you to come to me with such a message, especially after the way I acted. But I thank you for it. Knowing, I find, brings me a strange sense of peace."

"I struggled with delivering Andentine's warning. In the end, I felt you had to know and had to know it would come this day so you could be prepared."

"I understand. But enough of that. Do you feel he was in the hall?"

"Vantrill's presence was there," Brielle said. "I could sense it."

"Then he should believe he knows our plan, don't you agree?"

"I felt his presence withdraw as we finished speaking. I believe he left thinking so."

"Excellent, then we'll trap his army between us! Destroy them all, Brielle. Do what I cannot, and save our people. How soon can your group be ready to execute our real plan?"

"We will leave within the hour, with your blessing, my lord."

Tennington placed his hands on her shoulders. "I want to thank you again, Brielle, for everything you've done." He embraced her before stepping back and looking her in the eye. "Take care of yourself, High Protector. And take care of our realm for me."

Brielle stepped back and bowed deeply. "You have been a very good king to your people, they will not forget you. And you have taken excellent care in raising Willow. For that, I could never thank you enough. I will never forget you, my king."

Brielle set out immediately to meet with the small group who would be going with her. She found them spread out as planned in the palace gardens. Aria and Tanton waited as Vander and Brendan met with her first.

"I must confess something to you both before we go," Brielle said as she approached. "Years ago, I went to the swordsmith commissioned to forge your two swords. I entered his shop in the middle of the night for a very special purpose that I have until now kept secret. Your father, Vander, as you know, had your swords each specially made by the king's own swordsmith." Brielle could see the two young men were intrigued as to where this was going and were listening intently. "I went to the shop the night before your father picked up the finished swords to infuse Brendan's with magic," she said, waiting for Vander's response. She got it immediately.

"I knew it! I just knew it!" Vander said, throwing his hands up in the air, exasperated, before looking to Brendan. "Ever since we discovered the Blue Witch is your sister, I've said to myself, it's the only reason he bests me every single time. His sister did something to him or his sword!" he said smugly, feeling completely vindicated for his losses at the hand of Brendan. "Not only do you possess magic we did not know of, but so does your sword! No wonder you've always bested me! You're a cheater!" He laughed.

"Actually…" Brielle drew out the word, hesitating. "Your father had not yet decided who was to receive which sword as his gift, so I had to infuse them both equally," she said, smiling, enjoying her little joke on Vander. "And Brendan only recently discovered his magic."

Brendan looked at Vander, cocking an eyebrow at him. "Any more excuses?"

Vander, not finding it as amusing as the other two, grabbed Brendan around his neck playfully. "I still think you possess something I do not," he said as they wrestled about.

"I hate to admit this, Vander. I thought to never have to speak of it, but I do possess something you don't," Brendan admitted. He looked at Vander, deadly serious for a moment, and then placed his hand on Vander's shoulder. "It's known as…" He delayed a long moment, looking down at the ground as Vander leaned in closer, curious as to what it could possibly be. "Well, my friend, it is something you are sadly lacking in. I don't think there's anything you can do about it either," Brendan said, and then said no more.

Vander was all ears as he waited impatiently. "Well? What is it?" he finally burst out, unable to wait any longer.

"Skill!" Brendan shouted as he pushed Vander away and took off running toward the others with Vander hot on his heels. The two left Brielle standing by herself as they raced through the gardens. Brielle, however, beat them both to the supposed finish line, appearing out of thin air before the others as the two ran up. Vander and Brendan stopped and looked to each other, each shrugging his shoulders.

"Well, that's just not fair!" Vander exclaimed, to the laughs of the others.

Brielle gathered the small group to her before addressing them. "I will give us all protection when we first arrive, but be prepared to defend yourselves immediately when we appear. Tanton, I will be bringing you. Brendan, Aria, you will have Vander between you two, and, Aria, you will take my free hand. I want to make sure we all arrive at the same time and in the exact same place. Are we ready?" she asked one last time. Everyone indicated they were, and they were gone as one in the next instant.

Chapter 27

Brielle and those with her appeared on the road behind Vantrill's army, veiled by Brielle's magic. They could see the demon army stretched out before them, marching toward the palace, and the men and women prepared for their arrival there. Brielle looked around silently, making sure everyone was ready. They indicated once again they were, and she removed the veil concealing them.

They were now exposed but yet unseen. As planned, Brielle began the attack. She sent a heavy barrage of her fire ripping through the rear of the demon army. She hit them again and again as the demons were caught off guard and began breaking ranks.

Brielle advanced on the army's rear flank, which was now in utter disarray. Aria and Brendan moved into their respective positions, one to each side of Brielle, but spread further out to the road's edges. Tanton and Vander were still holding behind the attacking siblings. The three were cutting through the ranks of Vantrill's army and reducing its numbers with every blast of their magic's

192

searing bolts of fire. Brielle was sending blast after blast of blue flame into the horde, while Aria used her red and Brendan his wicked-looking green. Their surprise attack had its desired effect. The demon army stopped advancing as confusion ran amok.

With hundreds of the dead and dying littering the road before the three attackers, the sky above them grew ever gloomier. Thunder rolled across it, and it was evident there would be a major storm in the next few minutes.

Brielle had no sooner looked back to Tanton and Vander, pointing to the clouds, than a searing bolt of lightning tore across the darkening sky. A tremendous clap of thunder followed, shaking the very ground beneath their feet. At the same time, Vantrill appeared at the rear of his army and began to approach Brielle. His large, dark form stood out easily from his hideously deformed demons.

As he closed the distance between them, the storm's winds blew harder, howling down through the valley the road traversed. Lightning flashed across the sky again and again as thunder clapped and boomed about them. The smell of rain was in the air. Brielle stood firm as Vantrill approached.

Brendan and Aria stopped attacking at the sight of Vantrill and watched intently, knowing the confrontation Brielle had warned of was about to take place. All had been told to stay out of this fight, no matter what happened. Vantrill approached and stopped before Brielle.

"Blue Witch, you bested my demon spirit. For that, I thank you. I believe he intended to keep the pendants for himself and kill me upon his return."

"What a shame it would have been. We would have missed the opportunity to enjoy this fine weather while we visit. I certainly enjoyed our last chat."

"I was far weaker than I realized. I've remedied that unfortunate situation."

Lightning continued to flash across the darkening sky as the wind blew relentlessly and the thunder boomed, shaking the ground beneath them even harder.

"I'm happy to hear you're feeling better. Shall we call off this nonsense and let you find yourself another realm for you and what demons you still have left?"

"No, witch, I want this one, and so I shall have it. And then I will take Andentine's."

"Easier said than done, Vantrill. You should reconsider your options. Know this: Andentine has made me High Protector of this realm with King Tennington's blessing. As such, I will defend it to the bitter end, and with my life if necessary."

"How nice for you," Vantrill spat back. "You should have turned him down and stayed within the safety of his realm across the Dead Bridge, foolish girl. Your desire to protect the people of this land will be the death of you."

"I think someday it may, but it will not be this day."

"So confident you are, Blue Witch. I want to watch you die and see the look in your eyes as you do. We shall see how confident you are in that moment. But I have many plans for you before then." He said it so coldly and confidently, she was instantly furious.

"Perhaps I will watch the same look in your eyes, Vantrill, since you insist on dying this day." Her blue magic engulfed Vantrill's large figure, but he instantly freed himself, shedding the magic easily.

"Foolish girl!" Vantrill said, raising his arms and sending a powerful blast of energy toward her. The Blue Witch deflected it effortlessly.

"Oh, that was pathetic!" she called out to him over the howling of the wind. She sent a blast of her blue flames hammering into him, knocking him backward and sending him sprawling on the ground in front of the demons that had turned to watch the confrontation.

Vantrill was not only embarrassed, he was furious as he gathered himself and fired bolts of black fire at Brielle, charging toward her. The Blue Witch waved them off like flies. Vantrill opened a vast hole in the ground beneath her, and she disappeared into its depths, only to reappear again on the opposite side of Vantrill. The two glared at each other across the expanse.

"I assume we are somewhat evenly matched, dead girl," Vantrill taunted.

"You assume too much, Vantrill. You know how my brother took his time dealing with your Sintin. I did the same with your spirit friend. I also made a fool of you when I took my daughter back right out from under your nose. I rather like having my enemies think they have a chance against my family and me when they clearly do not. You lost in the past to my family, and you will lose to us again this time."

Vantrill was enraged and walked across the air of the open pit directly up to Brielle. He looked her dead in the eye. Brielle, just as confident, looked right back at him. Neither blinked as they stared one another down.

"I'm done with your little games, witch. You are going to be mine for the rest of your life. Perhaps even for eternity if I so desire, and I will do with you as I will!" Vantrill shouted over the storm. Four blackened and bloodied arms reached up through the earth below Brielle and latched firmly on to her legs. She grasped wildly for Vantrill, but he could not be reached.

"You are mine now, girl!"

The Blue Witch looked between Brendan and Aria, who were rushing to her aid. She held up her hands to the two, warning them to stop, as she was slowly pulled through the ground until she was gone. Vantrill watched until he was convinced she was, then disappeared.

Brendan and Aria both rushed to the spot of Brielle's abduction but found nothing to show she had ever been there. They looked at each other wordlessly as the wind continued to swirl about them. Lightning flashed repeatedly across the sky, and all around them, thunder still clapped, now even louder than before, as the storm overtook them.

Vander and Tanton, who had also witnessed the event, moved much closer to the two. Brendan finally took Aria's hand and led her silently to their companions.

"She's gone! Let's do what we came here to do!" he yelled above the storm. The four of them circled around the pit and began their pursuit of the enemy army.

Chapter 28

Willow ran through the corridors of the palace, racing to reach the king. She dodged and darted past others going about their business without slowing or saying a word. She found Tennington and Bear, along with Commander Stinson and a few others she did not know, at the council table preparing for the advancing enemy army. They each looked to her as she ran directly to the king.

"I must speak with you in private, my lord, it is most urgent!" Willow said, sounding so much older than she appeared. Tennington looked at her but a brief moment before responding.

"Very well, Willow." He stood, and they walked hurriedly across the ruined hall's floor until they were far enough from the council table to have privacy.

"Vantrill has captured my mother," she said, surprisingly showing little if any emotion. "His army is now advancing once again toward us. Brendan and Aria, along with Tanton and Vander, are in pursuit from the rear. The enemy army suffered heavy losses in the attacks before Vantrill took my mother, but their numbers still remain incredibly strong. Now that he has her, he leaves his army to fight without him. Vantrill believes having captured my mother, he will gain her pendant and the power of it."

Tennington looked at Willow, studying the child's face. "Please forgive me, Willow, but you seem very calm about all of this. Is there something I should know?"

Willow looked at him and smiled. "My mother told me before she left of her real plan."

"She wanted to be captured?"

"Yes. Vantrill wants her pendant so badly, he has abandoned his army. I came to tell you it's the time to advance."

"How were you able to see this, Willow?"

"My mother found the magic blocking my sight and successfully removed it before she left. I have my sight back fully." She hesitated, looking at him as tears came to her eyes. "I knew I needed to come to you. To say"— she hesitated, trembling terribly—"goodbye."

"So, you know?"

"Yes." Tears flowed freely from her eyes as she fought futilely to hold them back.

Tennington knelt down and scooped her into his arms. "I have never told you this, Willow, and I regret waiting until this hour to do so." He looked away and then closed his eyes, fighting back tears of his own as he held her. "I have always thought of you as a daughter. No. More than that, as my daughter. Though I have always treated you as my ward. I wish now that I had been strong enough to treat you as my own and tell you how much I love you."

Willow could no longer hold back as she clung to him, still shaking terribly, and sobbed into his shoulder. "I would have liked that very much," she said, and kissed him gently on the cheek. She pulled back, hesitating as she attempted to speak. Instead, she bowed deeply. "My king," she managed to say before turning and running from the hall.

Tennington rose, wiping tears from his eyes. He took a deep breath, letting the air out slowly as he gathered himself, and then he returned to the council table, deeply shaken.

"We will be riding out to meet the enemy as soon as possible," Tennington said, turning directly to Stinson. "Prepare to advance, Commander!"

Stinson came to his feet immediately. "We will be ready for your order, my lord." He bowed and ran from the hall to ready his men.

"Two runners are to be posted outside Willow's door, along with four guards. If she leaves her room, they are to stay with her. If she wishes a message sent to me or anyone else, it is to be delivered without question or delay."

"Yes, my lord," another man said, standing and bowing, before leaving the hall to carry out his orders.

"Bear, it is time," Tennington announced, looking to the big man. Bear rose and nodded. He rode beside the king moments later to join the men and women assembling outside the city walls.

"I know that you would prefer to be with the men of the Elite, Bear. But I must say it gives me great comfort to know that you are at my side this day," Tennington said, placing his hand on Bear's shoulder and stopping him. He reached into a pocket and pulled out a piece of paper folded up and sealed with the king's mark.

"I charge you, Baird Prow, with delivering this to my council should I fall," he said, studying the big man's face as he spoke. "There's a copy of this in my private quarters where none but myself would normally have access. Some members of the council may have a hard time with its content without more proof. Therefore, one additional copy has been left with another. They will come forward only when, and if, necessary. All copies are sealed, and none know the contents of the message within."

Bear looked at the paper and its intricate seal, then back to his king. "My lord, I know this is a great honor, but let's hope it is an unnecessary one," he said, smiling. Bear was not at all pleased with the look he found on Tennington's face in return.

The two men made their way quickly to their destination. When they arrived, they found, as Commander Stinson had promised, the men were assembled and ready to march.

"Excellent work, Commander," Tennington greeted his commander. "Advance!"

Stinson raised his arm and repeated the command. His officers could be heard calling the order to advance forward like an echo. Stinson nodded to his king and rode off toward the front to lead the fighters of the Elite personally.

The army began to move forward, and the king turned his horse back toward his city and his home. Bear did not turn with him; instead he watched him closely. Tennington finally closed his eyes and did not open them again until he had turned away and was advancing with the men and women of his army. Bear noticed that Tennington did not look back again as they rode off to war.

They marched for some time before the leading edge of the storm slammed into them. They marched on without stopping and eventually came out the other side of it soaking wet but otherwise no worse for having gone through it.

The sun was high overhead when they cleared the storm, and it began to both warm and dry them as its light glistened off beads of water on the soldiers' armor and chain mail. It was not long before a familiar face approached Bear and King Tennington. Bear recognized the man as Drake Fallon as he made his way closer.

"My lord, the enemy approaches, the two armies will soon meet," Drake reported.

"Very good, Drake. Stay with Bear and me now," Tennington responded.

Drake looked at Tennington, hesitating but a moment. "As you wish, my lord." He did not understand the order. This was not the place for a scout, but he had to assume his king had his reasons. Bear wondered at the order himself, but he gave no outward indication of it. Clearly, something was on the king's mind. His actions were not those of the confident leader Bear knew Tennington to be. The three men rode to war without speaking, enjoying the warm touch of the setting sun after weathering the storm.

At the front of the column, Stinson and the men and women of the Elite First could now see the enemy approaching in the distance. The two armies were quickly closing the gap between them. The enemy army stretched out far beyond Stinson's line of sight, and he could not see the attacks he knew were taking place at the rear of the enemy ranks.

Commander Stinson brought the army to a halt at the top of a small rise, giving them the advantage of the high ground in the area. They waited there as the hideous creatures of Vantrill's army moved ever closer. He could see the creatures in greater detail now. Their twisted and deformed figures were no longer just dark smudges in the distance. As the demons neared the bottom of the rise, Stinson gave the signal and the Elite First's battle cry rang out.

"First to charge...last to die!"

The Elite First charged down the rise, cutting a path deep into the demon horde, their charge decimating the front lines of the enemy ranks. The second wave, charging behind them, cut down even more of the demons, who'd been scattered by the first charge.

The demons countered with sheer numbers, breaking ranks and swarming out around them, cutting off their escape. The men and women of the Elite fought furiously from their forward position while those of the second wave fought to reach them. The enemy army continued to pour up the hill around the two groups locked in battle. They surged past in vast numbers as those caught in the center were trapped and fought for any room to engage the enemy effectively. They found themselves totally on the defensive as the third wave was now cut off from them and engaged with more of the enemy well beyond them at the top of the hill. The Elite and the second wave were fighting furiously and continuing to wreak havoc on the demon army, which fell in vast numbers before the skilled men and women of the Elite First. The demons were too many, though, and even by the highly trained fighting forces of the Elite, they could not be overcome. It seemed to Stinson the demon numbers never lessened, as they continued to appear as fast as they could be cut down. He could see and understand the trap they were caught in.

Stinson, and the rest of the Elite, soon found themselves completely surrounded and fighting on foot after their mounts had been cut down from underneath them. They fought boldly and gave their lives bravely in the face of overwhelming odds.

The demons showed them no mercy, stopping to feed on the flesh of the fallen men and women as others continued to fight on around them. Some demons carried heads, limbs, and other body parts torn or hacked from the fallen. They feasted on their flesh and waved the partially eaten limbs in the air as they cheered on their counterparts. Men and women both, wounded and no longer able to effectively defend themselves, were either dragged along the ground or carried above it screaming as they were passed around and their flesh was shared by the demons.

Stinson rallied his remaining troops in a final effort to breach the enemy's lines and get clear of the hopeless trap. He fought fiercely, repeatedly beating back the demons around him and calling for his warriors to stay with him. He called out the first half of the Elite's battle cry over and over to those fighting with him.

"First to charge!" he would shout.

They responded each time, as they fought, "Last to die!"

The regiments of Tennington's army farther up the hill and cut off from the remaining men and women of the Elite First could hear the battle cry over and over again, the sound diminishing until they heard it from only a single voice. Time seemed to stand still as long, agonizing moments passed before they heard the Elite's call fall silent. To a man, they were certain it was the singular voice of Commander Stinson they had heard calling it out as he fought alone in the end.

Chapter 29

Brielle's demonic captors had pulled her down through the earth into a vast, cavernous underworld. She had been taken to a haunting forest of dead, sickly, twisted trees thick with hanging moss drenched in mist and fog. Brielle could see a large slate pit of black liquid churning with demons and spirits struggling to be free at its surface. They would rise partway out of the black liquid, fighting, only to be pulled back again by others trying to take their place. The churning repeated over and over again, unending. The moaning and the screeching and wailing of the demons and spirits trapped in the large pit was maddening.

Vantrill appeared on the slate bank of the pit, motioning for Brielle's captors to bring her forward, and they obeyed, walking her to their master. They placed her in heavy shackles and secured her with a thick chain to a ring set in a large moss-covered stone no more than twenty feet from the edge of the black pit. Brielle noticed even the moss was dead in this gloomy place. Her captors stepped back from her and the pit to stand guard over her.

"Oh, my little blue toy," Vantrill said, reaching out and stroking Brielle's face. "I'm truly going to have…shall we say, a lot of fun with you." He bent in close, placing his wretchedly disfigured face so close to Brielle's that she could feel the warmth of his breath and smell the stench of it. He studied her for a reaction, but she gave him none.

"Do you still think you allowed me to capture you? Do you think your pendant is beyond my reach? Oh yes, Blue Witch, I knew of your plan. It is why I had you brought here, to this special place. This is the Shades Hollow," he said, waving his arm toward the black pit at its center, and its demons and spirits in their eternal struggle to be free of it.

"When I've grown weary of our new relationship, and you no longer please me, I will cast you into its black waters. Once there, you can never free yourself, as you can plainly see. I would advise you to never even think of refusing me anything I ask of you or displease me in the giving of it," he said, staring deep into her eyes, his face all but touching hers. "Have you nothing to say now, Blue Witch?"

"I will say only this, Vantrill. I know and understand my situation, and all that you have said, fully. I promise you this day and swear to you, you will be given nothing of me that I do not freely give, and give willingly and with great pleasure to you."

"See now! The powerful Blue Witch only needed the proper motivation to bend her will to mine." He said to her two guards, "The Shades Hollow tends to have that effect, I find. I have business elsewhere, and pendants to acquire, but I will return for you soon enough. We shall see then how willingly you give all that I desire," he said, stroking her hair. "Do not attempt to escape while I'm away, my pet. For if you do, I will burn your people and all those you love. I will destroy your world and all you hold dear. I will take everything from you. And when I've fully satisfied my desires with you, I will throw you in this pit to remain for all eternity."

She showed him no emotion or sign of fear. She simply looked at him for a time, as he did her, before he vanished. The Blue Witch looked around the boggy forest and then watched the demons struggling in the pit. Every now and then, one would stay above the surface long enough to look around and notice her. They did so before being pulled back beneath its surface, clawing and grasping as anyone drowning would do for but a piece of straw to cling to.

There seemed to be no end to the different forms and shapes of the demons. Their deformed, twisted bodies were sometimes a mix of different creatures patched together. Some were part human or perhaps elven in nature, and yet others were demons of a kind unknown to her.

After looking around further and getting her bearings, she gently tested her magic and found she had full use of it. She destroyed sections of her shackles, replacing them instantly with her magic. Her guards never had a chance to notice.

The guards were strange dark-gray creatures with blood and fluid slowly seeping from open wounds all over their elongated, thin forms. They had no hair anywhere on their dark bodies that she could see. The wounds may have been burns, but she could not be sure.

"Gentlemen, I would like some water," Brielle called out. The two glanced at her, then turned away once again, but did not respond otherwise. "I'm thirsty," she tried again. This time, they approached her, tilting their odd heads back and forth. When they got close enough to her, they each spat on her before turning away to return to their post.

"Well, I never! I was feeling sorry for you two and wasn't going to harm you, but that was completely uncalled for!" she said, wiping the spittle from her face. They were paying her no attention at all, keeping their backs to her, daring her to try something. Brielle gently stepped out of her shackles and walked quietly up behind them. The two turned with surprising speed and latched on to her, dragging her back to the stone and its ring, replacing her shackles. They slapped and kicked her repeatedly before returning once again to their post.

She was both shocked and angry. How were they able to do such a thing to her? Only one real way to find out, she thought. Again, she removed the heavy shackles, and immediately launched bolts of her fire at the two. They vanished before the flames reached them and reappeared behind her, both grabbing a handful of her hair and dragging her around by it. They slapped and kicked her repeatedly before placing her back in her shackles once again.

Brielle was furious now. Again, she sent the shackles to the floor, and then attempted to wrap the two in her binding magic. They were on her so fast, she could not react, and she took another beating for her efforts before being returned to her shackles once again. She waited, thinking things through and developing a better game plan for dealing with her two irksome captors. She studied the demons in the pit as she worked on her plan. Soon, she was moving in small measures closer, a bit closer, and ever closer still to the pit. She inched closer yet until she was at the very edge of the pit. She then sent her magic into the black water.

Her two captors, seeing what she was up to, moved in to punish her once again. Brielle reached out with her magic and latched on to more than a dozen demons from within the pit and hurled them from the blackness into her two captors.

The two frantically tried to round up the escapees of the pit with their incredible speed. As they did, Brielle used her magic to fuse them together before they could react. They stumbled and staggered, no longer able to use their unnatural speed, and the demons freed from the pit were on them. They took hold of the two and lifted them over their heads. They carried them to the edge of the pit as the odd pair struggled desperately to free themselves. Stopping and looking at the blue girl who'd freed them, the demons tossed her captors into the pit.

The pit began to churn violently as they went under the dark liquid's surface, only to reappear, attempting to escape it. They came to the surface time and time again but were pulled back down each time. She could see their desperation and their wild-eyed looks each time they resurfaced. Now bound one to the other, their flesh melted together, they fought the pit's black water, unable to escape its eternal grasp.

The group of demons Brielle had scooped from the pit stood with her, watching. Brielle was not sure of their intentions but sensed they meant her no harm. They approached her, and as one, they bowed to her. As they rose up, one of the demons stepped forward.

"We are not the demons we appear to be, my lady. Vantrill altered our appearances to what you see before you now. We are the lost elves of Andentine, banished by Vantrill and those two handlers of his to this pit when we refused to do his bidding. We were captured in this war, though we do not know how long it has been. There is no way of knowing time or place in the Shades Hollow. I fear it has been a very long time, though," he said.

"Are there others of Andentine's elves still in the pit?"

"None I know of, my lady. When I sensed your magic, I quickly held fast to it with my men in tow. I possess some magic of my own," he said. "Forgive me." He again bowed deeply. "Please allow me to introduce myself. I am Prince Trindentine, my lady. I am the younger brother of King Andentine of the elves, and second only to him."

Brielle gasped and stood in shock before finally responding. "I am Brielle Pandane, Prince Trindentine," she replied, smiling warmly, then bowed in turn. "I know your brother well."

The group bowed deeply as one before her. As Trindentine rose, he looked at the young blue girl before him and with great pride announced, "It is my pleasure to meet you, Your Highness."

Chapter 30

T he four companions chased down the enemy army, tearing into them over and over again. Aria and Brendan, with their magic hammering into the enemy, had littered the road and the ground to either side with the remains of the hideous creatures they'd destroyed. Now a new threat was approaching: two giant demons, clearly in a foul mood, were making their way toward them.

Vander stood on Tanton's shoulder, steadying himself with a handful of his huge tunic, as the giant ran into the fray to meet them. As they drew near, Vander launched himself from Tanton's shoulder into one of the two demons, who were every bit as large as Tanton. Vander drove his sword into the demon's chest and, letting the razor-sharp blade and his body weight do the work, sliced through the demon, cutting downward at an angle all the way to its lower thigh before pulling his sword free and dropping to the ground. The demon could only attempt to catch and gather its entrails before stumbling forward and collapsing, eviscerated by the devastating wound.

Tanton slammed into the other demon, bringing it to the ground and pounding it with his fists relentlessly before he was thrown off. The demon came to its feet, nearly stepping on Vander, and Vander did not miss his chance. He sliced through the back of the demon's lower leg, severing its tendons and crippling the giant demon with a single swing of his sword. The demon dropped to the ground in agony, clutching at its ruined leg. Tanton picked up a large boulder and slammed it down on the writhing creature's head, ending its suffering and eliminating the threat in the same instant.

Tanton lowered his hand, and Vander ran, leaping up into it. The giant raised him to his shoulder and then returned, gathering Aria and Brendan up as well before the four disappeared. They reappeared directly behind the rear flanks of Vantrill's army and attacked once again. They repeated this plan of attack over and over until they could hear the more conventional battle that was raging ahead of them at the front.

Vantrill's army found themselves fighting between Tennington's resilient regular army units at the front, and the four who had been decimating them from the rear, when Vantrill materialized in front of the four.

Tanton shouted a warning, but Aria, who was attacking the enemy's right flank, didn't hear it. Vantrill stunned her with a powerful blast of his magic, sending her flying through the air before she crashed back down, rolled across the ground, and finally lay unmoving.

Brendan raced toward Vantrill, firing bolt after bolt of his fire. Vantrill fought back with his own dark fire. Brendan blocked it and continued toward his target without slowing. He was nearly on top of Vantrill when the demon master unleashed a barrage of attacks from multiple angles directly at him.

Brendan let his magic absorb the energy of the attack, then unleashed it back at his attacker in a single massive blast. Vantrill was able to deflect the burst, but it knocked him off his feet. He was amazed at his young attacker's power. Vantrill rose from the ground, concerned by the amount of energy it took. It was strange to him that it should require so much of his effort to defeat this brash challenger.

Vantrill gained his feet just before Brendan was on him. Brendan was fully enraged, his emotions running wild. He tried to use his fire, but it did not work. He drew his sword as he attacked, spinning the blade in his hand. He swept a killing blow toward his enemy, but Vantrill caught the blade, tore it from his attacker's hand, and cast it aside.

Brendan tried to use his magic again, but nothing happened. With no other choice, he dove on his enemy, tackling him back to the ground. He grabbed the demon leader by the throat, attempting to choke the life out of him.

Vantrill rose up from the ground despite the fact that Brendan was using all his strength to push him down with both hands clasped firmly around his neck, and the two came face-to-face.

"You are very strong, young Pandane. Soon I will enjoy killing you," Vantrill hissed at Brendan, holding his gaze. Vantrill's face was nearly touching Brendan's. "But there are others who must die first this day. I look forward to seeing you suffer for what your ancestors cost me, but that is for another time." With that, Vantrill disappeared, leaving Brendan grasping nothing but air.

Brendan looked ahead and could see that the enemy army had continued its march forward unhindered and was now gone from sight. He gained his feet and recovered his sword, then ran back to where Aria lay, with Vander and Tanton tending to her.

"Is she okay?" he called out as he approached, panting heavily.

"See for yourself," Vander said, turning his attention from Aria to Brendan. Vander held out his hand, and Aria reached for it, clasping it firmly. Vander pulled her to her feet, and Aria kissed him on the cheek, then flashed him a smile. She blushed before turning and jumping into Brendan's arms.

"Are you okay?" Brendan asked her, holding her tight.

"I'll live. I'm sure nothing's broken but my pride," she said, laughing.

Brendan sat her on her feet and quickly looked her over. "You're a tough one, to be sure, Aria Pandane," he said.

The four companions came together quickly to discuss their options.

"I believe Vantrill intends to kill Brielle. As we know, she planned to end him today after allowing herself to be captured. She is very confident Andentine has given her the power to protect herself; I hope she's correct. I believe we would be better served at this point to end our attacks and report back to King Tennington. Vantrill's army is severely weakened now but continues to advance. I believe our protection and help may save lives at the front. I do not like Vantrill's coming here, after Brielle was taken. And I'm concerned for those at the front. Does anyone think differently?"

None did, and the four came together once again, prepared to teleport together, but Brendan and Aria found that their abilities did not work. They tried several times, but to no avail. They tried altering their magic, then combining it, but nothing worked.

"Clearly, Vantrill did something to block our abilities. That must have been his real purpose in returning here.

Brielle did not have time to teach us everything, and we cannot counter it. We are left to travel by foot, but we must move quickly," Brendan announced, looking to Tanton. "Would you mind taking us there, big guy?"

When the four finally arrived near the front, they found a scene of utter devastation. The dead were scattered everywhere, those of the king's army and those of Vantrill's demon army alike had been completely destroyed. Their burned and charred bodies were intermingled in the throes of death. The bodies of hundreds of dead horses littered the area as well. They witnessed the gruesome remains of partially eaten bodies of men and women strewn about the battlefield. It appeared to them that Vantrill had spared no one. The four moved through the grim scene looking for survivors but found none. Thousands upon thousands of blackened corpses littered the four's way as they continued to move toward the palace.

It was some time before they came upon the body of Drake Fallon. He lay burned badly with the remains of three burned horses. Tanton lowered his three companions to the ground. Vander recognized the king's mount and the remains of his saddle, as well as Bear's. Vander pointed out the animals and what he knew of them. He looked around for some time but could find neither Bear's nor King Tennington's body among the dead.

The four resumed their journey to the palace at a fast pace but in silence now, afraid of what they might find there as well. They exchanged worried glances from time to time as they moved up the road closer to the palace, but none spoke as they made their way through the carnage.

Brendan could not help but be concerned Aria was seeing so much death and dismemberment at her young age. He kept a close eye on her. But there was not much he could do to shield her from it.

"It's Bear!" Tanton called out, breaking the long silence of their march. He grabbed the others quickly and ran with them up the road to the large man, who was carrying another in his arms. Bear, feeling the heavy footsteps of the giant and hearing the voices of the others calling to him as they approached, turned back toward them and waited.

As they reached him, they could see that he was in shock. He was badly burned and having trouble walking as he carried another's burned body cradled in his arms. The man's injuries were severe enough they could not tell whether he was alive or not. Nor could they identify the man. Bear looked down at the man in his arms and then up at his friends.

"We have lost our king."

Chapter 31

rielle looked sadly at Trindentine. The war he spoke of had ended generations ago; he and his elves had been trapped in the Shades Hollow for many centuries.

"I am going to take you to Andentine," she announced. "Take my hand, Trindentine, and have your elves join hands with us. Hold on tight. Do not let go!" Brielle said, looking around at each one of them to make sure they were all holding on before taking them with her.

They were on the black slate bank of the Shades Hollow one moment and in Andentine's realm the next. The elves looked around, bewildered, staring in awe at the beauty of the world in which they now found themselves. The creatures of faerie could be seen all around them. They could see elves in the distance with gnomes and trolls. Dwarves and dragons roamed the lush land as well. The air and water were teeming with life. A tall elf with long silver hair and dark-green robes appeared before them.

"Andentine! My brother!" Trindentine called out as his men bowed deeply. "I have missed you so much!"

"Trindentine?" Andentine studied the grotesque demon before him. "How can this be?" He looked at Brielle, searching for the answer.

"I found Trindentine and these elves quite by accident, or, rather, they found me. Vantrill was holding them captive all this time. Unable to bend them to his will, he'd thrown them in a pit of pure darkness, where he expected them to remain for all eternity," Brielle said. "I will allow them to explain what happened beyond that."

"Brielle, I know you must leave, but the damage has already been done. Before you go, I would like to introduce you to these elves properly," Andentine said, raising his hand and waving it before the hideously deformed figures before him. The creatures began to transform into the strong young elves they had been in their youth. They looked at each other, clasping each other's shoulders and hugging one another, recognizing themselves as they had been before Vantrill had tried to bend them to his will. Brielle thought they were the most handsome young elves she had ever seen.

Trindentine stepped to his brother and bowed deeply once again. Andentine pulled him close and held him for a long time before releasing him. Trindentine's hair and clothing were darker than those of any elf Brielle had ever seen. He was bold and handsome, and she could not draw her eyes from him.

"Brielle, I would like to introduce you to my brother, Prince Trindentine."

Brielle attempted to bow politely, but Trindentine stepped close and hugged her instead. "Thank you, Your Highness. I can never thank you enough or ever do enough to repay you for this," he said close to her ear. Trindentine released her and held up his hand, and his elves lined up beside him. "Thank you, Your Highness!" he said once again. The handsome young elves bowed deeply to her, and she did the same in return.

"All of your families were brought here shortly after you disappeared. They are here in this realm, my loyal elves," Andentine said. "You will dine with them this day!"

The elves were overcome with emotion as they bowed before their king. Brielle turned her attention away from the group of elves and back to Andentine.

"You know I must leave."

"I do, Brielle. I, too, cannot thank you enough for this incredible gift," he said, wiping at his eyes. He hugged her tightly and then released her. "Go directly to the palace, Brielle. Vantrill has gained his full strength, and unthinkable damage has been done there."

Andentine reached out and placed his hand across the pendant meshed with her flesh and held it there firmly. "I give you now what I have given no other, Brielle." He bent close, whispering in her ear. When he finished, he stepped back from her and said aloud, "Now go! I will see you again soon." She did not hesitate; she was gone before Andentine's words fell silent.

Brielle arrived at the palace in Willow's room but did not find her there, and she quickly discovered four guards who were burned beyond recognition in the corridor outside the door.

Brielle moved quickly through the palace to the common areas and found nothing but the burned remains of the King's Watch and the palace's staff. Brielle fought off the panic that began to take hold of her and kept moving. She found nothing but the dead.

When she finally made it to the Great Hall, she saw it was littered with even more of the dead. King Tennington's body lay on the council table with a small pillow placed under his head and his sword in his hands. Brielle moved closer and bowed to him one last time.

"Goodbye, my king. May your spirit travel fast to meet those who've gone before you and who await you with open arms."

The bodies of the army reserves that had been left at the palace in its defense were scattered in the hall and throughout the gardens. Brielle found many more along the creek between the city walls. Nowhere did she find a sign of life. She stopped, surrounded by death and the smell of burnt flesh that still hung thick in the air. She closed her eyes and searched for Willow but was unable to find her. She turned her attention to Aria but failed to find her as well. She tried with Brendan, but to no avail.

Brielle went to the makeshift infirmary, hoping to find Drae or Starlin there helping the wounded. She found the two lying dead alongside their patients. Many of the wounded had never made it to their feet. Their corpses still lay in their beds, most burned so badly they were unrecognizable.

Brielle reached out again with her magic in an attempt to find anyone yet alive but was unable to locate a living soul. She stopped looking for survivors and searched for Vantrill.

"Foolish girl, I've been waiting for you," his voice said in her mind. "Did I not warn you against escaping? Did I not warn you of all I would do if you did? You have brought this death and destruction upon your people, just as you did once before. Isn't that right, Brielle Pandane, murderer of the miners? You seek to do good, but you are only capable of hurting the ones you love most. It's not your fault; it's simply in your nature. Stop denying your true self. It is your destiny to be with me, to be my queen. Together, we will rule this realm and all others I desire. Together, no one could stand against us!"

"It seems as though you have taken everything from me, Vantrill, just as you promised," the Blue Witch responded. "Why, then, would I agree to become your queen? I think you and I are destined to fight until one of us is no more, or perhaps one of us is spending eternity in the Shades Hollow," she responded.

"I wish to show you, my future queen, that I can be merciful, as well. I have your family. I have to this point spared them. I only ask for what you have already agreed to give me, that which you have sworn to me. You must return to me. If you do so, I will allow you to choose what will happen to them. I have your daughter and your sister, as well as your brother. So, I will give you two choices."

"And what would those choices be?"

"You disappointed me, and for that you must be punished. Your first choice will be to pick which of your three family members will die quickly and mercifully. With your second choice, you will pick another to be transformed into one of my demons, to serve me as I wish for the balance of their life—and I will make sure it is a very long one. The family member that remains will be thrown into the Shades Hollow, where they will remain for all eternity struggling to escape its black waters."

"That is your offer of mercy, Vantrill?"

"It is as merciful an offer as you shall receive after your disobedience, Your Highness," he said dispassionately. "If you choose not to accept my mercy, so be it. I will decide their fates after I have tortured them in ways you can't possibly imagine. The choice is yours, but you will make it now!"

"I must assume that you have possession of my brother's and sister's pendants."

"I do."

"Then I will make you an offer, Vantrill. But know this first: I will not return to you and give you all I have promised and lose my family in turn. If you choose to harm them, I will spend the rest of my life with but one purpose, and it will be to end yours. And I assure you it will not be pleasant or merciful. However, if you wish me to return to you, I will do so willingly, and I will give you all that I promised and swore to. But I will do so only if you release my family and neither you nor any in your stead ever harms them again. I know you will never give up their pendants, so I will not ask it in the bargain. Free them, Vantrill, and I will return to you. I will willingly give you all I have committed to giving you." Brielle said it firmly and with great confidence, but she knew she had only herself to bargain with. She waited several moments before she received her answer.

"I accept your offer. Come to me now, my queen!"

Brielle lowered her head, knowing what she must do, and then she was gone.

Chapter 32

Two figures dressed in travel cloaks with their hoods pulled up close about their faces searched through the dead of the palace. They moved quickly until they found who they were looking for. When they did, they each picked up a body and carried it away.

They moved through the palace until they reached the Great Hall and laid the two bodies gently on the council table near the body of King Tennington. They then unfolded thin blankets and laid one over each of the three bodies. One of the hooded figures hesitated before pulling the blanket over the face of the body he'd carried.

"Goodbye, my brother, until we meet again."

Tanton waited outside patiently for his two companions. His thoughts drifted to Tiden and the words Brielle had spoken to him. He missed his brother but was at peace and pleased to know that he was with their kin in a far better place than the one he currently found himself in.

"We must return to the council members and report what we've found," Vander said, pulling his hood off as he approached Tanton.

"We found none alive, Tanton. We found Drae's and Starlin's bodies but found none we could recognize as Vlix," Bear said, removing his hood as well. "We'll return as soon as we can."

"I'm fine. Do what you must," Tanton replied.

Vander and Bear retuned to the Great Hall and crossed through to a stone wall behind the dais the throne sat upon. Vander carefully placed his hand on a stone that did not stand out from the others as far as Bear could tell. He pressed hard on it, and locks released, allowing a small section of the wall to open. The two men stepped through the opening, and the wall closed behind them, leaving no sign of their passing.

They traveled through a narrow corridor, steadily winding downward until they reached another heavy stone door. Again, Vander used a hidden release, and they moved through the door, then closed it behind them. They stood in a large, well-appointed room filled with fine furnishings and a large table with several chairs around it. There were no windows, as they were in a vault far below the ground. The passages and the room itself were lit by an unknown source, perhaps some form of magic they were not familiar with. At the far end of the room was another hidden door, and beyond that door were smaller rooms and a tunnel that ran back under the palace to another hidden door and further passageways.

Members of the High Council of Andavar seated themselves around the large wooden council table upon seeing the two enter the hidden chamber. A distinguished-looking woman with dark hair and skin remained standing at the head of the table.

"Vander Ray, I am, as you may know, Danianne Olenfore, this council's leader. Before we go any further, we would like to recognize your bravery and quick actions when the attack began. I think we of this council," she said, looking about at the other members, "can safely say we owe our lives to your fast action." The council members stood and applauded. When they had finished and had seated themselves again, Danianne continued. "Please, tell us what you have found, Vander," she said before sitting herself.

Vander walked around the table and stood closer to Danianne before addressing those gathered. "I, of course, am aware of your service to our king. I regret we have both spent so much time here in the palace yet know so little of each other." He reached down, took her hand, and kissed it gently as she nodded politely.

"I am afraid my report to this council is a grim one," Vander continued. "As you all well know, you were being informed of the death of our beloved king when we were attacked. While we were able to get all of you safely here through the hidden tunnels, the attack raged on above us. I am sorry to inform you that after a thorough search of the palace, none were found alive."

An audible gasp arose from many of the council members. Some came to their feet with raised voices. Danianne remained stoic and held up her hands, silencing them and bringing them back to their seats. "We must remain calm and act decisively in this crisis, my fellow council members," she said, and then nodded to Vander to continue.

"The High Sword and his sister Aria are both missing, as is Willow. If not for Willow's warning, and the High Sword and Aria's counterattack, I would not have had the opportunity to get you to safety. And let's not forget Baird Prow, here, who is known affectionately as Bear. He is a highly decorated former officer of the Elite First and was also instrumental in helping us reach this room," Vander said, turning toward Bear. Again, the council momentarily stood and applauded before retaking their seats.

"We have lost our king, and we have lost our army, including all of the brave men and women of the Elite. We also have no idea where the Blue Witch is, the one most capable of defeating this new evil. With her and her siblings missing, and our army gone, we have lost all ability to defend the people of our realm." Vander finished speaking and stepped back from the table.

Danianne hesitated before she spoke. "Our king left us no queen or heir to ascend the throne. Our people do not yet know that our king is dead. I believe we should, for the moment, keep it that way."

Bear cleared his throat, drawing all those in attendance's attention. "Forgive me, but I have something from King Tennington that I believe should be presented at this time. Our king gave this to me before the last battle began. He instructed me to present it to his council members should anything happen to him," he announced as he approached Danianne. Bear pulled the sealed paper from within his cloak and handed it to her. She examined the seal carefully before breaking it and reading the message. She read it again, confirming its contents, before addressing the council.

"It seems that our king has named his successor, which was within his power to do. He has also left an explanation of his choice. Though he acknowledges no explanation is necessary, he felt it would be beneficial for to us to have it. He has left this same message in his private quarters, and another sealed copy has been given to an individual not named here. Should anyone on this council attempt to contest his instructions or their validity, this person will come forward. I believe, as I said earlier, we should make no announcement of this to our citizens at this time. Before I read our king's last command, are we in agreement on delaying this announcement, as well as the delivery of any information on the current state of the realm, to our people? I think it best to prevent widespread panic and allow us to regroup as best we may under the circumstances."

The council members conferred only a few moments before all confirmed they were in agreement and were sworn to silence on the matter. Bear and Vantrill also gave their word that they would remain silent for the time being.

"Very well, then. It is with great honor, and my deepest sorrow, that I now read before this council King Tennington's final command."

When Danianne finished reading, she looked around the table to the men and women assembled.

"Do any dare contest our king's final command?" She asked the question firmly, indicating that she did not expect any argument, and none came. "Very well, then, you are all bound to silence on this matter until such time as our new king can be crowned at his coronation and ascend the throne of our realm."

Chapter 33

The Blue Witch reappeared far outside the city gates in an area where she would not be seen.

"No, Vantrill. I will not come to you yet; you already have two of the pendants and the power you desire, but we are still working on trusting each other. Once I return to you, you may decide you no longer wish to honor our agreement and release my family. Release them and send them here to me now. I will say my goodbyes quickly enough and will appear before you shortly thereafter. I will not delay long. You have my solemn word on this. If I do not keep my word, I know now that you have the power, as you have already displayed, to punish me and take my family members from me forever."

"That is true. I am more powerful now than I have ever been before, my future queen. I will honor your request, as one last sign of my mercy and goodwill, as we embark on our new covenant. But I warn you, should you not come to me as agreed, it will not only be your family that suffers the consequences; I will punish every man, woman, and child of this realm. And you and you alone, Brielle Pandane, will be responsible for their suffering."

"I agree to your terms fully. You have my solemn word I will return to you with all I have promised and sworn to."

Her three family members appeared before her a second later. She grabbed Willow and Aria and pulled them to her, then reached out to Brendan. "Hurry!" she said. He took her outstretched hand, and they were gone. The four were in Andentine's realm a moment later, and Andentine appeared before them nearly simultaneously.

"I must leave my family in your care, Andentine. It is the only way I can be sure they are out of Vantrill's reach. I have promised to return to him. King Tennington is dead, and his army has been destroyed. I must go to protect those who remain. Vantrill has threatened to punish all, even women and children, if I do not," she said, hugging Brendan and Aria. She quickly hugged and kissed Willow, then hugged her one more time, before looking back at Andentine. "You were right; Vantrill desires much more of me. He wants me to be his queen. He has the other two pendants. I have no choice; I must return to him. Take care of my family for me, Andentine," she said as she looked back one last time at her loved ones. Her family members stood there, unsure of what had just taken place.

"Go, my child, you have that which you have committed yourself to," Andentine said. "Your family will be safe here with me." A moment later, she was gone.

"Aria, it is good to see you again, my child. I wish it could be under different circumstances," Andentine said, turning his attention to his three guests. He knelt down in front of Willow and looked into her hazel eyes. "Willow, it is my great pleasure to have you back in my realm once again as well." He hugged her before returning to his feet.

"Brendan," Andentine said, addressing him for the first time, "you and I must spend some time together. There is much I wish to discuss with you."

Brendan looked at the elven king, a bit confused. "How is it you know of me?"

"Your sister Brielle has spoken with pride of her family since she first ran across the Dead Bridge, as your people call it. You do not know this, but she spent time with you and Aria as you both grew up, just as she did with Willow." He looked at the young girl knowingly. "She could not spend the time she would have liked with you, but then, she did what she had to do."

"What'd she have to do that kept her away from us so much?" Aria asked.

"Brielle came to me quite by accident. She did not know what would happen to her when she ran across my bridge, and I don't think she cared. She came to me a broken young woman, full of regret and guilt. She was lost and consumed by her emotions," Andentine began.

"I gave her hope and a purpose in life that met with her own desire to use her magic for the good of her people. When I left your realm with the elven people and those of faerie, I knew I would most likely never return. I have always cared for the race of men and wished very much for them to join us when we left. I've watched their realm ever since. When I saw that evil was creeping back into it, it was clear to me it would soon be in great danger once again. I recruited Brielle to be a weapon against this evil. I gave her pendant, the one with the blue stone, additional powers and abilities to help her," Andentine explained.

"Brielle has saved the race of men several times from great evil. She has fought incredible battles to save her people from these threats, all completely unbeknownst to them. Battles that have taken a heavy toll on her, both physically and mentally. The Blue Witch has served to protect them since coming to me. I recently asked her to officially become the realm's High Protector, with King Tennington's knowledge and blessing, knowing that the danger there was about to increase, and she has become just that. I have given her powers that she has not yet discovered for herself, to help her in dealing with Vantrill and any other evil she may encounter. Willow, I know that she showed you her true appearance," he said, looking directly into the young seer's eyes. "I cannot begin to tell you how hard that must have been for her. She must love you very much to have done so."

Willow lowered her head, ashamed. "She did show me," Willow replied, embarrassed and saddened further that she had pressed her. "I wish I hadn't asked her to." She wiped at her eyes. "It wasn't fair for me to have done so."

"Do not blame yourself for wanting to know your mother, Willow. Brielle is much stronger than she realizes. I'm sure deep down she wanted you to know the truth of her appearance and for you to love her regardless. You gave her that, Willow, and I thank you for it." Willow looked up to Andentine and smiled as she continued to dry her eyes.

Brendan watched Willow's reactions to Andentine's kind words. "Where did she go?" he asked. "She didn't go back to Vantrill, did she?"

"Brielle made an agreement with Vantrill. In exchange for your lives, she agreed to return to him. He intends to make her his queen."

"And you allowed her to leave here knowing she was safe here with us! Why? Why would you allow it?" Brendan demanded. "Who cares what she was forced to agree to!"

"Vantrill warned Brielle that if she did not return to him after your release, he would punish the innocent men, women, and children of the realm for her deception. Vantrill not only intends to make Brielle his queen but expects her to join with him in achieving his goal to rule not only the realm of men but every other realm he wishes to invade, including this one. Brielle returns to Vantrill to save the very people she swore to protect."

"But Vantrill has taken our pendants and is stronger now than ever before!" Aria interjected.

"Brielle is very clever, and she knows this. She knows as well what she must endure to protect the realms."

"You would abandon her to her fate, then?" Brendan said. "You would allow Vantrill to force her to be his queen?" He was livid. "You can't stop this? You can't help her?"

"Brielle was willing to risk everything to save the three of you, to save her family. She is also willing to sacrifice herself to protect her people and mine."

"It's our fault, Brendan," Aria said. "We should have fought harder, fought smarter. If we hadn't allowed ourselves and Willow to be captured, Brielle would not be in this awful mess. We are to blame for this!"

"No, Aria, you are not to blame," Andentine said. "You did what you could, but you two are not nearly as powerful as your sister. Vantrill is a dangerous creature and knows how to exploit one's weaknesses. Do not attempt to take any blame for that foul creature's actions."

"But what can we do to help her?" Brendan asked.

"We can do nothing more for Brielle. It is beyond any of us to save her," Andentine responded. "But as I said, Brendan, you and I must speak of other urgent matters. Please join me." He stepped away from the two young girls, bowing politely to them before departing.

Brendan looked at the two and shrugged before reluctantly joining Andentine. He was not convinced that Brielle should be left to her fate, and he intended to press Andentine further to help her.

Chapter 34

Vander and Bear, with the council's blessing, left the vault room to organize efforts to clear the palace of the dead. First, they removed King Tennington's body and placed it where workers helping with the effort would not discover it. They left the bodies of the other two where they lay covered on the Great Hall's council table.

They left the palace and exited through the ruined gates of the city's outer wall. They were on foot but soon were able to move far enough away from the city to find a few people who had been brave enough to come out of hiding. They were able to borrow mounts, including one particularly large horse suitable for Bear's big frame. As they moved further from the capital city of Andavar, the two found more and more activity among the people. They were able to find young riders willing to spread the word that their king needed the help of those physically able to provide it.

With word spreading quickly, Bear and Vander returned to the palace. They were working on the plans for what needed to be done when helpers started to arrive.

And they arrived in large numbers. Bear and Vander met with the men and women at the outer gate.

Vander, speaking to those who had gathered, addressed the massacre and what would be needed from the living. He informed them that should any feel it was beyond their ability to deal with what they would be seeing and doing, they were free to leave with no shame and the king's blessing. Though, in truth, he knew those who'd made it to the city gate had passed awful scenes along the main road and would likely have already turned back if they could not stomach the bodies. The people who had come to the palace wanted to do their part. It was a massive undertaking clearing the palace, along with the grounds and gardens, of the charred bodies of the dead.

Horse-drawn wagons had been called for, and many were available for the workers to use. All of the bodies were loaded onto the wagons except for the two on the council table. They were left untouched.

Wagon after wagon, filled with the dead, was driven past the city walls and into the surrounding countryside to an area designated for the mass grave now being dug by a great many men and women. It was impossible to identify most of the dead, and the council had decreed that the communal grave would eventually become a memorial to the brave souls who'd been lost.

The council members would from time to time present new orders from the king to divert any questions about Tennington's whereabouts. They wished to give the impression that he was still in command and giving orders as normal.

The work was moving along swiftly with the amount of help that had arrived. Carpenters and metalsmiths were repairing the city gates. The cleansing of the corridors and palace rooms had begun, with dozens of people following behind the crews that were removing the dead.

Vander and Bear worked side by side with the members of the council to oversee the work. Repairs to the Great Hall were still to be delayed at this time, so no work was taking place there, though many had taken the opportunity to walk through it as the day proceeded, in order to witness the vast damage.

Food and drink had been prepared in large quantities to accommodate the workers at both sites as the day waned to night. Though many had trouble eating, they did so to keep up their strength. The amount of help and effort was truly impressive, and it appeared as though the bulk of the work would be completed by the end of the night.

By sunrise, most of the workers had run out of things to do and were leaving to make their way back to their homes. Vander and Bear had also worked through the night and were overseeing the last of the efforts. What had started as a massive undertaking had been completed by midmorning through the incredible efforts of those who had come to support their king and show their respect for the fallen. There had been many tears shed over the loss of life. Most had gone about their tasks in an eerily silent manner, in shock and stunned by the carnage. As the last of the volunteers left, a deafening silence fell over the palace, as it was now all but abandoned.

Repairs would of course still need to be made throughout the palace and the grounds. The city itself was unscathed for the most part, as were the homes and farms in the surrounding countryside. It was the army and the palace that had taken the brunt of the attack. Local workers had begun the grim work of clearing the road through the battlegrounds. Pile after pile of demon remains was burning along the road that traversed the land.

The remains of Tennington's army had been arriving by the wagonful throughout the morning at the mass grave site. The volunteers there had been the last to finish their work. They filled in the large grave after reports that all of the remains that could be recovered had been. They left the excess dirt and rocks piled off to the side for possible use in the memorial that would be designed and constructed in the future—assuming they could find a way to secure their future. Only a select few knew the threat was far from over.

Vander and Bear borrowed one of the wagons and its team for one last deed. They placed the two bodies that had been left covered and untouched on the council table in the Great Hall gently into the back of the wagon. They drove out into the countryside, not far from the city, to Vander's family grave site. There they began wordlessly digging two graves side by side.

When they had finished, Vander and Bear placed the bodies of Drae Tine, who had no known family of his own, and Starlin Ray in their final resting places. They said a few words in the men's memory and finished the job they had set out to perform.

"What will you do now, Bear?" Vander asked as they rode back to the palace.

"I have good men tending to my business in Ravens Burg. So, I think I will stick around and see what our new king is made of and whether I may be of any help. What about you?"

"I'm obligated to the new king. I'm bound by my duty until relieved. So, I will be staying as well."

Neither of the sweaty, exhausted men could think of anything else worth saying. And so they drove back to the palace silently, listening to the horses' hooves clopping on the road before them and the wagon's wheels creaking beneath them.

Chapter 35

Brielle watched dispassionately as Vantrill approached her. He sickened her, but she would not allow him to see it upon her face.

"So, you have come to me as agreed, Blue Witch. Smart girl!" Vantrill said, looking over his new prize closely, touching her face with the back of his hand and stroking her hair, lifting it and letting it fall again. "I was not completely sure you would."

"We have an agreement, and you kept up your end of it. I'm here to fulfill that which I have promised as well," the Blue Witch replied as she stood staring at the floor.

"And so you shall, my queen. You will join me in conquering many realms. And you will assist me in destroying any who oppose me. You will do as I command you. And you will bear me a son who will carry the magic blood of Pandane. You will give me all that I desire and more." He put a finger under her chin and raised her head to face him, then ran his finger over her bottom lip. "And you will please me in ways you never knew existed."

"I think you have misunderstood the nature of our agreement, Vantrill," the Blue Witch responded. "What did I promise for my part? I promised that I would not ask for the other two pendants to be returned, and I won't. I agreed to return before you, and I have. I promised that you would receive nothing from me that I did not give freely, willingly, and with great pleasure. Do you remember my words? I assure you, Vantrill," she said, slapping his hand away from her face, "I do. And that is all you will receive from me!"

"So, you have deceived me with your words?" he spat back.

"You let your greed and desire deceive you. I most certainly didn't. I spoke very plainly of what I would do and what I would give," she said.

"You do not know the power I now possess, or you would not attempt such a dangerous and foolish game with me!" he said, cocking his head and studying her, measuring her, searching her face.

"I do not know the dark realm that Andentine banished you to, Vantrill, but I fear it has turned you into a fool! Do you think I would make a deal that required me to return to you if I was not confident in the outcome of our game?"

"So, you do not intend to flee from me?"

"You have abducted my family; killed many of my people, including my king; and tried to hold me prisoner. Now you wish to force me to be your queen and bear your child. No, Vantrill, I'm not here to flee from you, you sick, twisted demon, I'm here to kill you!"

"Then it is you who is the fool!" He struck her face hard with the back of his hand. The Blue Witch neither flinched nor attempted to block the blow.

"Oh, Vantrill, do you think you could possibly hurt me with a coward's slap? Do you think me weak and afraid?" She dealt him a vicious backhanded blow in return, mixed with the power of her magic. It sent him flying into the wall behind him and then to the floor.

"You see, Vantrill, I know you're afraid. You're a coward, like all who attempt to harm those weaker than themselves. And you know nothing of my real power!" She struck him again as he rose from the floor, knocking him off his feet once more.

"Did you really think I would allow you to keep my family's pendants?" She struck him once again, so hard he crashed into the wall at the far side of the room. "The only people given real power by them are my brother and sister, and I've trained them on how to use their magic. You have no way to extract the pendants' power; I made sure of it. I will not ask for them back. I did promise you that. And I intend to keep my promise. But I am going to kill you and take them back."

"You lie, witch! I felt their power!" He stuck his hand out, grasping her by the throat, attempting to choke her with a strong measure of his own magic, but she brushed aside the attack.

Vantrill changed tactics, diving on the blue girl and taking her to the ground. He ripped and tore at her frantically before she threw him off and came to her knees, releasing bolts of her fire into him. Vantrill absorbed the blows and rose to his feet, pinning her to the wall behind her with his magic. She broke free of its hold and threw a large section of the wall at him, burying him in the rubble. He burst up through the debris and hovered in the air near the roof of the old castle's chapel like a specter. Vantrill rained fire down, filling the room with flames, heavy smoke, and ash. It was suffocating and burned Brielle's lungs as she countered the attack by bringing part of the ceiling down above Vantrill, pinning him to the floor.

Brielle moved in closer, burning Vantrill with her fire as he struggled to free himself. He screamed out in frustration and pain before he cast the rubble into the air with his magic, spinning it wildly into a funnel. Then, gathering the storm, he launched it at her. She was able to block most of it at the last moment but was hit by several pieces, which drove her to the floor. She attempted to rise before slumping back down and lying still before Vantrill.

Her enemy attacked again, engulfing her in his powerful black flames. Her robes were able to help protect her from the flames and shield her from the heat, but they were heavily damaged. Only tattered and smoldering remnants were left clinging to her body.

"Now you will pay the price for rejecting me!" Vander struck her with blast after blast of his searing black fire. The Blue Witch, finally able to rise to her feet, lashed out at her attacker, but Vantrill walked through the weakened effort unfazed. He snatched her up by the neck, raising her over his head.

"You could have been my queen, but you have chosen death instead!" He threw her roughly into the nearest wall. Then he picked her up again, pinning her to the wall with one hand firmly locked around her throat. Vantrill looked at her burned robes and scorched blue skin and laughed at her. "It is time to send you back where you belong, Princess."

He noticed something then. There, exposed beneath her torn robes and blouse, he could see the pendant fused into her flesh and its silver chain meshed around her neck. The pendant's clear blue stone was moving within itself.

"When I dig that pendant out of your corpse, Princess, I will be powerful beyond imagination. None will be able to stand against me." He squeezed her throat tighter, continuing to choke her. She tried to scream but was unable to do so, and Vantrill could feel her life draining away.

"What, nothing clever to say now?" Vantrill taunted.

She could move her mouth but not speak any words. Her sparkling eyes began to dim and then glassed over. Vantrill, sensing victory, squeezed her throat with both hands, using all of his strength, until the blue girl in his grip breathed no more.

"The powerful Blue Witch, dead in my hands!" Vantrill said, mocking his victim as he shook her limp body. Vantrill held her before him and, bending close, kissed her blue lips before letting her corpse fall to the floor.

Chapter 36

Andentine walked through his realm with Brendan at his side for some time before he finally spoke. "I have asked much of Brielle since she came to me. And when I asked her to officially become High Protector of the realm of men, I had her deliver a special message to King Tennington. Your king, before his death, knew that his time was coming to an end and that his fate was sealed. I warned him of this and asked him to consider carefully who would succeed him as king. As you know, Brendan, he had no heir. As I have asked much of Brielle, I now must ask much of you. You must continue to serve the realm of men, Brendan, but you cannot remain its High Sword."

"I would not wish to leave our new king at a time like this, Andentine. If you have need of me elsewhere, might it wait some time first?"

"No, Brendan. You will be needed as soon as Brielle returns."

"I like that you speak so confidently of her return. I fear for her."

"Vantrill does not know the danger he is in playing games with the Blue Witch. As I said before, she has no reservations about risking everything to win. And, Brendan, you must know this: in every situation she has faced, she has always ultimately won. The Blue Witch is an incredibly dangerous and powerful creature." Andentine noticed the look that Brendan gave him. It was a look Andentine understood. Brendan did not like his sister being referred to as a "creature."

"Brielle has seemed quite loving and pleasant to me in the short time I've spent with her," Brendan said.

"I'm sure she has, Brendan. Do not mistake me; I love Brielle very much and have enjoyed her company and counsel for some time. But Brielle and the Blue Witch are really two different people. As Brielle, she is an amazing young woman who has overcome much in her life—far too much, Brendan. Brielle, though damaged, feels and gives love as much as she is able to. Brielle is very much still the sister you lost all of those years ago. But I assure you, Brendan, you have never spent any real time with the side of her that is the Blue Witch. When your sister has come to you or spent time with you and your family, it has been Brielle that you have enjoyed spending time with and getting to know better. Brielle is confident in her abilities and is very powerful, to be sure; do not misunderstand me." He paused in thought before continuing.

"The Blue Witch is the complete opposite of Brielle. It's the part of her that has never recovered from what happened to her, the part that has suffered and lost so much, a very damaged and dark part. In truth, Brendan, the Blue Witch has kept your sister Brielle alive. That side of Brielle, the dark and loathsome side, you have yet to truly see. The Blue Witch neither seeks nor desires the company of others. She is supremely confident in herself and fears nothing."

"It does not sound as if you wish me to join Brielle, or as if she would have need of me if you did."

"You are wrong on both counts. I wish you to join her by taking on a much larger role in your realm. The Blue Witch does not need you, or anyone else, for that matter, but Brielle most certainly does."

"What would you have me do, then, Andentine?" Brendan asked, stopping and looking to him for an answer.

"As you now know, you are a direct descendant of the first king of men. Through time, death, and perhaps even fate, the Pandane name lost the throne and was replaced with the Ashford name. You are of royal blood, Brendan. By now, Tennington's final command will have been delivered to his council. His command is that the direct descendant of the first king of men, the firstborn male heir, shall succeed him on the throne as the realm's new king."

Brendan laughed. "I serve my people, Andentine, but I do not think I'm such a wise choice to be king. I hate council meetings and politics. What do I know of such things? It would seem another, one who cares for and is more practiced in politics, would be more suited for the throne than I."

"It is you, Brendan, who can heal your realm. Nobody can deny your blood, so it will end any claim by another. Your people will accept you because of your royal blood and the close relationship you had with King Tennington as his High Sword. Remember, Brendan, this was his last command. The very fact you do not desire this will help you succeed. You will act in the best interest of your people and not be misled by your own desires. For what it's worth, I believe you will be a great king," Andentine said, placing his hand on Brendan's shoulder. "I've known every king in the realm of men since the first and have been a king myself even longer. Do not sell yourself short, nor deny your people. Be the king your people need you to be."

Brendan stared at Andentine, lost in thought, for several moments before responding. "If I accept this, Andentine, if I agree, will you be willing to help me and advise me when I need you?"

"You are welcome to come to my realm anytime, Brendan, and you have the ability to do so quickly and easily. I'd consider it a great honor to assist you in any manner that you wish. If it is within my power, you'll have any help you require from me. Your kingdom needs you, but you must stay here until the Blue Witch has dealt with Vantrill. She will do so quickly enough. Vantrill is dangerous, but he has always been a fool, grasping at power beyond his reach. The Blue Witch will take advantage of this and exploit it."

"While we wait, will you tell me what I need to know to serve my people well?"

"That, Brendan, is why you are the right choice to ascend the throne. You think of others first. Walk with me, and I will tell you what you should know to start, at least."

Andentine spent the time with Brendan discussing many issues he would face as the new king. He spoke to Brendan in broad terms of the demands of being a king and talked about what to expect, as well as how to anticipate the unexpected. He spoke about how to deal with his subjects, from his council and military leaders to his staff at the palace and the individual citizens of the realm.

He spoke about the importance of treating the lowest of his realm as if they were the highest. He reminded Brendan to respect and love those whom he was meant to serve and protect, and they would love and respect him in return. Andentine warned him of the dangers and pitfalls of being a king and how to wield his power with patience and grace. He shared the importance of being decisive but knowing when to take the time to weigh options as well.

Andentine gave Brendan the knowledge he had acquired over hundreds of years of ruling and through the mistakes he had made along the way. He educated Brendan on the kings who'd preceded him, including their greatest successes and their biggest failures.

Brendan asked many questions, and Andentine was patient with him, answering each one thoroughly so Brendan would learn more than he'd even sought to about the subject in question. Time stood still as Andentine worked his magic, infusing Brendan with knowledge. What seemed a brief conversation had, in fact, filled Brendan's mind with a vast amount of information he would need to draw upon in order to succeed as the king of men.

"Will Brielle kill Vantrill?" Brendan asked, his mind wandering back to his sister.

"No, not as Brielle. Brielle is not capable of such a thing. You must understand, Brendan, Brielle has developed a side of herself that protects her and can do the awful things that she herself cannot. It's the spirit of this witch within her that will kill Vantrill, I'm confident of it."

Brendan looked at Andentine. "Does the side of my sister that's Brielle know and understand what's happening in these situations?"

"Yes and no, Brendan. She experiences and remembers it all. That's why it takes such a toll on her. The Blue Witch side of her—Brielle's alter ego, if you will—could not care less and is not affected by such things, but Brielle most certainly is. The Blue Witch takes over and is in complete control when Brielle is faced with certain types of danger, but Brielle is witness to all that takes place. At least that seems to have been the way of it so far."

"Does she understand the two sides of herself?"

"To a degree, but that's a complicated question, Brendan. I do not know the answer with certainty, but I think there may be more to her than we know. She understands that people long ago took to calling her the blue witch, and she embraced it. But she seems to have assigned that name to both sides of herself. I know that, at times, Brielle has been tortured by nightmares of the Blue Witch's actions and what she's had to witness. I know the Blue Witch side of her cares enough to serve the greater good and believes what she does is both necessary and justified. But she has never indicated to me how she sees Brielle. While Brielle knows the Blue Witch well, I do not think she is always capable of realizing she is actually a part of herself. Brielle sees the Blue Witch as another who is with her." Andentine paused for a moment.

"It seems that Brielle thinks her strength comes from what she endured in the woods as a teenager and the creature she believes she became there. She is very concerned about that part of herself. As I said, Brielle is very confident in her own abilities but has fought to shed that part of her. It is very difficult at times to know where Brielle stops and the Blue Witch begins. I believe as time has passed, those lines have blurred a great deal in her mind." Andentine paused again as he thought of the girl she once was.

"I'm concerned that if she were to ever discover the truth of herself fully, she would suffer irreparable damage and might cease to exist as Brielle altogether. I worry that we could lose her completely to the Blue Witch or another yet-unknown part of herself. I fear that more than anything for her. Brielle is far more damaged than you have witnessed to this point, Brendan. Even I cannot fully understand the depths of her complicated mind." Andentine stopped and stood with Brendan for several moments before speaking again. Brendan felt he was fighting back tears.

"That, Brendan, is how you, Aria, and especially Willow can help her. Brielle needs her family to love her, to help her and give her not only a reason to simply exist but, far more important, a reason to live. If she does not have that, Brendan, I do believe we'll lose her one day."

Chapter 37

Vander stood before the king's council studying the faces of those gathered around the meeting table as he concluded his presentation.

"And now, with this council's permission, we would like to start recruiting men and women to serve in the army and the King's Watch."

"We've spoken of the need for this as well, Vander. We were preparing to ask the two of you ourselves. The effort you put into the cleansing and repair of the palace did not go unnoticed by this council," Danianne informed the two.

"Thank you. We'd be honored to begin the process of recruiting and training for both the army and the Watch as soon as possible. However, I'm afraid it will be some time before the Elite can be formed again."

"That is understood by this council, Vander. You and Bear, with our thanks, may begin as you see fit," Danianne said. "We have discussed many options and believe that we must continue as we are doing until such time as our new king arrives, hopefully with the help we need to protect our people if attacked again. We can only hope that another attack will not come before then," Danianne concluded, and stood, signaling the meeting had come to a close.

Vander and Bear wasted little time. They left the palace and again found young riders to spread the word throughout the realm of King Tennington's need for men and women willing to serve, both those with and without experience.

The response was overwhelming as more men and women than the two could properly interview showed up wishing to serve. They started by addressing the crowd and asking for those who had served in the past to come forward.

Only three men stepped forward. Vantrill and Bear spent some time with them before speaking to those without experience. They found that of the three who had experience, none had held any high rank, but they had to begin somewhere and accepted all three. Needing to continue the screening process, they quickly schooled them on what to look for and what could be overlooked based on their desperate need.

The five men set about the job of vetting those wishing to join. It was a quick process individually, but for the five dealing with the masses, it was a long day. By the time they had finished, they had accepted nearly every man and woman who'd applied. Only a few brave souls not physically capable of the rigors of service had been thanked for their willingness and politely refused. In all, they now had over five hundred men and women to house, feed, and train. Bear and Vander relied on the council to arrange for the recruits' pay, providing them a detailed list of the enlistees' names and information.

Cooks and seamstresses had been recruited next. Orders for uniforms, including belts and boots, had gone out to multiple shops throughout the realm. Weapons that had been gathered from the fallen were now being cleaned and the edges repaired and sharpened. It was an exhausting undertaking, but one that Vander and Bear found much more to their liking, and they were truly enjoying the process.

"This new king of ours had better appreciate all of the effort we've been putting into getting his kingdom back in order," Vander joked.

"Brendan had better! Or should I say King Brendan?" Bear laughed.

"I think for you, it will be 'Your Highness,' followed by the deepest of bows," Vander teased.

"All I know is he better get back here soon. I don't know how much longer we can hide this situation. And the council is getting more and more nervous every minute he's not here."

"I know. I've been concerned about that myself. I sure hope they're safe," Vander agreed. "Bear, I'd like to select twenty of our recruits to train for the Watch as soon as possible."

"I have two selected I wish to promote to assist me, but other than those two, I'd give you the choice of the next twenty if you agree," Bear proposed.

"I think I know the two you're eyeing. I believe we'd be better served to have them with you; they're more suited for your needs than mine."

"Very well, then. We have much to do, Vander. But for now, I'm starving; let's get something to eat!"

"Food would be good. It's been far too long since we ate last, and I'm starving!"

The two sat in the dining hall eating, thankful for the few remaining cooks and kitchen staff who had been keeping them and the council members fed. When they finished their meal, Vander selected the twenty additional men and women he would begin to rebuild the King's Watch with and began their training. Bear selected his assistants and claimed the balance of the men and women for the army. He formed them into ranks, and their training began shortly thereafter.

While both Vander and Bear worked with their recruits, the new members of the palace staff were learning their roles and assignments with Danianne, who had taken charge of all the palace's day-to-day operations.

The palace and its grounds were abuzz with a flurry of activity at every turn. Repairs continued everywhere, with the exception of the Great Hall. The repairs to the hall were going to be extensive and were not considered critical to palace operations and the immediate needs of the realm's citizens, so they would have to wait.

"Well, if nothing else, Brendan will return to a functioning palace and council," Vander said to Bear as they took a walk around the palace grounds, inspecting the ongoing work. "And, in truth, your efforts in the rebuilding of the army have been invaluable. You know he'll want you to take full command of both the army and the Elite forces while we continue to grow them."

"I did not want to assume anything, but I must admit I've given it a great deal of thought," Bear replied.

"How would you answer him if he were to ask it of you?"

Bear stopped and looked at Vander. He closed his eyes for a moment, searching his own feelings. He had seen far too much death and too many battles, he thought. But he also understood that Brendan might very well request he accept the position. He was torn between the desire to serve and the desire to return to his home and his life there.

"I don't know. I honestly don't know."

Chapter 38

antrill studied the Blue Witch's body as it lay in a heap on the floor. Her scorched and tattered robes were partly open and loosely strewn about her. He walked around her several times, then stopped and kicked her repeatedly before finally shoving her over onto her back roughly with his boot. He watched her a bit longer as she lay on the floor at his feet, and then he waited no more.

Vantrill knelt down beside Brielle's body and tore at her robes and the blouse she wore beneath until he could see the most powerful of Andentine's three pendants once again. He watched something swirling and moving within the clear blue stone. His desire for it overwhelmed him.

Vantrill paused, watching the stone more closely, mesmerized by its beauty and movement. He reached down gingerly and ran his finger over the intricate design of the silver pendant fused into his victim's flesh. He then ran his finger over the blue stone itself, and it responded to his touch. The stone's center swirled faster, and its blue hues changed rapidly.

He desperately wanted the last of the pendants, certain it was the most desirable of the three. He hesitated, concerned that it might be dangerous to remove it from the blue girl's corpse. He ran his fingers up the silver chain, examining how it was fused with the Blue Witch's flesh. Finally, his desire for it consuming him, he could resist no longer and dug his long, thick fingernails into the blue flesh surrounding the pendant.

The pendant responded, glowing with a soft blue light radiating from the stone's center. He stopped but did not remove his fingers from Brielle's body. As he waited to see what would happen next, the glowing blue light receded back into the stone. Vantrill proceeded again, carefully digging further into the blue flesh.

As he continued to violate the Blue Witch, the stone flared brightly and shocked him with a violent burst of energy that was overpowering and unrelenting. He screamed out in pain, and as he did, the Blue Witch opened her eyes, fixing them on those of her enemy. She found them filled with hatred and fear as he screamed.

The Blue Witch grabbed the back of his neck with her left hand and shoved her right hand deep into Vantrill's gaping mouth, unleashing all the power she could in a single burst of blue flame. Vantrill's body shook, and his wild eyes locked on to hers as she dug her fingers into the flesh of his neck.

As the blue fire filled his body, Vantrill burst into flames, then shuddered violently before exploding into pieces of rent flesh and bone. The Blue Witch had not released her firm grip, and she lay on the stone floor of the castle holding nothing but the head of Vantrill by a small jagged piece of his spinal column. She pulled her right hand from his mouth and took hold of Vantrill's chin, working the hinge of his jaw open and closed like a puppet's as she mocked his words.

"'I'm going to make you my queen! You're going to give me all that I desire and more!'" The Blue Witch laughed as she continued to play with her gruesome new toy. "'You're going to bear me a son with the magic blood of Pandane in his veins!'" she said, still imitating Vantrill's voice and bobbing his head around as she did. "'I'm more powerful now than ever before.' Fool!" she hissed as she looked at Vantrill's hideous face once more before tossing his head nonchalantly across the floor.

The Blue Witch rose to her feet and, touching the flesh around her pendant, inspected the damage. She then straightened her hair and examined what was left of her robes before removing them. She shook them out firmly, and they were once again as good as new. She put them back on, then bent down and retrieved the other two pendants from the floor near her. The Blue Witch looked one last time around the room at the pieces of Vantrill's body and across to where his head lay, then disappeared.

Andentine was still speaking with Brendan, discussing the responsibilities that he would be taking on as king, when the Blue Witch appeared before them. She looked confident and strong, fresh from her victory over another enemy.

"I killed Vantrill."

"Brielle, are you okay, my child?" Andentine asked. The Blue Witch cocked her head and glared at him, seemingly confused. "Brielle." Andentine said her name again in his soothing voice. The Blue Witch said nothing as she stood defiantly before him. "Brielle, come to me. It is safe. Come speak with me, Brielle…please."

Brendan could see a change wash over her. No longer was she the confident and victorious Blue Witch; she was Brielle, and she was clearly still in shock at what she had just been through. Andentine stepped forward and wrapped his arms around her.

"Everything will be okay, Brielle. You are safe here with your family now. Your daughter's here; Willow is here waiting for you, Brielle, remember?" Brielle broke down sobbing in Andentine's arms. Her slight body trembled visibly as he held her.

"I can't do this anymore, Andentine. I can't. It was horrible. I had to be so still. She kept me from screaming, even when I was dying."

"I know, child, I know," Andentine said gently. "You are safe now, Brielle, and so is your family. She did what she had to, Brielle. She did what she had to, to save you all. You were so brave to go through that. It is over now. You and your family are safe thanks to the Blue Witch."

Brendan didn't say a word, stunned at what was taking place before him. He didn't know what he would have said even if he could have managed to speak. He felt so bad for Brielle. He realized now, to a small degree, at least, what she was forced to live through as the Blue Witch went about her business without fear or remorse. Brielle, on the other hand, trapped and frightened, could not retreat from it and was forced to witness the horror in the most intimate of ways.

He could see plainly now her terrible internal struggle. It broke his heart, and he turned away long enough to wipe his tears.

"Who is she, Andentine? Why does she always come?"

"She is a friend."

"She is a monster! You don't know her. You don't see."

Brendan stepped closer but stopped as Brielle began sobbing and trembling in Andentine's arms once again. "I'm so tired, Andentine, so tired. Make her go away. Please help me, I'm begging you, Andentine. Please help me. I don't want to do this anymore. I'm so tired, my head hurts. Make it stop, Andentine, please make it stop."

Andentine held her close, reaching up and placing his hand on her head. Brendan could see a soft glow emanating from his hand before he removed it. Brielle calmed, and a moment later, she pulled back from Andentine.

"I'm sorry," she said, wiping away her tears and drying her face as best she could. She looked back to Andentine and wiped at her eyes once again. "I'm sorry."

Aria and Willow ran up to them, completely unaware of what had just taken place. Brielle knelt down and hugged Willow as if her very life depended on it, and maybe it did. She held her daughter for a long time before she was willing to release her.

"I love you, Willow," she said.

"I love you too."

Brielle came to her feet, turned to Brendan with a knowing look, and bowed deeply to him.

Brendan walked up to her boldly and grabbed her, holding her close, speaking softly into her ear. "Never do that again. You are my sister. You are my family, and I need that more than anything."

Brielle did not pull away or argue but held her brother tight. "Me too."

"Okay! Something's going on here, and I don't like being the last one to know all the time!" Aria said. "So, somebody better start talking!" She flashed that grin that Brendan loved so much, and he winked at her over Brielle's shoulder.

"Oh, it's nothing, Aria. The Blue Witch has killed Vantrill, ending his threat to the realms. I'm guessing Brielle has recovered our pendants, and, oh yeah, one more thing, I'm the new king, or at least I'm going to be."

"That's more like it. Was that so difficult?" she said, looking around at the others. "Wait! Did you say you're going to be king?"

"Yes, Aria Pandane, I did. You may begin bowing and groveling at any time." Brendan winked at Brielle, and she smiled. "You may want to refer to me as 'Your Majesty' or 'Your Highness' from now on."

"Never gonna happen. Hey, that means I'm going to be a princess now!" Aria said, grinning from ear to ear.

"I suppose it does, Aria. I suppose it does indeed." Brendan laughed. "Andentine, I have much to do. I would like to thank you for all your help. But now I'm anxious to get home and get started."

"Of course, Brendan, I understand. I would, however, like for Brielle and Willow to remain here with me for a short time longer," he said, looking at Brendan with incredible compassion in his eyes.

"I think that's a good idea," Brendan agreed. Brendan looked again to Brielle, and she brought him his pendant, placing it around his neck. She then brought Aria hers and did the same.

"Willow and I will join you both in a few days. We'll be there for your coronation, my brother. Be expecting us."

Chapter 39

Brendan and Aria appeared in their small cottage outside of Andavar. They both took a few minutes to look around, making sure that everything seemed in order, and they found it to be so.

"Aria, we haven't had time to speak of this, but we'll be staying at the palace from now on. I'll either rent out or sell this cottage. I haven't decided for sure yet what would be best. Will you be comfortable staying at the palace?"

"Oh, I think I can manage." Aria laughed. "Who would have thought it, Brendan?"

"I can barely believe it myself," he said. "Let's take the time to clean up and get some much-needed sleep before we return. I don't know about you, but I'm exhausted."

"I agree. I'm a fright, but you look even worse," she said, teasing him as she walked off to her room, not bothering to look back for his response. Brendan could only smile and shake his head as he went off to his room.

When they were rested and had dressed in fresh clothes, they left the cottage for their new home. They had no sooner arrived than Vander ran up to greet them.

"We've been expecting you. While the two of you were off gallivanting around, Bear and I have been here working to get everything put back together, though we finally managed to find some time to grab some sleep." He gave them each a warm hug before leading them to see Bear. They found him hard at work helping with the newly formed army.

"Look who I found sneaking in the back door, Bear!" Vander announced as they approached.

"Well met, Brendan Pandane!" Bear greeted him before snatching Aria off of her feet and hugging her as she laughed. "And you as well, young lady."

"We should find a place to speak in private," Vander said. The four of them made their way to a more secluded part of the palace.

"Are you aware of the situation here, Brendan?" Vander asked.

"I've been informed of some of it, but I am sure I haven't been told all I'll need to know, my friend. I'm aware of the massive losses we've suffered and of King Tennington's last command. Who else is aware of his final command?"

"All of the council members—they're all safe—and Bear and I. No one else knows. Danianne suggested we not announce anything until your return. Though, in truth, some were concerned whether that would actually happen."

"What about Tanton? We didn't see him when we arrived."

"He's here. He's out in the lake bathing and washing his clothes," Bear responded. "It made the most sense. We don't need a naked giant on full display in the garden's creek again."

Aria blushed, and Brendan smiled. "Vander, if you will inform Danianne and the council that I've returned, I'd like to meet with them right away."

"Certainly," Vander responded. "You should know, we lost a great many here, my friend, including Commander Stinson and all of the Elite First. I'm sorry to say we lost Drae as well as Drake and Vlix." Vander stopped and looked at Brendan as tears came to his eyes. "And...and Starlin."

Brendan and Aria were heartbroken at the losses and looked at each other, stunned. "I'm truly sorry," Brendan offered.

Vander stepped back wordlessly, nodded, and then darted off to inform Danianne and the council of Brendan's request.

"Vander, wait!" Brendan called after him. "The Blue Witch has killed Vantrill," he called out as Vander came to a stop. "I thought you might like to know we're safe now."

Vander walked back and stood before Brendan. He glanced to Bear and then back to Brendan.

"Brendan, you do know it wasn't Vantrill who attacked us and destroyed the army, don't you?"

"What? What do you mean it wasn't Vantrill? Who else but Vantrill could have done this? Of course it was Vantrill!"

"It wasn't him. I caught a glimpse of her, at least I believe it was a woman, but it was definitely not Vantrill. This was done after Vantrill captured you and left. This was an attack by another, I'm sure of it. We need Brielle. She's our only chance. I assume she came back with you, but I haven't seen her."

"She's still in Andentine's realm with Willow. I'm not expecting them for several days yet."

"We're still very much in danger, and we need her! Bear and I've begun rebuilding the army and forming a new King's Watch, but we're in no position to protect our people or make any kind of stand against another attack. Not that we could against that kind of power anyway. We've done what we could to keep our citizens from full panic by acting as if the threat is over and Tennington still lives."

"Then while we meet with the council, Aria, I need you to go get Brielle. Explain to her and Andentine that this is not over. Tell them it was not Vantrill's attack that did this damage, and we have no idea who or what it was. Let them know we're in no position to withstand another attack."

"I'll get her!" Aria said. And she was gone before Brendan could say another word.

Brendan and Vander, joined by Bear, made their way through the passageways that led to the council members' chamber; they were still hidden away in the safety of the underground rooms. Brendan, walking the secret passageways for the first time, could not help but notice the strange light that appeared to have no source.

"Where's the light in here coming from?" he asked.

"We don't know," Vander answered. "We assume it must be some form of magic put in place long ago when the palace and these passageways were first constructed. I knew of the passageways and had been shown their security measures along with the hidden controls for opening their doors some time ago. I asked the same question about the light source then, but nobody knew, not even Tennington."

"Well, it's a mystery for another time, then," Brendan replied.

Vander guided them to the meeting room. The three entered to find the council already seated and Danianne standing at the head of the table. The council members came to their feet and bowed as Brendan and his two companions crossed the room to stand with Danianne.

"Welcome, Brendan Pandane, former High Sword of the realm. We welcome you back as our king, Your

Highness," Danianne said, bowing again. The council members bowed as well, then clapped loudly. "Your council is at your service, my lord," she said.

"As you all know, our realm has suffered massive losses, including the loss of King Tennington. I have been informed that those in this room, along with my sister Aria, are the only ones who are fully aware of this. I've sent my sister to bring the Blue Witch here to help us. For those of you who may not yet know, the Blue Witch is my sister. Her name is Brielle Pandane, and she is a direct descendant of the first king of men, Ethan Pandane, as am I. I have met and spent time with the elven king, Andentine, in his realm across the Dead Bridge. Aria and I were taken there after the Blue Witch rescued Willow and the two of us from Vantrill. I will also have you know that Willow is the Blue Witch's daughter, and therefore my niece and of our royal blood as well. She is to be treated as such from this moment on."

Brendan looked intently at those seated around the table before continuing. "The Blue Witch has killed Vantrill. I learned only moments ago that Vantrill was not the one who attacked us so devastatingly here. We are still in danger and very vulnerable. I'm aware of the efforts of this council, along with those of Captain Vander Ray and Baird Prow, in mobilizing our citizens. Our army consists of less than a thousand men and women, and nearly all have never served or seen battle of any kind. The King's Watch has also been reestablished, but again, with very inexperienced men and women. Their training has begun, as you are aware, but we are a long way from fully rebuilding our forces." Brendan looked around at the faces of the council members once again before resuming.

"I am very proud of what this council has already accomplished under Danianne's leadership. But we have much to do to secure our realm and our way of life."

Brendan paused and looked directly at Danianne. "I call on Danianne and this council to continue their excellent service to our citizens. Our people will need to be informed that they have lost their king and of his last command. I will leave any such announcements and arrangements, including the timing of them, to this wise council's discretion."

Brendan paused again, taking the measure of the council members seated around the large table before him. He made sure to make eye contact with each of them as he did.

"Until such time, you are all still bound by your promise to remain silent. No one is to address me by anything but my name outside of this room. Danianne, I wish to have a word with you in private before I must leave to tend to other matters." All rose as Brendan stepped from the room into the passageway beyond with Danianne.

"Danianne, you gave wise counsel to King Tennington during his reign. I would like to count on your counsel as well, but I must know you have no reservations in continuing your service." Brendan looked at her intensely as he waited for her answer.

"My king, it would be my honor to serve you and the council of this realm in the same capacity in which I served our former king."

"Then I have but one condition, Danianne. Be as you must be in front of the council and others in speaking to me. But when we speak in private, you must speak to me freely, holding nothing back from me, without fear of any rebuke from me for speaking your mind. I must be able to count on you for this, Danianne. Can I be assured you will not fear speaking to me in this way, and will always do so?"

Danianne was impressed by her young king's request. "You can be assured I will give you my honest feelings and true counsel in everything we discuss. You have my solemn word on this."

"Very well, let's begin with this. We need a man to take over as commander of the army and the Elite First. I believe there is an obvious choice if he is willing, but I will not command it of him."

"You speak of Baird Prow," she responded.

"I do. What are your thoughts?"

"I think he's the obvious choice as well, and I can assure you, based on what's transpired in your absence and his actions in that time, the council and those already recruited for service would agree and support him fully." She paused a moment in thought before continuing. "Should Bear steadfastly refuse, there is another who would serve you well."

"Very well. I will speak to Bear on the matter. If he refuses, we can discuss that option. Vander is currently the commander of the King's Watch. Do you see any reason he should not remain so?"

"I do not. The other members of the council and I owe our lives to Vander."

"Danianne, you may not have been aware of this, but King Tennington named the Blue Witch High Protector of this realm. The elven king, Andentine, suggested this to him. I support this as well, though it was never announced to our people. How do you think they will respond?"

"The Blue Witch is known to be incredibly powerful and is feared throughout the realm, though she has never harmed a citizen to my knowledge. Because of this, I think our people will be relieved to know she has agreed to act as their High Protector. Knowing she is committed to protecting them, and has the ability to do so, will help in this transition. However, I believe there's one glaring question we must be able to answer when this is announced."

"And that is…?"

"If King Tennington made the Blue Witch our High Protector before his death, why wasn't she here to protect us when we needed her most?"

Chapter 40

Brendan walked with Bear through the palace, waiting patiently for his decision. He knew this was not easy for Bear. He also felt Bear was the only man for the job—he had spent time with him and knew him to be someone he could count on without reservation. As they walked, Brendan's mind was working on who besides Vantrill could have attacked them and why. He hoped Brielle and Andentine would have some answers for him.

He had already spoken with Vander and secured his commitment to the Watch, but there had never been any doubt about that. It was Bear who concerned him, but he had already decided that he would not command Bear to serve. Bear had already given too much of himself for Brendan not to respect his wishes. As they walked out of the palace, they found Tanton sitting on his large bench in the gardens.

"Tanton, my very large friend, it's good to see you!" Brendan called to him as they approached.

Tanton came to his feet and then knelt down. "Brendan, my young friend, it is good to see you as well.

I've been concerned for your family's safety. I assume all is well?"

"It is, Tanton. We're safe. The Blue Witch was able to save us, and she's put an end to Vantrill."

"A creature far more powerful than Vantrill has been unleashed on this realm. I do not know much, Brendan, but while I was being held in captivity by Vantrill, something happened that may shed a little light on this matter."

"Anything you can offer at this point would be helpful."

"Vantrill broke out of the realm Andentine banished him to. We know this, but we do not know how. I'm thinking this other creature may have helped Vantrill escape. I once overheard Vantrill speaking aloud, though I could not see who he might be speaking to. But I remember Vantrill saying, 'I will fulfill my promise to you, I swear it!' He seemed quite nervous, if you ask me. I now wonder if he was speaking to this other creature. That's all I heard, but I felt you should know my thoughts. Wait, maybe Vantrill made a deal to give it one of the pendants. Maybe that was the promise he made."

"You may be right. It would make sense. Andentine said that Vantrill was very powerful at one time but had grown weaker in the dark realm. Finding a more powerful being in the dark realm and making such a promise to gain his freedom would make sense. I've sent Aria to bring Brielle back to help us. I'm hoping she'll have more information from Andentine when she arrives." Brendan had no sooner gotten the words out of his mouth than Aria and Brielle appeared before them.

"I'm sorry I had to ask you to return like this, but so happy you're here, Brielle," Brendan said. "Do you bring any information or advice from Andentine?"

"I do. We're facing an enemy not yet known to Andentine—though he has warned me the dark realm he banished Vantrill to contains evil unparalleled in any other realm known to him. He believes Vantrill must have brought something or someone back with him. He does not believe Vantrill or this other creature would be capable of escaping on their own. Andentine believes they must have combined their powers in some way to break free."

"Andentine may be right. Tanton has suggested that perhaps he made a deal to provide one of our pendants to another from that realm in order to secure the help he would have needed to escape."

"Andentine made virtually the same warning. I think, until proven otherwise, we have to assume this is what happened. And if it is, when this creature finds Vantrill is dead, now that it has been freed, it very well may come back seeking the pendant it was promised. Vantrill had two of the pendants in his possession, so he did not give one up to this thing. Andentine thinks Vantrill may have planned to betray the creature and use the power of the pendants to overcome it." Brielle paused and looked at her companions.

"There is a far more troubling possibility Andentine discussed with me as well. Vantrill may have feared this thing so much that even with the two pendants he possessed, he would not dare challenge it until he obtained the third," Brielle said. "Either way, we will be dealing with an unknown entity of incredible power bent on obtaining more."

"We were hit so hard and fast by it that I have spoken to no one else who saw what this creature looks like, but as I said, I'm sure it wasn't Vantrill," Vander interjected.

"Clearly, we have no idea what we're dealing with; all we know is that it destroyed both our army and Vantrill's, so we know it possesses immense power already, and the confidence to carry out such an attack,"

Brielle added. "I think it intended to turn against Vantrill and came here expecting to obtain a pendant or pendants itself. Why else would it destroy Vantrill's army along with ours?"

"What do you think we should do, Brielle?" Brendan asked.

"It could be anywhere, preparing for its next move," Brielle began. "Clearly it has little fear of our ability to stand against it. I believe we have only two options. We can wait for its return and risk more loss of life here, or we can hunt it down and end the threat."

"It doesn't sound like we have much of a choice," Brendan responded. "How do we go about hunting this thing down?"

"I will find it, wherever it is. I would normally say I will go alone, but this thing may be beyond my ability to defeat by myself. I think we must form a group, a small group, to confront and kill this thing."

"I insist on going with you, Brielle," Brendan stated firmly.

"As do I," Vander added.

"And I," Bear said. "I wish to see this through."

"I will be going," Tanton announced.

They all looked to Aria, who had remained silent. "What?" she said, stretching her arms above her head and yawning. "Do what you want, I'm gonna take a nap." She looked around at the others stoically before grinning. "There's no way I'm staying behind!"

"Then we have our group," Brendan announced, turning to Brielle.

"Very well, I will search for whomever or whatever we're looking for. Stay together and be prepared to leave at once when I find it."

"Brielle, I have to address the council before I leave. It will not take long. While I do, the rest of you can prepare yourselves. Except for you, Vander; I'll need you with me."

"Of course, Brendan. It may take some time for me to find this thing. I'll begin my search, but I will not leave here before your return."

"We'll be back as soon as possible."

Brendan and Vander made their way back to the secret rooms where the council remained safely secluded. Brendan addressed the council as they took their seats once again around the large meeting table.

"I will be joining a small group hunting down and ending the threat of the creature that attacked us so savagely. Vander and Bear will be going with my sisters and me. Tanton will also be joining us in this endeavor. We will have to continue to hold off on our announcements until I return. While I am away, Danianne will speak for me on all matters. You will consider any order or request from her a direct command from your king. Danianne, please join me."

The two left the room and entered one of the passageways that led back up to the palace, stopping a short distance within.

"I know we did not have a chance to speak of this, but I need you to remain in charge while I am away. We must keep our people calm, and unfortunately, that means we must continue to withhold the death of Tennington from them. You must make your decisions as you see fit, based on what you are facing, not as you think Tennington or I would make them. Lead decisively, Danianne, as I know you're capable of doing. Do so in the best interest of our people, and I'll stand firmly behind your decisions. I give you my word."

"I'll do my best for our people. You be careful, Brendan Pandane. We need you to return; we need you as our king. I have a feeling you're going to be a very good one."

"Then I shall do my best as well."

Chapter 41

B rielle searched for the creature using her magic and special sight to reach out and track the unknown entity. She became lost in her effort, and time no longer registered or mattered to her. She began at the palace and spread her search out until she picked up a trail she could follow. Having found the stream of magic she sought, she followed it quickly but very cautiously. She did not want to accidentally alert this thing to her presence.

When she finally caught up with it, the creature was in what she assumed was the dark realm from which it had come. She could not see the creature as she wished to, but Brielle was certain that she had found their enemy and was concerned by what she could see. She brought herself out of the trance, checking herself and her surroundings as she did. All those who'd agreed to go with her were there and patiently waiting on her.

"I found it," she announced to the small group. "But I must leave for a few moments to consult with Andentine. I won't be gone long; wait for me here." She left before anybody could question her need to go. True to her word, Brielle was not gone long before she reappeared, and the others gathered around her.

"I must warn everyone, we will be traveling to another realm. The dark realm that Vantrill was banished to, and the one this creature has now returned to. Andentine was able to provide me some basic information about this place. It was once thriving with life. A devastating war, unlike any we have ever known here, tore their world apart and drove it into great darkness. It's a lost world, a world full of evil, now. It's a world of criminals and creatures banished from other realms, and it serves as a prison for them."

"We have no idea then what dangers there will be," Vander interjected.

"No, we do not," Brielle agreed.

"How will we be able to enter or leave this realm?" Brendan asked.

"That was one of the things I needed to speak with Andentine about. Any one of our pendants will act as a key to the realm. I explained to him what I saw of the creature we are after. Andentine did not offer any advice beyond this: he agrees we should not wait for it to return here. He believes if we do, it will bring more evil back into this realm with it. Having found a way to escape, it could open the floodgates, allowing those banished to the dark realm to devastate this one."

"Then we go?" Aria asked.

"Yes, if all here are still willing," Brendan answered, looking to his companions. All stood firm, resolved to go. Brendan looked to Brielle. "Vander and I have secured plenty of supplies, not knowing what we may need or how long this would take. Tanton has agreed to carry them for us. What would be a heavy load for the rest of us, the big guy here won't even notice. We're ready when you are, Brielle."

"Very well. I will warn you all again, be alert and stay together. We do not know what we will face in this dark realm. We must all join hands and hold tight; I will take us there. I intend for us to arrive a safe distance from the creature we seek." They took each other's hands, and Brielle looked at each of them, confirming they were ready, then took hold of Tanton and they were gone.

They arrived moments later in a world darkened by a thick black mist swirling above them. The mist filtered out a good deal of the natural light. It took a few moments for their eyes to adjust to the gloomy world they now found themselves in, but otherwise, they did not delay in beginning their search.

The group stayed close together, with Brielle in the lead and Tanton in the rear. They moved along cautiously but maintained a good pace. Brielle led them without slowing or stopping to rest. They passed strange structures ravaged by the war that had destroyed the world long ago. Some of the structures were so tall that they disappeared into the dark mist high above. Clearly, these were the skeletons of a once-great civilization, they agreed.

"What kind of force could cause this amount of devastation?" Brendan asked as they passed yet another of the impressive towers, one that had fallen to the ground. The massive structure's remains snaked along the ground between several still standing defiantly, though in ruins as well. No one in the group even hazarded a guess at Brendan's query.

They walked on, picking their way through the rubble strewn everywhere about them. They moved deeper into the midst of the great structures and soon came to one that stood out from the others. It sat apart from the rest and was much smaller. It was a dark, sleek-looking thing that captured their collective imagination. While it was heavily damaged, it had survived the war far better than the larger structures looming over it.

Brielle stopped, studying the odd structure. Her companions were equally interested in what was before them. The dark form was shaped unlike anything any of them had ever seen before.

"What is it?" Aria asked.

"I don't know for sure," Bear answered. "But I do not think it was built here for this spot. It appears to be a vessel of some sort, though it couldn't be for traveling on water, or even land, with this design. It looks like it was designed to fly like a bird—see the wings here, though these wings certainly could not flap like those of a bird. I believe this was used to fly in. Think of it as a Zaroe," Bear added.

"It has windows up here," Tanton announced, looking closer at what appeared to be the front of the object. "And there's at least two seats in here," Tanton said as he peered through the windows. "I think you're right, Bear, they made metal Zaroes."

"Andentine told me the inhabitants of this realm built many fantastic things, and they had creations capable of flying and carrying passengers enclosed within them," Brielle offered. "This must be one of those."

"It's impressive, isn't it?" Vander said.

"We must continue on," Brielle announced as she started off again. The others fell in line as she did. Their journey quickly took them past many more strange and wondrous sights. But they found the hazy darkness a noticeable distraction that affected not only their concentration but their mood as well. Brielle seemed to be the only one who was not bothered by it.

Brendan could not help but notice Aria was staying very close to Brielle. Perhaps, he thought, it made her feel a bit safer in this dark world. Though, in truth, all had stayed closer to her than normal, perhaps for the very same reason.

It was not long before they came across a series of large trenches dug into the ground stretching out a great distance before them. All had been filled over, except one. They approached the edge of the one left open and were aghast at the sight within. Several thousand and perhaps even tens of thousands of skeletons—it was hard to tell not knowing the depth of the trench—were piled up to a level several feet below the rim. It was, however, easy enough to tell the trench contained the remains of adults, as well as children and even babies. All lay together in their open grave. Trench after trench stretched as far as the eye could see in the dim light. No one uttered a single word as they stood before the horrific sight.

A row of heavy wagons of some kind sat near the edge of the open trench, a few with a great claw at one end and a heavy shield at the other. Larger ones had only the single claw. These things had chairs as well, they noticed. Some were open and others were enclosed by large windows, though most of those were broken, with only jagged shards remaining.

"These things must have been used to dig and move the dirt," Bear said as he studied the one closest to them.

"But how?" Brendan inquired. "How could they move on their own?"

"I don't know, but if they could build things capable of flying, like the one we saw, they could've discovered a way to make these things work as well," Bear replied.

The group moved beyond the trenches, and Brielle brought them to a stop. "Whatever killed those poor people is not our enemy. Do not dwell on it. This realm was destroyed long ago. It is the creatures that have been banished to it we must be cautious of now. Andentine and I believe that the one we hunt is the most powerful of them, though we may be wrong in this. Do not let this endless gloom dull your senses. You must stay alert; the one we seek has been moving not too far ahead of us for some time now."

"Does it know we're here?" Brendan asked, stunned by the revelation.

"Yes. And she has shown no fear of us. She is, in fact, leading us," Brielle answered.

"Leading us? Leading us where?" Vander asked as he moved closer.

"I don't know. Into a trap perhaps, or she's simply curious and studying us. Of course, Vander, there's always the chance she just isn't hungry yet." Brielle looked at him gravely, then looked at Aria and gave her a wink. Aria lowered her head and bit her lip.

Brendan noticed that spending time close to Aria seemed to help Brielle stay in a lighter mood and remain herself. Aria often had such an effect on people, though. Her sense of humor was unbridled. Aria was fearless in being herself and found humor even in dire situations.

Brendan had been considering what Andentine had shared with him about Brielle and the Blue Witch. The Blue Witch, he thought, was the dark side of Brielle that protected her but repulsed her, and surely frightened her as well. He looked ahead to where Aria walked with Brielle and observed the blue girl in her black robes. He could not help thinking about Brielle's past and the tortured life she'd led. He thought of the guilt she'd carried for so long, and her self-imposed exile from her loved ones, a choice she'd made to protect them. He thought about the loss of Willow's father, Brielle's love and the man she'd planned to marry, lost to her in another tragic accident. It saddened him deeply that Brielle had known so much loss and pain in her life. He fought to change his train of thought as the group continued on but found he was unable to do so.

Brendan could not help but feel for his sister and the loneliness she'd suffered. It was Aria's and his biggest fear, and Brielle had lived it most of her life. It was crushing to him, and he could not shake the thought of her being so young, only a year or so older than Aria was now, alone in those mountains for so many years. He thought as well of how she had faced and fought untold evil alone. According to Andentine, Brielle had done so many times, with nobody there to help her, or witness her death and care for her remains if she had fallen. Brielle's life had been fraught with death, disappointment, and unbearable loneliness. Her having to leave Willow time and time again in search of evil she was to extinguish in some far-off part of the realm had done as much or more damage to her as the evil things she'd faced.

He thought suddenly of his own battles fought alone in distant parts of the realm, and the time he'd spent away from his home and Aria. He could not help but think that, in some ways, his life and his sister's had taken similar paths. Though he knew he had faced nothing in comparison to what his sister had.

He wondered about how different their lives could have been. He thought of how young they had been when their lives took such a tragic turn and what they had all lost to a single innocent mistake, and he wanted it all back, especially his mother. Brendan thought of the last time he'd seen his mother alive and the guilt he still carried to this day from his childish actions and what he'd denied her. He could still hear her calling to him and see the tears falling from her eyes before she turned away and walked out their door for the last time.

"Are you okay?" Vander asked.

"What do you mean?" Brendan snapped, shaken from his thoughts.

"You have had tears running down your face for some time now. Forgive me, I was concerned."

"I'm fine. I was lost in thought and dwelling on the past; I didn't realize," Brendan replied, wiping his face with his sleeves.

Vander put his hand on Brendan's shoulder and leaned in close to him.

"It is often what's known and certain of our past that haunts us more than the unknown and uncertainty of our future."

"What? What are you babbling about?"

"I was trying to sound profound."

"Well, you sound like an idiot."

Vander stumbled back, feigning being wounded. Brendan began laughing, and Vander could not keep from doing the same. "It actually was quite profound, Vander," Brendan conceded, squeezing his friend's shoulder. "Thank you."

Brielle stopped, and her companions gathered near her.

"What is it?" Brendan asked, stepping closer.

Brielle held her finger to her lips and pointed ahead in the direction they'd been traveling. She looked back at the group and held her hand up, palm facing them. She took a single step forward. Those behind her stared ahead with her but could see nothing. Then Brielle spun about, wide-eyed.

"She's coming for us!"

Chapter 42

ndentine walked the corridors of Elveshenge alone. He had searched once again after speaking to Brielle of what she'd seen, and found what he was looking for, confirming his worst fears. His thoughts were now of Brielle and what she and her companions would be facing in the dark realm. Perhaps it is time the realm of men know the truth of their past, he thought.

Andentine saw Willow approaching. "Willow, how are you, my child?" he greeted her.

"I've seen my mother and those with her. They're in danger, Andentine!"

"I know, child. Vantrill unwittingly unleashed a creature of incredible evil and power on the realm of men. Your mother is my weapon against this creature."

"Then you must help her, Andentine!"

"I cannot help her any more than I already have, Willow. I've trained your mother and given her immense power and abilities, knowing this creature would one day resurface."

Willow looked at the elven king for a moment,

working out in her mind what he had just said. "You know this thing! Don't you?" she asked.

"Yes. It has taken me some time to confirm its identity, but I have done so."

Trindentine, approaching the two, interrupted their conversation. "Excuse me, Willow," he said with a polite bow. "My brother, you wish to see me?"

"I do. Please join us." The three continued through the corridors as Andentine spoke. "A great evil from our past has reemerged, Trindentine. Our family was once a victim of her incredible cruelty and evil ways. I think you know of whom I speak," he said, looking directly at Trindentine. "I was just about to talk with Willow about the one who murdered my daughter and cost me my wife."

"No, Andentine! You mustn't!"

"It is time, my brother. Circumstances have brought us to this point. We knew long ago this time would come. I will wait no longer; I cannot."

It was several moments before Trindentine spoke again. "Very well, Andentine, the time has come."

"Willow, I will not attempt to explain everything now. I must speak to Trindentine in private, but I will tell you this much. Trindentine and I do know this creature. Her name is Saphira. She is our sister."

"Your sister!" Willow exclaimed, scrunching up her face. "I can't keep up with you people!" she said, throwing her hands in the air and shaking her head. The two brothers watched the girl as she walked away mumbling, "Demons, men, witches, elves, you're all crazy!"

"She has a lot of her mother in her," Andentine said, shaking his head.

"Will the Blue Witch be able to stand against Saphira?" Trindentine asked. "Our sister is a creature of untold power and evil; she will not be easily defeated, as you well know.

"It is not certain. I have given Brielle everything within my power to assist her. But it is up to her now," Andentine replied. "The Blue Witch is a very powerful creature herself, Trindentine. I have helped make her so, knowing this time would come."

"So that was your purpose in raising that poor girl and keeping her alive all along." Trindentine gasped. "Oh, Andentine, how could you?"

Andentine gave him a quick, sharp look. "Do not presume to know my mind, Trindentine. But in part, what you say is true. It was not my intention originally, I assure you. It was an awful mistake. But now she is the only one who may be able to defeat Saphira."

"Our sister may come to realize who Brielle really is."

"Yes, Saphira may discover the truth. It is of great concern to me, and it may very well be the Blue Witch's only weakness."

"Andentine, I owe my life, as do my men, to Brielle. We would be willing to join her in this dark realm you speak of to face Saphira."

"No, my brother, she will succeed or fail now without further help from us."

"How, Andentine, how could we have a sister of such pure evil?"

"I don't know why some who have the power to do good choose evil instead."

"What will you do, Andentine, should the Blue Witch fail to destroy Saphira? You must know if she does, now that Saphira is free, our sister will come for you seeking revenge."

"I do," he answered. "Saphira will seek to destroy me and this realm, and I will not be able to stop her. The Blue Witch must prevail, for if she fails and falls in battle, the realms of both men and elves will fall with her."

"I do not have the gifts the two of you do, but I say again, let me go to her aid."

"Trindentine, my brother, you have just been given back to me; I could not bear to lose you again. If Brielle fails, all those who stand with her will be lost. You know Saphira will leave none alive. She does not care to take prisoners, except to torture them before killing them. Brielle already has Brendan and Aria Pandane, along with three others who stand with her in the dark realm."

"She does not have me or my skill with a sword. And what will it matter, if she does not succeed, whether I die here or there?"

Andentine looked at his brother, thinking for some time before speaking. "You are the greatest warrior I have ever known or have even heard of, my brother, but your magic is very limited and will not in itself save you. Especially from Saphira." He hesitated, then went on. "Very well, you alone, Trindentine," he said reluctantly. "I will give you something to assist you. But know this: Saphira does not walk her realm alone. She may have creatures of untold strength and power under her control that will fight for her."

"I assumed as much. That is where I may be able to help most. I believe I'm back to full strength now. Give me the last pendant, Andentine, and I will go do what I do best. I know that you wish it could be you to stand before Saphira, but you know it cannot be."

"Of course I wish to stand before her! It should be me for what she did to my wife and daughter!" Andentine went quiet for several more moments. "Very well, Trindentine." He reached into his robes and removed a silver pendant. The pendant, with its intricate design and markings, did not have a brightly colored stone but rather a black one. The stone was haunting, changing from solid black to a translucent darkness that shifted as faces, one after another, appeared at its surface, peering outward, before receding back into the darkness.

"Do not attempt to stand against Saphira, Trindentine. You do not have the power it will take to do so, not even with this pendant," he said, handing it to Trindentine. "Help Brielle and her companions if you can, but she alone has the power to face Saphira, and she alone must face her, Trindentine."

Andentine held his hands out before him, and a sheathed sword appeared in them. "Take this sword, Trindentine. It is without compare in any realm. It will feel as though it is a part of you. But do not be fooled. Its only power is against spirits of the dead and its ability to bond with its master. It will not add strength, speed, or skill to you, Trindentine. But it will know your thoughts and intentions and will act as one with you."

Trindentine strapped the sheathed sword around his waist and drew the blade. Its design was amazing, the polished black blade flawless. Trindentine looked closer and could see fine designs running the length of the blade ghosted into the finish. Then, stunned, he looked again. The images were changing within the sword. He felt its weight and swung it gently at first, then switched it from hand to hand.

The sword was incredible, its balance perfect. He swung it more aggressively and found the sword was bonding with him in a way he could not explain; he felt himself bonding with it in turn. Though he did not wish to, he forced himself to sheathe the sword. Amazingly, he could feel his bond with the sword growing ever deeper with each passing moment. He reached down and gripped its handle lightly without drawing it again.

"Thank you, Andentine, it is truly magnificent. Does it have a name?"

"The sword has had many names over many millennia. I think you will have to find it a new one, as each of its owners before you has had to do. Your relationship with the sword will be unique to you, Trindentine, and in time you'll find your own name for it."

"Very well, my brother. Please explain to my elves that I could not take them with me. They will not be pleased I left them behind."

"As you wish. If you are ready, I will send you to Brielle and her companions."

"Wait!" Willow screamed as she ran to them. "Wait!" she called out again. "Trindentine, when the swordsmen come for you, you must face them alone. Do not let another fight with you. You must not! They are immune to magic and serve Saphira of their own will. She tricked them long ago, but their honor binds them to their word. They cannot be defeated in battle by any form of magic. You must face them alone."

"Who are you talking about, Willow, what swordsmen?"

"I've seen them. Heed my words, Trindentine. They will come for you. When they call to you, you must face them alone! If you do not, all with you will perish, and all will be lost. Promise me, Trindentine. All of our lives will depend on it."

"Listen carefully to Willow, Trindentine. Heed her words; her gift of sight is very strong," Andentine said.

"Very well, Willow, I will face them alone, I promise you. I'm ready, Andentine."

"Do not forget Willow's words, and remember my warnings as well!" Andentine said, then Trindentine was gone. Andentine stood where he was a moment longer, troubled by what he had seen, and then he looked down at Willow. "I have seen something myself, Willow, and I must seek the help of an old friend."

Andentine passed through the corridors of Elveshenge alone, a conflicted soul. He climbed to a room higher up and to the back of the great castle. He crossed the room and walked out onto a large balcony overlooking the sea. Once there, he closed his eyes, calling for the great winged beast in his mind. Moments later, a dragon of immense size landed before him.

The dragon was magnificent to behold. His scales changed color as he moved; he was white one moment, then blue, then green, and then a kaleidoscope of colors all at once as he continued to transform rapidly before Andentine. His size belied the idea he was capable of flight. The dragon turned, facing the elven king.

"Andentine, what need do you have of me?"

"Drazmoss, I have called you here to help Brielle. She will be facing Saphira soon in the dark realm—"

"You know I can't save her from Saphira, Andentine, I do not have the power to do so. Brielle must face her alone," he said, cocking his head. "Though I sense she does not yet know the truth of herself or why it falls upon her to face Saphira."

"I know this, and you are correct, Drazmoss. I have not revealed to Brielle who she really is. And I do not intend to. I fear it may destroy her to discover the truth."

"It may indeed, Andentine. I will not judge you for what you did to that girl, nor will I judge you for what you are doing to her now. It is not my place to do so. But I cannot help but feel a great sadness for Brielle. I am one of the few who knows her real story, Andentine, and I know it weighs heavily on you. What is it, then, that you ask of me?"

"Moments ago, I sent Trindentine to help Brielle. As I was doing so, I saw something disturbing. One of Brielle's companions will soon be killed. I wish you to go to the dark realm, Drazmoss. As you know, I cannot assist you in getting there, nor can I join you. You will have to go on your own. Even with your incredible speed and magic, you cannot prevent this death."

"What would you have me do, Andentine?"

"I want you to retrieve their body. We will not leave our fallen to rot in the ashes and dust of the dark realm."

"As you wish," the dragon said, then he flew off into the darkening sky as Andentine watched him wing away, the pieces now in place for a battle that may be impossible for them to win—but one they must.

CPSIA information can be obtained
at www.ICGtesting.com
Printed in the USA
LVHW021552140422
716194LV00001B/46